TO FOLLOW A DREAM

CHANDRA LYNN SMITH

TO FOLLOW A DREAM

CHANDRA LYNN SMITH

This book is lovingly dedicated to
the Master Storyteller
who stepped into my story
and invited me to create with Him.

It is also dedicated to my sweet mother,
Betty Davis Overman.
Mama, you taught me to love stories.
This one's for you.
I love you and I miss you.

ACKNOWLEDGMENTS

Thank you my Savior Jesus Christ, Who writes every story WITH me and in Whom I trust with all of my heart and soul and mind and strength. Thank You for helping me find joy in the middle of every life circumstance.

I was blessed to live only fifteen minutes away from my mother most of my adult life. She was a huge part of our lives. We traveled together, watched my four sons' wrestling matches, baseball games, soccer games, and musicals together. We had many wonderful times sitting in front of the fireplace with a roaring fire, or on the porch, or on the swing by the pond reading books. I treasured those long times of silence, each of us in our story world, but doing it together. One of my most special memories is our weekly lunches where we shared our love of books, stories, talked about my writing, and solved the problems of the world. Thank you Mama. Without your love of reading to me when I was a child, my love for books would not have developed.

Thank you to my husband who has put up with my quirkiness

for 37 years of marriage. Thank you for understanding—at least trying to understand—the hours sitting at my desk writing, or not writing. Your support is a treasure.

Thanks to my four sons for blessing my life and encouraging me in my writing even when you know my romances are not something you have any real interest in reading. Your belief in me helps me on the days my words are 'stupid.' Thank you also for bringing your lovely ladies into our family for us to love.

Thank you to my editor for your hours of painstaking reading, marking, and making excellent suggestions. I'm sure you sighed at my writing as often as my characters sighed—which they do less of now, thanks to you. Your editing has blessed my heart and my writing. Thank you.

Thank you Carolyn for your excitement and joy in my writing. Your encouragement is huge. Thank you for loving my stories even while going through and marking them up in track changes. Thank you for being such an amazing friend.

Thank you Lisa for the laughter and reality checks at our brunches. You do bless my heart, not in the southern sense of the words, but for real.

Thank you to my beta readers, Amy and Heavenly. I love you two.
   Thank you to my proofreaders. Eunice, Johnnie, and Ruth. Your keen catches were lifesavers. I called it a victory when I find five consecutive pages with no correction needed.

Thank you, Ken Raney, for designing another beautiful cover and formatting my manuscript. I especially thank you for your patience with my myriad questions through the publishing process.

Thank you to my critique partners in Penwrights, Imagine That Writers, Sharpened Pencils, and Scribes. Each of you challenges me to stretch and grow. I appreciate your candor, encouragement, and toughness all at the same time. This writing journey would not exist without your help. I love all y'all.

Thank you to my dear friends in West Virginia for the weekend getaways, your friendship, and love, and the joy I have each time I visit. We've had some great hikes and picnics and fun exploring the mountains, lakes, and four-wheeling on the back roads. Thanks for the tlc.

And the dogs. I thank every dog I have ever owned, and each of the thousands I have trained since 1985 for bringing me joy and providing inspiration for my canine characters.

"My brethren, count it all joy
when you fall into various trials,
knowing that the testing of your faith produces patience."
James 1:2(NKJV)

"I pray that God who gives hope will fill you
with much joy and peace
while you trust in Him. Then your hope will overflow by the power of
the Holy Spirit."
Romans 15:13(NKJV)

CHAPTER 1

*M*aryRose Elliott closed the trunk of her VW Bug, brushed her hands together and faced her step-grandfather, Papa Shane Macloud. "That's everything. I left enough room for Dapple on the front seat. You'll come see me won't you?"

"Moving to another state won't be chasing me off, lassie. I'll make a regular pest of myself. You know you don't have to be going so far away don't ya?"

"I don't have to, but it is the best for me right now."

MaryRose lifted her one-year old Miniature Wire-Haired Dachshund onto the passenger seat and fastened him into his doggie restraint. She looked one last time at the black water of the creek in her back yard and the now-empty house in which she'd grown up. Her heart hitched. Who was she kidding, the house had been empty for months, ever since her family died, and her heart was about as black as that creek water. The VW made the familiar sound of a vacuum sealing as she closed Dapple's door.

"It's time, Papa Shane."

He frowned at the dark clouds in the western sky. "Storms are brewing that way. Ya may be driving into the tempest."

She shook her head. "No matter how bad the storms are, they cannot beat the ones inside my heart."

"Aye, but those storms will be going wherever ya go. Moving won't be stopping them."

"I know that, Papa, but I have to give myself the chance to find my history."

Papa Shane touched her shoulder. "There is one more thing I have for ya. Wait right here."

MaryRose leaned against the car and watched an egret wade into the creek. The bird was pure white in the swampy blackness. Was there any purity left in her soul? She didn't have much time to ponder before Papa Shane hustled back to her. He carried what looked like a wrapped boot box.

"If you're gonna be tracing your family history, this box might come in handy. Don't be opening it now. Wait till ya get there and have a moment of missing home. Maybe it will be cheering ya up."

He opened the back door and wedged it between the bentwood rocker and a box of clothes. His hearty chuckle warmed her heart.

"You beat all, lassie. If I were a betting man, I'd a lost. I figured you'd nary get all your stuff squeezed into the car, but ya did."

"You forget Pa was the king of efficient packing."

"That he was."

She cleared her throat.

Papa Shane pulled her into his embrace.

"Don't be swallowing those tears. Ya need to let them flow. There's healing in it. But God will be helping you with that. I know it."

She inhaled the lingering scent of the cherry tobacco from

his pipe and absorbed the love flowing from him to her. Phew, this was tough.

"I love you, Papa."

"I know ya do. I love you too. I'll be missing you. You will call me when you get there?"

She nodded. The lump in her throat blocked her words and threatened to take her breath too. As she closed the door and started the car, the first big drops of rain hit the windshield.

MaryRose slowed the VW before rounding another hairpin turn. A white flash of lightning instantly followed by a crash of thunder startled her. She steeled herself and gently accelerated up the mountain. Eyeing the rusty guardrails, she shook her head. There was no way they'd keep her from careening over the edge of the mountain.

She stretched her neck and rolled her shoulders. Nine hours of driving in storm after storm had given her too much time to think. What made her think moving would help her heal? At the top of the mountain she pulled into an overlook of sorts. Of course all she saw was a guardrail and a black void beyond it.

Each lightning strike lit the forest around her transforming trees into tall shadow monsters. Thunder cracked so loud her car shook. Dapple burrowed into the blanket on his seat. Mary-Rose reached over and rubbed the back of his neck. Poor guy. It had been a long day for him too.

"It's okay, Dapple. The map you're sitting on says we'll be there when we reach the bottom of this mountain."

He thumped his tail once and shivered.

"I agree." She slid the map from beneath him and looked at it under the dim dome light. So much for GPS, it stopped working when she left the interstate. Thank heavens Papa insisted she

3

take an atlas too. Lake Nolan Drive should be at the bottom of this last mountain.

Thankfully.

In answer to her relief another deluge of rain and hail struck the car. She put the car in gear and tried not to hydroplane as she descended. White knuckling the steering wheel at the final curve, she made the left turn onto Lake Nolan Drive, then snaked around three more curves until a mailbox numbered 675A came into view. She exhaled the breath it felt like she'd held for hours.

"We made it."

Dapple whimpered.

MaryRose turned onto a gravel drive that circled a huge Victorian house with a wrap-around porch. A row of rocking chairs invited her to relax—when it wasn't storming. The drive continued downhill past the house and ended behind a small log cabin surrounded by a white picket fence. Lights from the windows glowed through the watery windshield like those in a Kinkaid painting.

A man ducked as he exited the cabin and stepped onto the little back porch. After pushing thick brown hair from his forehead he looked up at the black sky then headed her way.

If he was the owner, oh goodness. The tall man coming through the gate was not much older than she—or else he was aging to perfection. He stepped around puddles as he approached her car and opened her door before she had a chance to. A whoosh of wind blew into her face.

Dapple growled.

MaryRose looked up into eyes lit by the dome light. Even in that dimness she could tell he had the bluest eyes she'd ever seen. Her breath caught.

He offered his hand. "You must be Ms. Elliott. I'm Randall Cobb. Sure picked one heckuva night to drive in from the coast."

"It appears I did. If the mountains are this rough to navigate in rain storms, I might have to hibernate during the winter." More thunder rumbled as she accepted his hand and stepped out of the car.

"Please call me MaryRose."

"It's nice to meet you. When winter comes you'll learn the skill of car-skiing." He chuckled.

Dapple leaped out and landed in a huge puddle. He splashed mud over the bottom of her gypsy skirt and Mr. Cobb's jeans. If she'd hoped to make a good first impression with her new landlord, this was probably not the way to start.

"Dapple is not used to being cooped up in the car for so long."

As if cued, the pup plopped in front of him and wagged his tail.

"So this is the little guy you told me about over the phone." He bent and scratched underneath Dapple's chin.

"Cute." He straightened up and looked at the ominous sky. "How about we get inside before the next wave hits? And I go by Randall. People who call me Mr. Cobb usually want to boss me around or take my money."

MaryRose followed him through the gate, onto the porch and into the cabin. Dapple zipped right up the steps and tracked mud into the kitchen. She'd be lucky if the puppy didn't get her evicted before she moved in. But a sideways glance at Randall showed him smirking at Dapple. A really cute smirk.

She stopped inside the door and stared into the sunshine-yellow kitchen. The white cabinets and butcher-block table in the center of the room looked fresh and homey, not rustic as she'd expected. God knew, she needed that.

Randall pointed to a document on the table. "That's the lease. Feel free to look around the house before you sign."

After the day she'd had, she didn't care if the house was less than perfect. And if the rest of it was bright and cheery like this kitchen she would love living here. She sat down to read the lease. Straightforward, except—she looked up at him, standing beside her, smelling way too good—her brain went blank. She shifted in her chair and focused on the lease.

"Um, it says nothing about yard maintenance."

He turned a chair backward and straddled the seat. "My dad does the mowing and trimming around here."

"Could I tend to the flower beds?"

"Sure, if you want. They're a mess. Flowers were my wife's job."

But not anymore? She swallowed the lump that returned whenever he smiled at her. Time for a mental subject change. MaryRose peeked into the next room and admired the cozy pine furniture. Yes. This house was perfect.

"I love it already. Did you furnish it?"

"My daughter, Andrea, took care of that. Feel free to change anything you wish."

"I doubt I'll need to." MaryRose dug into her purse, retrieved the check, and held it up. "This isn't local."

"I think I'll know where to find you if there's a problem." He raised his eyebrows and gave her the most charming crooked grin.

MaryRose swallowed—hard—as she signed the lease and then slid it and the check across the table. His hand brushed hers when he reached for them. It felt like an electric current raced up her arm. She jerked her hand back.

"You okay?" He gave her the much too charming grin again.

Oh no. He felt it too. She slid her chair back. Most definitely time to get lover-boy out of there. "I'm fine, a bit tired." Yeah, right.

The sideways grin remained. He folded the check inside the lease, pushed the papers into his shirt pocket and then stood. "I planned to have a dishwasher here by now. I'll let you know when it arrives."

"Thank you."

MaryRose stood and rubbed shoulder muscles taut as guitar strings. Bone weary and tense, she would give the house a once-over, and then grab her overnight bag. The rest could wait until tomorrow. After all, it was Friday, so she could take all weekend to move in.

Dapple ran to the door and barked. MaryRose turned and saw Randall stepping back on the porch. Her breath caught. Was this going to happen each time she saw her landlord? That could be problematic.

"Is-is there anything else?"

"I wanted to let you know I'll install it when it gets here."

"Install—the dishwasher?"

"Yep. It'll work better if it's installed. Oh, and the washer and dryer are in the closet in the bathroom."

"Not sure I've ever seen the laundry room in the closet."

He kept standing there. How was she supposed to concentrate?

"Is there anything else?"

"I thought you might like help unloading your car before it storms again."

His eyes, the color of Nana's blue topaz ring, almost implored her to need his help. But she didn't have the energy to make nice right now, especially with someone who looked as good as he did.

She squared her shoulders and set her jaw the way both her father and Papa Shane always had when they met whomever she dated. "I think I'll get my overnight bag for now. I can do the rest tomorrow."

"Suit yourself. Call if you need me." He hustled up the hill.

As MaryRose stepped off the porch a big fat raindrop smacked her cheek. She rushed to the car and grabbed the overnight bag and Papa's gift. By the time she made it back to the porch the rain began again with a vengeance. She locked the kitchen door, and then stepped into the front room. A wall of windows overlooked the lake. Probably a lovely view on a moonlit night, but now it looked like a black abyss lit by an occasional white strobe of lightning. She closed the curtains to keep from looking into the darkness.

MaryRose walked around her little cottage. Three rooms and a bath, simple but cozy. Mr. Cobb's daughter must have a keen eye for detail.

The furniture was casual but immaculate. It complemented the rustic pine paneling in the living room. The sunny yellow in the kitchen and the sky blue in the bedroom brought a touch of the outdoors inside. Everything was perfect.

MaryRose lifted Papa Shane's gift and crossed the living room to the big fluffy chair by the front door. Setting the box on the floor in front of her, she dropped into the chair. Dapple curled in a tight ball on the rug beside the box.

She opened the card first.

Dear Lassie,

The day you told me you had to move it grieved my heart so much.
I tackled the garage shelves with the energy of a man gone mad. Surely I threw away some things I should have kept. Thank the Lord; I didn't toss the old box tucked behind my tax records. Your nana and I thought this was lost in the attic fire. Guess it was here all along. I opened the old box and found your great-great-gramma Rose's missing journals. You can bet I'll be looking more care-fully on my shelves now. Figured you might get a smile

opening this box. Time for you to follow your own
dreams, it is.
And it's praying for you I am,

Papa Shane

MaryRose traced her fingers around the edges of the box.
Sweet tears trickled down her cheeks. She opened the box and
inhaled the scent of old leather. The journals. Her family history
was intact.

CHAPTER 2

*M*aryRose stared inside the non-descript cardboard box in front of her. It might as well have been a treasure chest filled with priceless jewels. There were six journals. Nana had only ever talked about one. Maybe that was because the one on top was the only one labeled and dated.

The journals had been stored in an old cardboard box in Papa Shane's garage and yet they were well preserved—which would make it easier to transcribe them onto her computer. Sometime soon she would have to purchase a fireproof safe.

Reaching into the box, she lifted the first journal out and hugged it to her chest. There was time to read a few pages before calling it a day.

~~~~

Rose Emily Thomas, Sunday, April 23, 1865

Today was my sixteenth birthday. Momma gave me this

book. Papa shook his head and grumbled. He told me I should be sewin, doin my chores, learnin how to cook. Always did say I had no need of learnin. After church he got the confoundest look on his face.

He stared up the road and told me to stay in my Sunday dress and go fix my hair, company was comin. I didn't see a soul. And Momma didn't know what he was talking about.

I did what he said. Then I went out back and sat on my swing under the big oak tree. Wasn't long till he called me back in.

This day I won't be forgettin. When I got in the house, he wiped a smudge from my cheek and told me to go into the parlor.

And there was a man, couldn't be a lot older than me, but he was a man. He stood as I entered. Goodness gracious, he looked scared half to death. I still don't know what the regular pallor of his skin would be if he wasn't about to pass out.

"Miss Rose, my name is Patrick Elliott. With your father's permission, I've come to court you."

I don't know what happened next. Honest. Maybe God will help me remember someday. I hope I didn't embarrass myself. Because the next thing I knew, I was on the settee and he was handin me some of Momma's tea.

I could hardly believe what he told me. Supposedly this man, Patrick, had a dream about me. What kind of man dreams about meetin a woman, gets up in the mornin, dresses in what he wore in the dream, walks to a stranger's house, introduces himself and says he's there to court the man's daughter? Evidently, my intended does.

What kind of father allows this? Evidently mine. Papa says he also had a dream—so my future is determined by two men's dreams? Was that really you, God?

While I admit the man is pleasant to look at, and everyone over in Hertford says he is a wonderful circuit preacher, I don't know about this. I asked Momma if I could go spend the summer with Gramma in Aracoma, West Virginia. First she said no, cause they's still too much unrest on account of Mr. Lincoln's War. Then she kissed the top of my head and said she'd talk to Papa.

I need to get away. I need to think. When I come back, there will be a November weddin out on the river. I'll be a preacher's wife? I'll be a wife? I'll be—I am frightened.

I like this book. Will my betrothed think it's silly? I think Mama is the only one who understands me. Some days I sit here in a house full of family and feel alone. Will it be that way when I am married too?

Lord, help me. Amen.

~~~~

MaryRose closed the journal then wiped her eyes.

"Don't know which is worse Gramma Rose—your loneliness in the midst of family or mine without family."

MaryRose sat on her back porch sipping mint tea. She'd spent all day Saturday unpacking and arranging the house. Everything looked in order and she should be ready to start her new job tomorrow.

She shook her head. *Almost* everything was in order. She'd shoved the last box into the corner in the kitchen behind the pantry door. Six months ago, if someone had told her a box labeled 'family pictures' would unravel her day she'd have laughed. But six months ago most of the people in the pictures still lived. She blew the air from her lungs and looked toward the lake. Tackling that box could wait for another day.

The fence gate creaked as a young lady stepped through it into the backyard.

"I'm Andrea, Randall's daughter. I wanted to meet you on Friday, but I was in Morgantown, registering for vet school."

Andrea stopped at the porch and extended a slender hand. "It's nice to meet you."

Andrea was taller than MaryRose's five-foot-eight frame and had eyes as blue as her father's.

MaryRose shook her hand.

Dapple ran around the yard and skidded to a stop on Andrea's feet. His whole body wagged. Andrea scooped him into her arms and was rewarded with sloppy puppy kisses. "He's quite affectionate, isn't he?" She held his mouth closed for a moment. "I know you're barely moved in, but we're having our Sunday cookout. Why don't you come on down to the lake and meet everyone?"

Hang out with a happy family all afternoon when she'd so recently lost her own? She couldn't even open a box of pictures. Her throat tightened, and her eyes welled.

"Thanks for the offer. I'll take a rain check. I want to finish unpacking."

Andrea put Dapple down. "I could help you."

A tidal wave of melancholy washed over MaryRose. She couldn't look at Mom's and Dad's smiling faces, Nana's wink, Sean on their wedding day, or little baby Heather by herself, much less share those moments with someone she'd just met.

Her chest burned. "Thanks again. But I am a bit fatigued. Plus I start my new job tomorrow."

"Okay then. You'll miss a good time, but I understand." Andrea opened the door then faced MaryRose. "Daddy's stopping by in a few minutes. He has something for you."

Andrea scooted down the hill as Randall arrived. He stepped onto the porch in one stride, and then pulled the largest bouquet of daisies she'd ever seen from behind his back. "Got a jar?"

Daisies. Of all the possible flowers, why them? Sean—their wedding flowers—her flowers. Her mouth went dry. She couldn't speak but managed to wave him inside before grabbing the countertop to get her balance.

"MaryRose?" Concern etched his brow.

"I'm a bit tired. The flowers are lovely, thank you." She placed them in a pitcher, added water, and set it in the center of the table.

"They grow along the road near the construction site where we worked yesterday. I thought of you when I saw them." His cheeks reddened. "Is—is there anything I could help you with?"

"I have it all in control." Kinda.

Randall opened the door and stopped mid-step on the porch. "MaryRose, you're welcome to join us all at the lake."

"Some other time maybe."

"See you around, then." He walked off.

She stared at the daisies. No matter how hard she tried to block them out, Papa Shane's words fairly screamed in her mind. "Lassie, God has another for ya. And you'll know 'tis him

15

when he shows up at your door with an armful of the daisies you love."

She wiped her sweaty palms on her jeans.

Dapple's frantic bark interrupted her thoughts. After the Cobbs had finished their cookout and all was quiet by the lake she'd let the puppy loose in her yard. Didn't take him long to get into trouble. She hustled outside.

"Dapple?"

Another growl. But it had a different sound, almost panicked.

"Hey, Buddy, where are you?" She rounded the front of the house. Another growl, then he barked in a tone she'd not heard before. She circled the yard. Where'd he go?

"DAPPLE!"

She pushed aside old rosebushes at the front of the house and ignored the thorns tearing her flesh. Something was wrong. She called him again.

A harsh staccato, almost like maracas, erupted from beneath the porch. Dapple's tail jutted out from underneath the front steps. She squatted and peered into the blackness, clicking her tongue.

"Dapple, what are you doing under there? Come back."

He yipped and crawled farther under the porch. Growls continued and a strange musky smell wafted from beyond him. Something was wrong. It sounded like a thousand cicadas chirped nearby, but she didn't think it was bugs. She wiped her brow and licked dry lips with a sandpaper tongue.

"MaryRose, don't move." Randall's voice boomed behind her. "Forget the dog."

Was he crazy? Dapple needed her. She scooted closer to the porch. Dapple yipped again. This time something moved. Mary-

Rose froze. A black rattlesnake slithered out of the ground a few feet from her legs.

"D-d-dapple, stay."

The puppy howled.

A second snake lunged. Pain speared her ankle. The snake pulled back and struck again. Another shot of teeth-gritting agony sent sharp, burning pain up her calf. She tried to kick the snake away, but her leg wouldn't work. Venom seared her foot as nausea rose in waves. Had to escape. Legs wouldn't obey.

"I said, don't move."

A gunshot exploded in her ears. Rocks and dust splayed around her feet.

Thousands of pins pricked the back of her skull, and heavy fingers squeezed her brain. The trees and sky spun in rapid circles as her world inverted.

Strong arms scooped her up, and she rested her face against a warm chest that smelled of spice and sawdust. Sean—no, he's dead—Randall—a shroud cocooned her and darkness overcame the light.

CHAPTER 3

*M*aryRose shifted the pillow under her leg and a zinger of pain stabbed her ankle. She remembered little about the past ten days, but everyone told her she'd almost died. Everyone said rattlers don't strike twice. The one under her porch did. She got enough poison in her system to kill her. It had knocked her out for four days. But it didn't kill her. Thankfully.

Randall visited daily. Andrea took care of Dapple and called Papa Shane and the boss at MaryRose's new job. Five days later, Friday afternoon, Randall brought her home. A week of her life gone like that. A family she had only met last week taking care of her. And her landlord rescuing her from the pit of vipers. So much for having a calm and peaceful first week at her new home.

Then there was the home care nurse, Trudy Trumble, coming over to do wound care today. That lady was a character. Her hair was dyed and fingernails painted the loudest neon turquoise MaryRose had even seen. Trudy's personality was about as bright.

The landline on the kitchen wall rang. Ugh. Why in the

world did she choose the one place in the country her cell signal didn't exist to settle down? Even on the coverage map it showed Lake Nolan as a dead zone. Yet everywhere she went she saw others on their phones. Probably time to change carriers.

She limped to the kitchen and answered the phone in time to prevent the call going to voice mail.

"Hello?"

"Hey, it's me." Her best friend, Missy Greene, chirped in her ears. "You said you'd call me by the end of last weekend and let me know if you got all moved in. Now math isn't really my forte, but that weekend was eleven days ago. And what's up with this new number? Your cell phone goes straight to voice mail."

"I have to get a new cell service. This week became more complicated than I ever imagined. I got home yesterday."

"What are you talking about?"

"This could take a while."

"I got the time."

MaryRose relayed the story.

"I can't believe you went through all of that by yourself. If I'd known, I'd have ditched rehearsals and been there to help."

"I couldn't let you do that. Your show opens in a month, and you couldn't miss rehearsals. I'm okay. Randall and Andrea got me home. Papa Shane managed to smooth the delay with my editor. And, I have Trudy Trumble."

Missy burst into laughter. "What's a Trudy Trumble? Sounds like a character from a children's show."

"Trudy is the hospitality lady-slash-nurse at Charleston Memorial who sat with me every day, even when I was sleeping. She's coming here for wound care. Honest, I think she'd move in and be my mother if I let her."

"Sounds like our seventh grade Sunday School teacher. Remember her?"

"Exactly." Phew. One mention of home and MaryRose's

chest hurt. Her ankle might be screaming for her to sit, but her heart yelled escape.

"MaryRose? What's wrong?"

"Nothing."

"Liar. Don't you shut me out. Sorry I mentioned home. I know what you're thinking—"

"Then you'll understand why I'm hanging up now."

MaryRose ended the call and slid to the floor. The emptiness sucked her in and she found no reason to fight it. She massaged the swollen skin around the wound. At least her ankle was soothed.

Footsteps across the porch startled Dapple, and he charged the door like an angry Pit Bull Terrier. Then he stopped barking and jumped at the screen.

Trudy peeked through the door. "Well, honey, what in tarnation are you doin' on the floor?" MaryRose waved her in but didn't move to get up.

Trudy lowered herself to the floor and opened her medicine bag. "Personally, I always took more to chair sitting. But since we're here, we're here."

"You're a character."

"That's what I tell my Walt every day." She tilted MaryRose's chin up and gazed at her. "Those eyes get greener when you cry. Tell me what broke your heart today, dear?"

MaryRose looked away.

"Okay then. I'll get started on this wound. But, honey, remember you talked a lot in that delirium. I probably already know whatever it is you don't want to talk about." She wrinkled her nose and sniffed. "What in the world is cooking?"

"Honey and violets."

Trudy cocked her head. "And you think *I'm* a character. I'll take the bait. What's honey and violet soup for?"

"The bite. Today I mixed it in my tea. Tomorrow I'll start

applying it to the wound. It helps with circulation and reduces scarring."

"Um-hm. I'm to be put out of a job by honey and violets?"

"That's one way to look at it."

"All righty then. I best do a good job of doctoring you today."

Trudy removed the bandage and applied the antibiotic.

The only evidence that the bite was improving was remembering how horrid it looked the first time MaryRose saw it. Two stiletto-sharp fangs sunk in the ankle twice. Now her lower leg and ankle looked like they got caught in a machine that chewed on them.

Trudy's feather-light touch soothed as she cleaned the wound. She applied ointment, then stretched MaryRose's leg out. She touched the wound, making soft circles with her fingertips. Warm, tingling energy flowed into the wound.

"Ahh. That's amazing."

"It's called healing hands. Learned it in one of my massage classes. It helps a body heal itself."

MaryRose concentrated on the circling sensations in her ankle. Trudy slowly changed position and massaged her foot and leg above and below the bandage. She rested her head against the wall and closed her eyes. "You have the gentlest touch."

"Comes from years of helping my little poodles birth their babies. Got good ears, too, if you want to unload what's tearing you apart."

She looked away.

"I'm just saying."

MaryRose flexed her ankle, pleased to find it wasn't as stiff as yesterday.

"Sometimes it's a lot. I moved here for a new start, was supposed to start work this week. Instead, I met a den of rattlesnakes and got stuck in the hospital. I was expecting to have my first assignment to work on this weekend. Seems a long weekend looms ahead."

"You got flower beds out there in need of a makeover. And the outdoors will do wonders for a healing body." Trudy clicked her tongue. "How about I go with you to Charleston on Monday when you check in at your new job? I'd be happy to show you around some."

"I couldn't ask you to do that."

"Didn't hear you ask, heard me offer. Sometimes we get a little too much alone. Why not let me be that old lady friend who nags you to death?"

"You don't nag me."

"Give me time, girl, give me time. Call me anytime you need me. What time shall I pick you up on Monday?"

"Ten o'clock?"

Trudy stood and kissed the top of her head.

"Nana used to kiss me like that."

"Yep, it's a mom thing. I'll let myself out now."

Company and a bit of sight-seeing on Monday sounded grand, actually. It gave her something to look forward to as the quiet weekend loomed. Working on the flower beds was an excellent idea. It would keep her busy enough to ignore the carton of photos in the corner like a Pandora's Box mocking.

Long after Trudy left, MaryRose remained on the floor. Dapple paced between her and the door. Poor guy wanted to go out and play. But before she could get up, Andrea tapped lightly on the screen door and peeked in.

She winked at MaryRose. "Got room on that floor for me?"

MaryRose stretched her legs and managed to stand without her sleeping feet giving out. She waved Andrea in. "I think I've had enough floor time."

23

"I brought you a treat." Andrea stepped inside and placed a foil-covered plate on the counter. The aroma of brownies filled the kitchen. She then scooped Dapple into her arms and received his customary kisses.

"Did you brush his teeth?"

"No, he did. Knocked over the basket of mint I gathered and ate a bunch before I got it all picked up. He is such a brat. Yesterday Trudy brought her poodles with her, and he cornered the white one in the only mud puddle in my flower bed. This puppy may well be the ruination of all order in my life."

"Isn't that what puppies are supposed to do?" Andrea set him back on the floor. "Don't you love Trudy?"

"She is a most interesting woman."

"What color is her hair this week?"

"This week?" MaryRose picked up two glasses from the dish drainer and set them on the counter. "You mean it isn't always that strange shade of turquoise?"

"You met her on a mild week. She breeds and shows those poodles. Her hair is always the same color as the dogs' toenails and ribbons. She takes accessorizing to a new level."

"Well, I'll be."

"She's a dear. Every time she comes into Doc's office she tells me she can't wait for me to be a *veterinarian*. That's another four years away."

"Who is Doc?"

"He's the local vet. I work for him. I'll probably come back and work for him after I graduate."

Andrea removed the foil from the plate. "Got milk to go with these brownies?"

"Yep."

MaryRose poured milk into the glasses and placed them and the plate of brownies on the table.

Andrea spoke between bites and gulps of milk. "I love this house. For years this old place was falling apart. Mommy always wanted to fix it up. I think Daddy did it as kind of a tribute to her." She wiped at her milk mustache. "He did a good job."

"And you decorated well."

"Early American yard-sale décor is pretty easy to find."

"I've always liked milk crates."

"Then you and Daddy will get along fine."

Get along? He was her landlord. She didn't have to do anything but pay him the rent. Why was warmth spreading across her cheeks? She cleared her throat and sipped her milk.

"I do love this little cabin. I wonder if it's log underneath the sideboards."

"Nope. It was a tack shed long before the lake was dammed."

"It reminds me of the stories I heard about the log cabin my great-great gramma Rose lived in."

"Where was that?"

"Not real sure. Pa used to talk about visiting when he was a little boy. He always said he didn't know if he could ever find it all tucked back in the hollers of those huge mountains. I know it's around here somewhere. Gramma Rose moved here right after the Civil War. West Virginia hadn't been a state long."

"What was her last name?"

"Elliott."

Andrea's brow furrowed. "That sounds familiar."

"What do you mean?" MaryRose's heart skipped.

"There's something familiar about that name. You'll have to ask my grandmother. She'll know who to ask."

Andrea got up and walked around the kitchen. "I like the way you arranged." She peeked in the open cabinets, ran her fingers across the row of small bottles lining the bottom shelf, and then picked one up. "What are these?"

MaryRose chuckled. Keeping up with Andrea's subject changes was like trying to catch a hummingbird. And it was almost as entertaining as watching the little birds at the feeders Nana had in her garden.

"Do you always do that?"

"Do what?"

"Change subjects without warning? I'm never sure which question to answer."

A blush spread over the girl's cheeks. "Daddy says I need to breathe between subjects, or at least say new paragraph. I'm sorry. I shouldn't be so nosy." She placed the bottle back on the shelf then sat at the table.

"Curious is not nosy. There's a difference." MaryRose picked up the bottle and handed it to her. "This is rosemary. I use it to flavor chicken, spice a salad, steep for tea to help me sleep, or make a hair rinse."

The girl's blue eyes widened. "One herb does all that? How do you know this stuff? Are all these bottles filled with herbs?"

"That's a lot of questions all at once. I grew, dried, and harvested these from my garden back home. Ma and Nana taught me all about them. They used plants for everything."

"Oh, you mean like spells and stuff?" Andrea sat back down at the table. "I read all about New Age stuff in my friend Jamie's life book."

"Life book? I don't know what that is. And, no, I don't mean witchcraft or New Age. This is actually biblical. Long before pharmaceutical companies, people used plants for medicine. Are you familiar with the Bible?"

"Not much. Used to go to church, but not since I was ten." Andrea twirled a strand of hair around her index finger. "Not since Mommy died. Once she was gone, church wasn't important to me and Daddy anymore. My Grandma goes, though."

"I look forward to meeting her." That closed the subject of the young lady's mother. MaryRose reached for a brownie. "Mmm. They're still warm."

Andrea grabbed one and popped it into her mouth. After wiping the crumbs and swallowing, she grinned. "I left a plate on the counter for Daddy. Knowing him, he won't see them.

He'll smell them, see the mixing bowl in the sink and come straight down here all upset that I didn't leave any for him. He's such a man. Mommy used to say even if there was a rattlesnake in front of him he wouldn't see it.

"Daddy hates them, really doesn't want them on his property. Probably blames himself you got bit, because he didn't find that nest before you moved in."

"It's not his fault."

"I know that, and so does he, but he still blames himself. That's my dad for ya."

MaryRose picked up another brownie. "Are there a lot of rattlers around here?"

"Yes. Some people claim they're the state reptile."

MaryRose shuddered. No comfort in that answer.

She studied Andrea. Except for the eyes, she didn't resemble her father much. "Was your mother blonde?"

"Yep." Her brows furrowed. "I'm sorry. I should say, yes ma'am. But you feel more my age—more like a friend."

"How old are you?"

"Twenty-one. You?"

MaryRose winked at her. "I'm thirty-two."

"You're not as old as Daddy. He's forty-one. By the way, he's all gaga over you."

That last statement clogged in her throat as she tried to swallow her last bite of brownie. MaryRose reached for her napkin after coughing on crumbs and knocked her milk over. She jumped up to stop the milk from running into her lap, but balancing on her good ankle didn't work. She grabbed the table to prevent falling, but her chair fell backward with a thud.

Dapple yipped and backed under the table where he discovered the milk puddling on the floor.

Andrea reached across the table to wipe the milk with her napkin and knocked her own glass over.

Andrea laughed so hard she snorted, and MaryRose couldn't

catch her breath. She was holding her side as she turned toward the counter for more paper towels.

And saw Randall at her back door.

Words got stuck. She barely got her breath out. Her landlord looked like a construction Adonis. She waved him inside willing away the blush on her cheeks.

"Hey, Daddy." Andrea's spoke through the brownie mouthful.

As he entered the small kitchen, MaryRose stepped towards the counter. A zinger of pain buckled her ankle. She staggered into his strong arms.

Not again. She looked into his face and saw concern—and something else. Ducking her head, she whispered, "Thanks."

"Is this to be a habit?"

If he didn't release her soon, her brain would turn to mud.

Dapple chose that moment to realize someone had entered the room. He raced from under the table, tracking milk across the floor, and charged Randall. He stood at the man's feet barking and growling. Each bark raised his tiny feet from the floor.

Randall released his hold on her. His eyes glinted. "Maybe you should call off your guard dog." He righted the chair and reached for a brownie. "Were you planning on letting your old dad have any of these?"

Andrea elbowed MaryRose. They started laughing again.

He frowned. "Did I miss something?"

"There's a plate of them on the counter by the microwave. Did you even look?" Andrea got up and hugged him.

"Nope. Followed my nose. Are you coming home soon? I have supper ready."

MaryRose wiped the last of the milk off the table and tossed the towel into the sink. "I didn't realize the time. I won't keep your daughter any longer."

"It's only supper because I stopped at Sarah's Diner and

picked up takeout. Good food. I'll have to take you there sometime."

"I—um—I'd like that." Was he asking her out or being polite?

He stepped away from the table and tripped over the chair he just righted. Andrea grabbed his hand. "Come on, Daddy. We better get out of here before one of you gets hurt." At the door she backward waved. "MaryRose, I can't wait to find out what to do with all of those herbs."

Randall held the door for his daughter and flashed a heart-melting smile towards MaryRose. "Are you feeling all right today?"

No. Can't think straight. Cologne smelled too good. "I'm a little better each day, thank you." If only she could catch her breath.

Andrea leaned against her dad as they stepped outside and walked up the hill.

MaryRose pressed her hand against her chest. She'd been with her dad like that.

CHAPTER 4

$\mathcal{M}$aryRose leaned against the doorjamb long after father and daughter had topped the hill. Closing her eyes and inhaling the fragrance of late blooming lilac, she could easily be in Nana's backyard. Crickets chirping from the flower beds took her back to summer days at Hertford. The soft rumble of a motor boat in the cove was like hearing Pa and Papa come in from a day of fishing in the sound.

Instead of filling her heart with pleasant reminders, her memories left it hollow. She stared at the sky. Why were things so unfair?

Silence. Again.

She stepped inside. The old wood screen door banged shut like Ma's always did and plucked her last nerve. She dropped into a chair and sobbed.

Once the deluge stopped, MaryRose wiped her eyes and admired the vase of daisies in the center of the table. She touched the velvety petals. What made Papa Shane say what he did about a man bringing her daisies? It was a coincidence. Her step-grandfather didn't know what he was talking about.

She'd spent most of the day avoiding journals and photos.

She had a whole weekend to focus on the eighteen hundreds and Gramma Rose. A mug of chamomile tea with honey would go well with journal reading.

The phone rang. It would be easy to let it go to voice mail, but it might be important. She picked it up on the fourth ring.

"Ms. Elliott?"

"Yes."

"Please hold for Mr. Little."

Who? Before she could ask, the phone clicked.

Then a strong voice spoke, "Ms. Elliott?"

"Yes?"

"This is William Little from *Mountain and Country Life*. I was sorry to hear about your tangle with the rattler. I trust you are mending by now?"

"I'm doing quite well, thank—"

"I've been assigned as your editorial supervisor, but . . ." he cleared his throat, "To be perfectly honest, I don't share the same enthusiasm about your whole Kitchen Cosmetics articles as the rest of the staff. Sure hope you're prepared to wow me. You will be here Monday as planned, correct?"

Her face felt as hot as the fire burning in her chest. Arrogant man. No cause for his rudeness. She ran her fingers through her hair and they snagged on a tangle.

"I assure you, sir, your boss—"she emphasized the word, *boss*, "—most definitely believes in the column. He told me he's thrilled with it." She bit her tongue. It would feel good to give this man a piece of her mind. She puffed out a deep breath. "And since he placed you as my editor, he must also have confidence in you. I look forward to meeting you on Monday, Mr. Little."

"Likewise. Good day."

After his phone clicked off, she threw hers on the floor.

The whole magazine thing was Ma's dream, a plan for spending her free time in retirement. Thanks to that drunk driver it never happened. She would honor her mother's dream and make it happen. Not even a snooty editor would stand in her way.

She plopped on the sofa and wrestled the afghan around her shoulders, then opened the journal.

~~~~

June 8, 1865

Today Papa rides with me to Gramma's. I was surprised Momma convinced him I need this trip. He wants me home to work all summer. And escortin me here keeps him away from his cotton crops. Ma told him James Paul is old enough now to help.

I wish Ma had taught me how to make a man see things her way. It might help me when I become a—wife. Not sure I like that word to describe me.

I cain't write much. Papa is tending the horses and I am to be makin our beds. He will be displeased I brought this book.

Lord, please keep us safe. Make the Indians we meet be friendly. Keep my family safe while I am away. And, help me prepare to marry.

Oh, be with Patrick too. Amen.

~~~~

July 1, 1865

So much has happened. So much to write about but
Gramma wants me to conserve lantern oil. I have never
seen country like this. The mountains are as high as the
clouds. Why, sometimes the clouds are lower than them.
I never thought Papa's wagon would make it through the
pass much less up and down those steep mountains.

Then there's the way they talk. I got the meanest look
yesterday when I forgot and called this Virginia. It's hard
to remember that part of my family was on the other side
of the war. Papa says I best be mindin what I say because
still waters run deep. Never did know for sure what that
meant. And sometimes, I cannot for the life of me understand them. Gramma says I will fit in, but sometimes I do
not know if I fit anywhere.

I am the only person I know who loves books the way I
do. And who ever heard of a girl writin like I do? No, I
don't fit. I wonder if Patrick will decide I do not fit him
either . . .

I guess I should write Patrick a letter every now and
then. How long will it take the letters to even make it to
him from the church offices? And more than that, what
will I say?

Lord, help me learn from Gramma and find a way to fit
in somewhere. Anywhere will do. Amen.

~~~~

MaryRose ran her fingers over the words. She could feel
Gramma Rose's loneliness. The page crinkled as she turned it.
The smell of old leather and dried paper filled her sinuses.

Dapple jumped onto the sofa and curled into a tight little circle in her lap. She wiped a lone tear from her cheek.

~~~~~~

July 2, 1865

Just walkin around here wears me out. Nothin is flat. Everything is up and down. Why, I never saw gardens growin on the side of hills before. I caint decide whether these mountains or the ocean are prettiest. Why, I caint even decide where I'd live if I could choose.

But that don't matter. I don't have a choice. Papa made it for me. Papa says it's God what made it. I guess I'm not so sure bout that. Gramma says if I keep prayin God will make sure my heart knows what's best.

There are so many plants to learn, plants we don't have in North Carolina. Course, it won't matter much when I go home, but still. God created so much. I think Gramma is tryin to teach me a lifetime of knowledge in one summer.

I know something new. Poison ivy makes me as itchy and blistery as poison oak. I never knew they was two of them. But when I was out pickin violets I reached into the plant on the ground. Shiny leaves of three. Ain't never gonna touch that stuff again. My arms have been itchin somethin fierce. I used up all Gramma's witch hazel tryin to kill the itch. Guess I have to gather some more of that too.

This mornin I was on the porch watchin the sun come up over the mountain. Pink like I never saw before. And lo and behold a bear walked right into the yard. Was all I could do not to scream. I sat there and watched it steal the fish Grampa had hangin outside the smoke house. It saw me and walked off. Gramma says we better watch. Now that it's found the food, it will be back. Don't know as I want to see that thing at night.

I wonder how Ma and Pa are. Gramma gave me a letter from Patrick after supper tonight. The neighbor, Mr. Estep, brought it from town with him. Gramma says if I write him back tonight we can post it when we go in town tomorrow. I read his letter out by the river before dark. He didn't say much, but I think he is a mite anxious about marryin too. I wrote him back. Had no idea what to write, so I told him mostly about things here. I pray for him every night now. Maybe that will help my heart be ready for a weddin. I did send him a poem about mornin too.

This mornin I think a piece of heaven
Came down here and touched earth.
Sunlight shinin in the grass
Dew like diamonds of great worth.
Birds and chickens sounded happy
Made me want to sing along.
It's mornins like this I hope
My summer here is long.

I need to sleep. Tomorrow we go into Aracoma to sell the eggs and milk and get some supplies. Gramma says we'll surely see the Indians. I'm afraid of that, but she says they are friends. Sometimes there's too much new stuff for me to sort.

Be with me, Lord Jesus. Keep my family safe. And keep
Patrick safe on his circuit journey wherever it takes him.
Amen.

p.s. I will put Patrick's letters in here and save them too.

~~~~

June 10,1865

~~Dear miss~~My Dear Rose,

May I call you that? I will, after all, be your husband in a
few short months. The hours I passed in your company
the day of our first meeting were the best of my four and
twenty years. I feel your destiny and mine have been
forever entwined.

It was with deep regret of heart and spirit I left your
sweet company that day. And as I pack my saddlebags, I
know not when I shall return from this circuit. But I go
with a new joy in my heart that upon my return we shall
be wed. I shall pray for you each day of my journey.

It is my hope that I will make you happy and in so doing,
be made happy myself.
Until next we meet, I am yours affectionately,

Patrick Michael Elliott

~~~~

MaryRose closed the journal. Joy and sorrow battled for
control in her heart. She dragged the photo box out of the closet

37

into the center of the room. All she had to do was open it to see Mom, Dad, Nana, and Grampa again. She could absorb the mischievous light in Sean's eyes on their wedding day and view Heather's ruddy face the day she was born.

What good would it do to stare at lifeless pictures? The longing to look at the familiar faces and hold the photos to her heart was overshadowed by the reminder that everyone she loved was eventually taken from her.

She kicked the box. Glass shattered.

The phone interrupted her sulk. She never got this many calls in Hertford. She limped into the living room and eased onto the sofa before answering the call. Hopefully the new cell carrier's signal would work.

"Hello, Lassie." Papa Shane's voice tickled her ear. She could almost hear his smile and smell the cherry aroma of his pipe tobacco.

"Hey, Papa."

"How are ya farin'?"

"I'm doing better." She lied. "I was taking a break from reading the journals when the phone rang." Kind of.

"Are ya sure I'm not needin' to come and care for ya?"

"I really am fine. Andrea and Randall keep checking on me. And the lady from the hospital, Trudy, is taking me to Charleston for my first work meeting."

"I've been prayin' for ya."

"Thanks. Other than a lonely moment here and there, I am good. Feel like I belong."

She looked out the windows overlooking the lake. The setting sun cast dancing sparkles across the water. If she tried hard enough maybe she'd believe her own words.

"'Tis a good thing to find a place to belong."

"Papa, I couldn't stay there anymore."

"I do know that. And if ya have need of me, I'll be there in a heartbeat." He took a deep breath. "You'll stay here with me when ya come next month, aye?"

"I hope to see Missy next weekend. Haven't seen her since she started rehearsals. I can't imagine her living in a cabin in a state park all summer."

"Aye. There's a city girl if ever I knew one. Give her a hug for me, will ya?"

"I sure will."

He puffed his pipe, which she knew meant he was planning his next words.

"And what will ya be doin' about next month? You'll come back, aye?"

She swallowed. "Why would I do that?"

"Lassie, you need to. You must bring this to an end."

She made a fist and punched the arm of the chair. "Bring it to an end? Really? That happened out there in Route 17. I'll not be back for the trial. I have no need to see that man."

"Anger grows dark, bitter roots. He took my wife too, ya know."

She gripped the phone till her knuckles turned white. It took every ounce of self-control to refrain from screaming in his ears. "Your wife. My Nana. How can you be so kind and forgiving? Go ahead. Forget Nana's horrid death if you want. I'll stay here, thank you kindly."

He exhaled slowly. "I'll keep prayin' for ya."

"I'll be okay. God guides me."

"Does He now? And would ya be tryin' to convince me—or yourself?"

"What's that supposed to mean?"

"Lassie, it means I know God's leading ya to move on. But things must be accounted for first. He canna build upon hate and anger. You canna run from them."

"I'm not running. I moved."

She heard him breathing. He probably had the pipe clenched in his teeth as he rubbed his chin with his index finger.

"Don't be lettin' that accident take your life too. Listen to the Holy Spirit and do what He tells ya to do. I'll be prayin God will remove that heart of stone from ya. You come back for the trial in June."

"That won't happen, Papa." She could almost hear her heart slam shut.

"Be watchin' which doors ya close on the Lord, child."

Did the man have the luck of the Irish or was he reading her thoughts? "I'll pray. That's all I promise."

"That's all ya need to do. Now I best be goin'. The Lord be with ya, MaryRose."

"You too, Papa."

MaryRose dropped the phone on the coffee table. He was probably right. But she couldn't even unpack a bunch of photographs. How could anyone expect her to sit in that courtroom? Let Papa Shane go and be all kind and pastoral to the man. She'd not go back to North Carolina to hear anything that drunk driver had to say.

MaryRose walked to the kitchen and grabbed Dapple's leash. A walk would be good for both of them. The dog almost dragged her to the lake. She slowed along the fence. The flower beds desperately needed tending. A few daisies peeked through the rails. And there, suffocating in the weeds, was a pink rose. She touched a tender petal. That bush needed drastic pruning to survive.

She bent down and pulled a few weeds. The dandelions stubbornly held firm. Jaws clenched, shoulders tight, she yanked once more. The weed gave way. MaryRose lost her balance and stumbled backwards. Fine. This was not a good time to try and salvage a rosebush. One prick from a thorn would tweak her last nerve.

Once they made it to the shoreline, she released Dapple from his leash so he could run along the water's edge. She followed behind him.

The mountains, the lake, her cabin, her yard, and everything about her new home was lovely. How she longed to show it all to Ma and Nana.

CHAPTER 5

*M*aryRose hit Select All and deleted the entire page she'd just written. So much for having her first column written and ready for tomorrow's meeting. Thank heavens for this new computer. For all the deleting she'd done that morning, a tree would have been sacrificed by now in the days of typewriters.

Maybe her pitiable writing was God's way of telling her she should have gone to church. But she couldn't do it, not today. A new church and new people on Mother's Day, of all days? She had no mother or grandmother anymore and had never had a chance to enjoy motherhood before they lost sweet Heather. No way could she have borne the celebrations at church on Mother's Day. Even though the little private worship she tried was hollow like the log across the creek where she and Sean used to sit, it was better than being in church.

She didn't think about Sean as much. No, that wasn't entirely true. Now she was able to remember happy memories without it breaking her. Yet not thinking about him created a new kind of emptiness inside. Maybe that was the natural process of mourning.

Leaning back in the chair and closing her eyes, she saw him sitting on the log beside her. Proposing. He'd gotten so excited when she said yes that he dropped the ring into the creek. His green eyes lit up when he fished it out of the crawdad's pincers. Mom and Nana had stood on the porch waiting for them to return, since he'd asked for their blessings first.

Mom, Dad, Nana, Grampa, Sean, and Heather. That last one wasn't fair, not at all. She and Sean hadn't planned to have a baby but were overjoyed when she got pregnant. And then they lost her. Why God? How in the world does one make sense out of something so totally senseless?

And that's why the box would remain unpacked. So many happy memories frozen in time in the photos. But sadness leached into them, sadness that was dark like the black waters of the creek back home. She stood and shoved her chair under the desk. Had to get out of the house, couldn't stay there.

She clipped her hair in a twist, tucked the T-shirt in her shorts, and slipped on a pair of duck shoes. Grabbing the basket of garden tools on her way off the back porch, she headed to the struggling rosebush and that monster dandelion.

"I told you I'd be back." No dandelion would get the best of her. Of course, the fact that she was talking to the plant could mean it already had gotten the best of her. The flower bed extended the entire length of the picket fence around her yard. It would take all day or more to weed and condition the soil. But she actually had all day. And if her editor got his way, she might have every day to work on her garden.

She walked along the fence, pulling weeds, looking for tender plants, and turning the soil. It was like a botanical treasure hunt as she found perennials struggling to grow through the weeds. She discovered black-eyed-susans, daisies, peonies, and a couple of old rosebushes. By early afternoon her hands hurt from the spade handle and thistle thorns, but the beds along the fence were clear of the noxious weeds.

She moved to the front of the house. The cutting from Ma's favorite purple Rose-of-Sharon sat in a pot on the stoop. Uprooted from its home, struggling to survive. It didn't ask for this. An innocent victim. She gritted her teeth and slammed the pick she held into the ground. Each swing had more force than the one before. The soil broke into clumps which she smashed with the blunt edge of the hand pick.

Digging in the soil and smelling the moist clay normally comforted her. Not today. The soil clumps became enemies she had to crumble. She beat the dirt, punching it over and over. She'd have laughed at her sodden punching bag if the anger coming out wasn't so strong.

The gate creaked and startled her. She fell backwards landing with a thump on the grass. Wiping sweat from her brow with the back of her hand, MaryRose looked up into eyes bluer than Randall's.

"Sorry, ma'am. Didn't mean to startle you none. Are you all right?"

She nodded.

An older man tipped his hat at her. "Jeb Cobb. I came to mow the lawn. Miss Ruth is all-fired mad at me for doing this on Sunday but me and the boys celebrated with her at brunch yesterday. I figured if she could get busy in the kitchen cooking up a storm on Mother's Day, I could get this yard mowed for the new tenant."

He extended his hand. "Let me help you up."

How much of her weed and soil abuse had he witnessed?

"I was, um, working out frustration." She brushed her hands on her shorts and took his. "MaryRose Elliott. Pleased to meet you."

She kicked at the cracked mound of dirt. "This is kind of my therapy. Guess it didn't look like it."

His laughter boomed. "Appears to me like it worked fine. It's my fault you're working so hard. I've neglected these beds for too long. Least I could do is offer to help. Since you want to do it on your own, how about you come on over for supper tonight when you finish?"

"I'd hate to intrude, especially on Mother's Day."

He shook his head. "Now, Miss MaryRose, I know my wife. If I went home and told her I didn't invite you, I'd be in trouble." He pulled a dandelion and tossed it on the pile of discarded weeds. "You wouldn't want me in trouble, now, would you?"

She wanted to agree but wasn't sure how much company she could possibly be.

He touched her shoulder. "Miss Ruth serves at six-seventeen."

MaryRose frowned. "Six-seventeen?"

"Yes ma'am. Miss Ruth knows I am more likely on time if it is an unusual time. So supper is at six-seventeen on the nose. She's got a roast cooking that would feed a small army. It's up to you. Come if you want and if not, we'll invite you again another time."

He ruffled Dapple's fur, then stood tall and headed out of the yard. "Ours is the stone pump house at the end of the road. I'll go on home now and tell Miss Ruth we may have us company for supper."

He walked with the same confident gait she used to love in Dad. Maybe it came with age.

She squatted again, picked up the trowel and resumed gardening. A lone tear tracked down her cheek and dropped into the soil.

MaryRose pulled her VW into the driveway and stopped beside a small stone house. She smoothed non-existing wrinkles out of her skirt, tucked a few loose curls back into her French braid, and willed her heart to stop racing. Goodness, this was only dinner with the neighbors.

Jeb opened the door for her. "Welcome, welcome. I knew you'd come."

"I tried to call, but your phone was busy all day." She walked into the kitchen.

"I am sorry for that. My boys will be all kinds of mad at me. I forgot to turn the ringer back on after church." A woman a little older than Ma greeted her with a hug then held her at arm's length. Her dark eyes appraised.

"Well, aren't you a slight thing. I am so glad to meet you. I've heard my Randall talking all about you."

She hugged MaryRose again.

"Call me Ruth. I've been praying an awful lot for you since that snakebite. How are you doing?"

"Very well, thank you."

Jeb playfully pulled on Ruth's braid. "How long till supper?"

"I'm not on a time clock, am I? You got time to get washed up and set the table." "Yessum."

MaryRose waited in the doorway until Jeb was gone and Ruth turned back to her cooking. "May I help?"

"Sure. My kitchen always has room for more hands. The dough's ready so you can roll out the biscuits."

"I'd—be happy to." Oh great, of all the things she could ask her to do. Long ago, MaryRose stopped trying to make perfect biscuits like Ma's and Nana's and started making drop biscuits.

She blew stray hairs out of her face. Funny, she could make about any kind of bread, so biscuit dough should not defeat her. Yet she stood at the counter, looking at the bowl, and wanted to run home. She managed to get the biscuits rolled out after several restarts and getting flour all over her blouse, face, and the floor. Finally, she stood before beautifully rolled dough.

Where was a biscuit cutter?

Ruth opened a drawer and pulled out an old jar lid. "Here you go. Cut them with this."

"Peanut butter lid?"

"Yes. Randall used my biscuit cutter outside once and it never came back in. I grabbed this lid that day. I've been using it ever since. Guess I could get a real biscuit cutter, but it wouldn't have the same charm."

MaryRose liked Ruth Cobb. She was down to earth like Ma and Nana.

After cutting the biscuits, MaryRose placed them on the baking sheet andthen set them on the countertop. Ruth opened the oven and removed the most luscious-smelling roast, then placed the biscuits in.

"Would you hold that platter right here so I can slide the roast onto it? Randall tells me you're a widow. How long?"

She could hardly think of anything other than the aroma emanating from the roast. Which was a much better thing to focus on than her sad times. But she mustn't be rude. She swallowed the lump in her throat.

"Seven years."

"You married young."

"Sean and I were eighteen—grew up together. His grandpa married my Nana when I was fourteen. Sean was always a part of my life. It's still hard to deal with the empty place in my heart since he died. Sometimes I wish—I don't know—it wasn't enough time."

Ruth crossed the room and enveloped MaryRose in a hug. "Aw, child, you're right. It wasn't enough. Hard to see God in those times. But you're young. Lots can happen."

"Maybe so."

"I'm sure God has things ordered for you. It's what I always believed for my boys too."

Her boys? That's what Jeb called them. They were a long way from boys.

"Course, Jonathon has mountain-moving faith. He doesn't date. The boy believes God will plop his future wife right down in front of him."

"Oh my."

She nodded. "I figure He will too, because God honors that kind of faith. I'm looking forward to seeing it happen. There's only two years difference in their ages. But Jonathon has the dark hair and eyes like me. Randall is his father's son right down to those sapphire eyes. They'll draw you like a siren's call before you know what hit you."

MaryRose had already noticed that. She touched her cheek. Way too warm.

"Um-hm." Ruth clicked her tongue as she began carving the roast.

Before MaryRose could think of a way to change the conversation, the door burst open.

"Hey, Mom. Who's here? That looks like MaryRose's car—"

Randall stopped inside the doorway. The scent of spice blew in with him. Wow.

Before he got all the way inside, the door opened again, hitting him between his shoulders. "What the h—"

"Randall Cobb!"

"Sorry, Mom." He rubbed his shoulder and glowered at the darker, but equally handsome man standing behind him who was stifling a laugh.

Ruth placed her hands on her hips. "I invited you boys here for dinner, and each of you told me you had plans. I should have known once you got wind a pretty lady was coming, you'd both show up. Go wash your hands and set two more places at the table."

Randall trudged to the dining room. What was eating him?

Jonathon kissed Ruth's cheek. "Happy Mother's Day again. Nice to meet you, MaryRose."

"Least one of my boys is polite. Let's eat."

Jonathon made a point to sit beside her, and Randall plopped in the chair across from her hard enough to jar the table. She chose to enjoy Jonathon's conversation rather than ponder the grump across from her.

Once the delicious meal was served, everyone was too busy eating to talk.

As they finished with a deep-dish peach cobbler, Randall finally spoke up. "MaryRose, tell Mom and Dad about the journals. Dad was a history teacher, and Mom knows about everyone in town. She might know someone who'd help you research."

He graced her with his first smile of the evening. And she couldn't find her words. She had to stop acting like a giddy teenager around that man.

Breathe.

Then speak.

"I have my great-great-grandmother's journals. I'm transcribing them for now and when I finish, I hope to write a novel based on them. I know she was from around this area somewhere, but not sure where. Her name was Rose Elliott."

"Rose Elliott. Maybe I can help you with that." Ruth polished off her cobbler and stacked her plate on the others Jeb carried to the kitchen.

"That would be much appreciated." She glanced at her watch and stifled a yawn. "But right now, I think I should head home. Dinner was wonderful. I'd love to have your biscuit recipe."

"Sure, child. You're welcome to stay longer."

"My puppy is probably starving by now. Plus, I start work tomorrow. I should go."

Randall and Jonathon both stood.

But Jonathon jumped to hold her chair and walked her to the door.

"I'll walk you to your car."

If only Randall had offered first. They walked through the

kitchen where Jeb stood at the sink, dishwashing. He put the pot down and hugged her with the kind of strength Papa Shane did.

Jonathon held the door open. He lightly touched her back and guided her down the steps. Certainly not the electric touch she felt around Randall.

"Aren't my parents fun?"

"I feel like I've known them forever."

"They have that effect on people." He opened her car door. "Do you have any plans for next Saturday?"

"Shopping. Writing. Why?"

"I'd be happy to take you shopping and maybe even show you around some."

"I'd love that. I can be ready around ten."

"Perfect." He patted the car after he closed the door. Why did guys do that? Jonathon waved as he walked to the house. And Randall stood on the porch, watching them.

Scowling.

CHAPTER 6

$\mathcal{T}$he sun hadn't topped the mountain behind her house yet, but the sky was lighting with soft pastels. Mary-Rose had been up for hours. Nerves over her appointment with the belligerent editor kept her brain too busy for sleep. She'd told herself a hundred times this was her dream. But it wasn't. It was Ma's. Honoring it would require a change in her editor's attitude. And hers.

She poured the last of the honey-violet balm into her hand and massaged it onto the wound. The balm did a better job of minimizing the scar than the prescribed medicine. She flexed her ankle. Not too sore and flexibility was returning.

She washed her hands and opened the journal. There was time to immerse herself in Gramma Roses's life before Trudy arrived.

~~~~

July 4, 1865

After shoppin yesterday Grampa said we was stayin in town another day. He already made plans for Mr. Estep to care for the animals. Gramma was so tickled to get a night away. He even took us to a little restaurant by the river for supper. I got to eat cornbread, beans, and fried chicken. Then we went to a boardin house and stayed the night. I aint never been anywhere so fancy. I want a bed like that one. It had big posts, almost as big as the log beams that hold Grampa's house up. And it was soft as heaven. Yep, I want a bed like that.

This morning we got up bright and early and went to church. There were people everywhere. There was food and all sorts of sweets. Yum. And I saw Indians too. One was real pretty and actually married to a white man. I never woulda thought. Gramma said she is a princess married to white man. She has a pretty name, Aracoma. I wonder what it means.

Then Grampa's pastor rang the church bell to gather us all. I figured it was for blessing the food. I guess it was. But he told everyone he had an announcement and an introduction. Said, he was leavin in the spring on a wagon train to the west. Oh my goodness, such wailin and fussin followed. I guess they all love their preacher.

After he got them all settled down, he said he wanted to introduce the preacher who would be takin his place. He said this new preacher was fixin to get married and comin off the circuits.

I think my jaw dropped plumb to my stomach when Patrick stepped up to be introduced as the new preacher.

Before I got my wits about me, they was callin me up too and introducing me as his fiancie. Oh Lordy, I thought I was gonna swoon right there. Patrick walked to me as proud as you please and took my hand in the crook of his arm.

Gracious if that didn't start a whole new kind of patterin of my heart. When he smiled at me, well, I cannot explain what happened. But after that, when he said that sweet blessin over all the food, I think I may have fallen right in love with him.

Tomorrow Patrick is pickin me up to take a carriage to where the church people are building us a little house. My head is spinnin like that tornado we had three summers ago.

Dear Jesus, Thank you for a good day. And for keepin Patrick safe. And, well, it is kinda embarassin, but thank you for what happened to my heart when he smiled at me. Help me be ready. Sure seems things is gonna happen faster than what I expected them to. But it's what you want God, not me. Amen.

~~~~

July 5, 1865

I cannot sleep. I may not sleep ever again. I am too happy. Papa would say I need to come out of my cloud. But why?

Patrick came over this mornin in his wagon. We rode to this place beside the creek, a purty spot. He showed me where there was already trees chopped down to clear a spot for a house. Our house. We walked around and he showed me how it would have two rooms. Two rooms! Oh, and a loft too. Then we walked beside the creek. He held my hand and my stomach did that flutter thing. Oh, we talked and talked.

Then he took me home. Before he left, he prayed for me, for us. He has to do this last circuit and then he comes back here. I have to write Momma all of the news. I don't guess I will go home. Well, this is home now.

I told Patrick about my journal. He smiled at me and brushed my hair from my cheek. He said, "You keep writin, my Rose. Write about everything and maybe when you get letters from me you can save them in the book too. I hope you will let me read your words sometime."

I looked in his green eyes, green as the winter wheat when it first comes up and nodded. I don't reckon I will ever be able to say no to that man. It was hard to watch him ride away. I felt like part of the air I breathe rode away in that wagon.

Dear Jesus, Keep my Patrick safe. Bring him back here soon. And help Momma and Papa understand things. Help my heart slow down so I can sleep. Amen.

~~~~

July 7, 1865

I am in a mood today. Gramma says I don't talk like a

lady. Papa always told me I had enough learnin. I can read and write and that is all I need. But Gramma says they is more for me to learn. She told me to practice writing right and it will help me talk right. Mercy. That will make writin in here be like school. I guess I will start tryin tomorrow.

Gramma says she figures the weddin will be in November after harvest is done and before winter sets in. And it will be here instead of back home since Patrick will already be workin here. Maybe Momma and Papa and everybody will be able to come then. So, I will be married by Thanksgiving. Land sakes, I know most girls my age are married by now, but, oh my, a couple of months ago I was still catchin bullfrogs in the pond with little Jay Jay. I miss him. I bet he's getting into all kinds of trouble without me there to catch it for him.

God's gonna have to do a heap a work on me to make me ready for a weddin. Gramma bought some pretty white linen for my dress. I aint never had something so fine before. Seems a shame I only get to wear it once. I got all tickled when she measured me, nobody never touched me in some of those places.

Oh my goodness, then she scolded me. She told me I'd better not be getting tickled like that when my husband touched me. I cannot hardly even imagine the ways of a man and a woman, let alone think it will be happenin to me before long. My face is hot as a summer day right now thinking about it.

I better go to bed, this kind of thinkin messes me up.

Dear Jesus, I'm out of words. Help me tonight, please. Amen.

~~~~

July 17, 1865

I ~~aint~~ have not had time to think in more than a week, much less write. Gramma has me ~~sewin,~~ sewing my dress. My fingers have a thousand tiny holes in them from the needles. She's making a quilt for us. It's pretty colors, and all made of rings interlocking, there, that is a word she would be right proud of. She calls it a wedding quilt or something. While we sew she talks. She tells me about my family, about canning and fixing all ~~them~~ those herbs she grows. She even told me how old Papa was when he went to North Carolina to the university and never came home. I never knew he grew up right here.

~~They's,~~ There are still some secrets she will not talk about. She mentioned something about Papa and a girl by the name of Hatfield and said it was just as well Papa married Momma and stayed in the east because them Hatfields and McCoys are ~~brewin~~ brewing trouble.

I asked her about marriage, about my wedding night, and she frowned over her glasses at me. "That is no talk for a lady. God will be showing you and Patrick what to do." Then she blushed. I never seen her blush before, and she whispered, "And you be sure to listen to God. Marriage is good."

I wish I knew what she meant. But if the flutters I get

when I think of Patrick have anything to do with it, well —I better write something else.

After supper every night we take a walk and harvest plants. Then she sits with me on the porch until dark and makes me practice my writing and talking. I don't get any time to myself until after that. And most nights I am too tired to write. I have to do better.

Dear Jesus, Does Patrick think about things the way I do? Is he safe? Keep Patrick safe and maybe put me in his mind sometimes. Amen.

~~~~

August 1, 1865

The heat here is as bad as at home. But there is no ocean for refreshment. I did take a walk yesterday and found a river. I think it is the same river that leads into town. I sat by the edge and sang to me and the birds. Then I couldn't bear it. Oh Gramma would be so ashamed.

I was all alone so I went in the water. It felt so good to swim and float. I dare not stay long though for fear of getting caught. When the wind whipped up and about blew my dress away I figured I better get out. Also, I had to give my unmentionables and my braid time to dry before I went back.

The scolding Gramma gave me for ignoring my sewing was worth it. What would she say if she knew the new preacher's future wife was swimming around in the river? Land sakes, I must be daft.

Maybe next summer, in the evening when it is me and Patrick at home, he will not be cross with me if I at least stick my feet in the cool water.

But then the day got real bad. Grampa woke us after we went to bed to go over to the Estep's place. Little Jacob got bit by a rattler. Now those snakes give me a fright. Poor boy was sick as I have ever seen. Gramma put one of them ugly leeches on him and then rubbed the wound with her honey and violet salve.

I held his little hand and prayed for him and he said it made the pain go away. Poor boy. He's about Jay Jay's' age and I think I would die if something like that happened to my little brother.

Dear Jesus, Please heal little Jacob. That's about all I can write with these tears dripping on the page and smearing things. Amen.

~~~~

August 10, 1865

Jacob Estep will be fine.

I got a letter from Patrick today. I held it in my apron pocket all day and built up so much excitement over reading it I thought I would bust wide open. After supper I begged Gramma to let me go for a walk and read it.

So I went to the river. I never been so excited to read something in my life. I think he does feel things for me too. The words he tried to cross out, well, I squinted my

TO FOLLOW A DREAM

eyes and worked hard and I could read them. I think I blushed clear down to my toes. Then I went back and Gramma was sitting inside sewing. I asked her why she was not out on the porch and she winked at me.

"Child, some things best done inside. This nightdress is for your wedding night and no one sides you and me needs to see it until your new husband does."
That time I think the blush went down to my toes and straight out my shoes. I ran to my room and couldn't capture my thoughts.

Dear Jesus, Help me control myself better. Keep Patrick safe and strong. Thank you for Gramma and this time with her. I miss Momma, but I think I needed Gramma. Help me learn to handle this heat and do all my chores right. Oh, and thank you for saving little Jacob. Maybe me and Patrick will have a sweet boy like that one day. Amen.

~~~~

MaryRose regarded her foot. It was a bit eerie how a snake bite connected her to Gramma Rose. She carefully unfolded the letter inserted in the journal.

~~~~

July 7, 1865

Dear Rose,

I inform you that I am well at this time. Was it a mere two nights ago I took my leave from your grandparents' house? The emptiness in my heart makes it feel as if much more time has passed. However, I did leave with fresh joy after time spent in your company. Your smile is etched in my mind as is the sparkle of sunlight in the green of your eyes.

This will be my last circuit. I shall be saddened to bid farewell to some of the families I have come to know these past three years. I have much to anticipate, do I not?

The turmoil around me grows. There is still so much hatred from the War. It about breaks my heart. 'Tis hard to figure where our Savior is in the midst of the arguments.

~~And some nights thinking of you, my thoughts sure need to be captured and made obedient to Jesus Christ.~~

I hope to finish this circuit by the end of the summer. Then I shall go back to Carolina, sell my parents' home-place, and pack my belongings. May the Lord grant me safe travels and a rapid journey to the mountains where I start a new life with you.

Your Husband to be,

Patrick Elliott

p.s. I keep your letters in my jacket by my heart. I read them often. And it pleases me that you pray for me before bed, as I do you.

~~~~

MaryRose almost felt like she was intruding on a perfect love story. She kissed the book cover as she closed the journal before sliding it back into the protective cloth cover.

CHAPTER 7

*M*aryRose took Dapple to the lake for a little romp before time to leave for Charleston. She walked barefoot along the path as the puppy splashed in the water. The ripples he made invited her to join in the fun. If her scabs were gone by the weekend she'd be able to enjoy the water like him.

"Halloo, MaryRose?" Mrs. Trumble trilled from the house. "Where are you, child?"

Tension spread across her shoulders. Was it already time to go?

"I'm coming, Trudy."

She hustled up the path and Dapple reluctantly followed. Rounding the bend in the trail she almost bumped into Trudy— standing with hands on her hips and a scowl on her face.

"Barefoot and no bandage. You said you would take care of that foot."

MaryRose lifted the hem of her long skirt and held the foot up for Trudy to see. "It's doing great, don't you think?"

"Well, I'll be. I have to make me a batch of that honey-violet stuff. It's working a miracle on you."

"Come on in. There's coffee in the pot. All I have to do is

wash my feet and put my sandals on. Really, I think I could drive myself today."

"Sure you could. But I figure you had yourself enough alone time this weekend. I might as well go with you. We'll have us a time seeing the sights."

"That is a great idea. But I can't leave Dapple here alone too long."

Trudy poured a cup of coffee and sat at the table. "Bring him along. I can walk him while you're in the office. There's a park by the river right next to that office building."

MaryRose slipped her sandals on and grabbed the leash. "Dapple, we're going for a ride."

He scurried between their feet barking. "Don't trip us. Back up and sit." He obeyed but quivered like he would shake right out of his skin when she grabbed her purse and keys.

Trudy touched her shoulder. "You look like a ray of sunshine with that gypsy skirt and blouse. And that auburn hair of yours —well you should wear it down all the time. If my hair was as pretty as yours, my pups would have bows and toenails to match me for a change!" Trudy laughed at her own joke.

As Trudy drove away from Lake Nolan, she reached across the seat and patted MaryRose's leg. "We have about an hour and a half of driving, but it's a fine day for it. I know a lot about you, but what I don't know is how in the world a girl from the coast of North Carolina finds herself in our mountains."

"My family comes from somewhere between here and Logan, far as I can tell. Back when it was called Aracoma, before West Virginia was a state."

"Sure enough?"

"Plus my best friend, Missy, is acting in the summer theatres at the state park this summer. Seemed like a good time to come here and start over."

"Starting over sometimes is a good thing. Long as you're not running from something. Things we run from have a way of chasing us."

Why did people keep mentioning that? She wasn't running. She stared out the window at the mountains. On either side of the interstate, they rose like earthen skyscrapers. There were at least twenty different shades of green on those trees.

"Wait till you see them in the snow. Ain't nothing like it. Course, you don't want to be driving' this highway then, no amount of plowing' makes it safe. Guess you don't know much about snow out there on the coast."

"Not too much." She had to look straight up to see the tops of the mountains.

Trudy turned the cruise control off and the car began a steep ascent. "I'll pull over when we get to the top. When you turn around and look, I swear you can probably see your home place in North Carolina from there. Tell me about your family."

MaryRose eagerly shared the family stories and what she'd read in the journal.

"You're serious about that man dreaming about his bride?"

"Yes, ma'am. It is actually in the county records."

"I'll be."

Trudy slowed down and pulled onto the shoulder. "Okay, hon, look out the back window."

MaryRose craned her neck. Nothing prepared her for how high they were or the distance she could see. It did seem as if she could see all the way to the ocean if she knew where to look.

"Wow."

"That's what I always say. You sit back and relax now. Rest a bit. I'll have you in Charleston in about forty-five minutes. You, me, and Dapple will have us a picnic down along the Kanawha River."

Trudy reached over and switched on the radio. Soft music drifted to MaryRose's ears. She stretched her foot out and closed her eyes.

MaryRose couldn't get out of the magazine office fast enough. William Little was full of himself.

"That man isn't even God's gift to himself." When he'd explained his disdain at being assigned her column she wanted to slap the smug look right off his face. How in the world was she supposed to write articles about herbs and natural cosmetics for an editor who sniggered and shook his head at each thing she proposed? He flat out told her she'd be lucky if the column ran more than one issue. He doubted people would care about that stuff.

Trudy and Dapple sat in the shade of a maple tree by the car.

She wiped angry tears from her eyes before catching up to them.

"MaryRose, you need sunglasses, honey. This sun is too bright for you to be unprotected. I know a little store at Marmet where we can buy a cheap pair."

"It's not the sun bothering me. My editor is a hateful man. I almost quit right on the spot. Might be better off waitressing."

"Awe, you got to give it time. Dreams take time."

She glared at the office building. "It wasn't my dream. Was Mom's."

"Honey child, who told you to follow your mama's dream?"

"Nobody. I thought it might help me heal if I did this."

"Well, I guess it might. But not if you have to work for a total pain in the butt. Nothing says you have to keep this job."

Dapple jumped and yipped and tugged Trudy from the spot under the tree. "Calm down, puppy. Me and your ma are having us a serious talk."

Trudy picked him up and handed him to MaryRose. Then, in a motherly gesture, wiped a tear from MaryRose's cheek.

"You pray about this, and God will show you what he wants

you to do. If your editor doesn't believe in what you write, it might not be where you belong."

"Not sure I belong anywhere."

"Sure you do, but you're carrying too much baggage around. Why not let me go with you to that trial next month?"

She froze then spoke through clenched teeth. "I'll not be at that trial. Why is it so important anyway? First Papa Shane, now you. Who else wants to jump on me about that?"

She turned away. Fine, let the woman think on that. She'd go to the car and wait. Her tote bag slid from her shoulder and dragged on the pavement. Great. She couldn't even have a tantrum right. Hard to make a point when she couldn't even stomp to the car.

Might as well repent. She called across the lot, "I'm sorry, Trudy."

"I'd be way more concerned if you didn't have any emotions about the man who killed your family. Put your bag in the car, and then come back here. While you were in your meeting I bought us a picnic lunch. That park I told you about is down the hill to the river. I have everything set up already. We can watch the boats and barges while we eat. We don't have to talk about nothing you don't want to talk about."

MaryRose acquiesced. She caught up to Trudy and hugged her. "I don't deserve you."

"That's what I tell my Walt every day. And that sweet man kisses my cheek and tells me nobody loves me like he does. He's right too."

"I expected I'd be married forever like you. But God takes away those I love the most. You might not want to sit too close to me. Maybe I'm contagious." The joke might have been funny if she didn't believe it.

"Don't you rattle on about nonsense. I don't know lots of things, but I do know this. We don't have to understand why

God lets things happen. He's big enough for your anger. But He asks you to trust Him to get you through."

MaryRose sensed truth in the words but wouldn't let them root. "It's that, well, sometimes I wonder if there are any more dreams for me."

"What kind of dream, honey?"

"I don't know. I'd just like a dream to follow."

"Well then, we'll be praying for that dream."

They walked down a tree-lined lane to the riverfront. Small gazebos dotted the water's edge. They actually hung out over the water. Some had benches in them while others had tables. MaryRose loved the quaint little park. Close to the business district of Charleston but with a country feel. The songbirds welcomed her. As they approached the first gazebo, she stopped beside a row of hummingbird feeders. A hundred or more of the little birds flitted from feeder to feeder. A few hung back and waited their turns, while others flew up and knocked others off the little perches.

"I've never seen so many at one time." She sat down near the feeders. "Nana would have stayed here all day. She always had two hummingbird feeders along with other feeders, suet boxes, and anything she could find. I remember her sitting in her garden in the morning and watching them. Said they sang hymns to her."

"There's a woman I would have liked. Let's eat our picnic right here."

They ate sandwiches and apples. MaryRose was mesmerized by the movements and brilliant colors of the little creatures. One female kept flying up hovering in front of them MaryRose was sure she could touch it.

After Trudy finished her lunch, she began humming "How Great Thou Art."

MaryRose's favorite hymn. She sang along. When Trudy

switched to "Amazing Grace," she did too. The sunlight filtering through the trees made her smile.

Trudy stopped humming. "Do you believe that?"

"What?"

"What you just sang."

She frowned. "Of course I do."

"Hmm. Which part?"

"We were singing 'Amazing Grace.'"

"No, honey, what words did you sing?"

"Umm. You mean about grace relieving my fears?"

Trudy nodded.

"I told you I believe them."

Trudy grasped MaryRose's hand and held firm. "Then why are you afraid to go back to that trial next month?"

"I'm not afraid." Was she?

"God needs you to go. He knows the spot in your heart that isn't going to heal until you put the past few months behind you. Maybe the dream you are waiting for is on the other side of forgiveness."

"I see no purpose in going back. I rehash it enough all by myself without sitting in court and seeing that man."

"But that is the purpose. It's time to finish it so you can move forward. Until you do, you're running away."

Unwilling to listen to any more, MaryRose wadded up her sandwich wrapper, grabbed her apple core and slammed them into the garbage can hard enough the hummingbirds flew away.

"We weren't going to speak about this again, remember? I'm ready to go home. I'll be fine on my own."

"Sure you will."

Trudy rose and walked to the car. That woman didn't appear the least bit upset that she'd been rude once again. Well, this time MaryRose had no intention of apologizing. Trudy had butted in one too many times.

CHAPTER 8

For the fourth night in a row sleep eluded MaryRose. She was used to crickets, cicadas, and locusts on summer nights. But when the owls, tree frogs, and bull frogs started their night songs, the volume kept her awake. She tossed and turned. If that wasn't enough, a fox somewhere in the woods screamed a warning and coyotes moaned. She pulled her sheets up over her head and tried to hum herself to sleep.

When sleep finally came, other noises woke her—noises in her head that closed windows couldn't silence.

Sirens, screams, police knocking on the door, "we're sorry to inform you, Ms. Elliott..." Lives gone, she forever changed. Twisted in a tangled mess of covers and nightgown she kicked at the linen prison. She grabbed the sheet and tried to free her legs. When she stood, a zinger of pain in the wounds caused her to jump and buckled her ankle. She hit the hardwood floor with a thud.

She pounded the bed's sideboard and pulled herself onto the chair by the nightstand. As the first rays of sunlight pushed through the gap between the drapes, she opened her journal and, with shaking hands, wrote.

I miss Mom, Dad, and Nana. How can they be gone? That drunk killed the three most wonderful people in the world. Wasn't losing Sean enough? I have no one. I'm alone. Scared. Angry at the drunk. At You, God. Help me. Please.

MaryRose inhaled deeply and closed her eyes. It took more effort than last time, but the anger was finally shoved back into the dark corner in her heart. Maybe He wanted her to face it, but not today. Yesterday she canceled the shopping trip and lunch with Jonathon. And Missy hadn't been able to get away from rehearsals either. When Trudy checked in last night and offered a ride to church, she flat out refused. Not ready for peopling.

She wrapped her cotton robe around her shoulders and cinched the belt tight. Coffee time. After sipping the hot liquid, she glared at the closet. What was so intimidating about a stupid box of photos?

Everything. Dragging it into the middle of the kitchen, she opened the box and picked up the picture that was on top. Her parents' happy faces mocked her. Nana and Papa Shane stood in the middle of the herb garden on their wedding day. Glass from the frame covered the faces. That's what broke the other day.

Her hands shook. She put the picture back into the box before dropping it and breaking the frame too. With a hard push she shoved the box into the corner beside the refrigerator. Not today. Maybe not ever.

MaryRose finished her coffee, then got dressed in shorts and a sleeveless T-shirt, twisted her hair in a bun, and headed outside. As she walked along the fence toward the lake she stopped to pull the few weeds she'd missed the other day. She grabbed yet another dandelion that refused to be uprooted. Anger flowed into her hands.

The drunk driver was like an ugly weed. She'd rip him from her life, from her mind the way she would this stubborn yellow flower.

Jaws clenched and shoulders tight she yanked with all she had. The weed gave way, but she tumbled backward and hit the ground hard enough to bite her tongue when her mouth slammed shut. She choked the flower, ripped it into pieces and scattered the remains on the ground.

A car pulled into the driveway. The engine rattled and sputtered as it wound down.

"MaryRose, are you home?" Missy called from the side of the house.

Wiping her eyes with the back of her hand, she called, "I'm around front."

Missy rounded the corner and stared at her. "I should have known I'd find you sitting on the ground digging in the dirt." She reached down and helped MaryRose stand, then pulled her into a bear hug.

Missy, who always dressed to a T, looked at MaryRose's smudged clothes. "If you're waiting for your knight in shining armor, you're hardly dressed for the part."

"Ha-ha. That would have been a long wait."

Missy touched her cheek. "You've been crying."

"I'm better now."

"Yeah, that's what it looks like. Let's go inside."

She shook her head. "No. I've been inside writing all week. I want to go to the lake and relax awhile. Thanks for coming. I needed to see you."

"If you weren't as stubborn as your dad was you would've called me."

Missy was right, but she'd not admit that.

MaryRose led the way to the dock. "It's like being on a private lake here." She pointed across the water. "The cove extends inland far enough you can't even see the biggest part of the lake. I come out here a lot and sit on the dock. Can't wait to swim some."

"A lot? You've lived here a little over three weeks, and one of them was in the hospital. You make it sound like it's been forever." Missy elbowed her. "I'm supposed to be the actress."

MaryRose lowered herself to the dock, and Missy followed suit, placing her arm loosely around her shoulder. "Want to talk?"

"Not really."

They sat for minutes or hours. Neither cared or tracked the time. How often had they spent entire afternoons in the tree house Grampa built, never talking? Sometimes they held complete conversations without saying a word.

Missy slipped her sneakers off and dipped her toes in the water. "Aah. This is nice."

"I wish I was this calm and peaceful."

"Time heals a lot of things, MaryRose."

"Times heals nothing. Only God can, and He's been pretty silent with me recently."

"Are you actually listening for Him?"

Before MaryRose came up with an answer, three vehicles came down the hill from the main house and parked by the boathouse. Andrea and a handsome young man raced to the tree by the boathouse and grabbed the rope swing. Jeb and Ruth eased out of the next SUV while Jonathon climbed out the back and grabbed a huge ice chest.

Missy squeezed MaryRose's shoulder. "Oh my. He is gorgeous."

"I don't see Randall."

Missy pointed to Jonathon who waved at them. "Then who is he?"

"His younger brother."

Before they could stand and make their exit, another vehicle, a mixture of golf cart and ATV, pulled down the driveway. MaryRose's heart fluttered. "That's Randall."

"Shouldn't be legal for two brothers to look that good. I have to meet them." Missy was up and walking across the dock toward the family before MaryRose could say she'd rather not.

Jeb was fussing as they approached the dock.

"Randall, is this how you drive every time you see a lovely lady? You almost crashed into the boathouse. It's okay, son. A man would have to be blind to miss the scenery at the lake today. I'd appreciate help with the food if you'd stop staring for a few minutes."

Missy covered her mouth but still couldn't squelch the giggle. "Oh, this is going to be good."

MaryRose grabbed her hand. "Maybe we should leave."

"I wouldn't miss this for the world. MaryRose, it's time to live a little."

Randall and his father lugged supplies to the grill at the dock.

"Hey, MaryRose."

"Randall, this is my best friend, Missy Greene."

He placed the cooler on the picnic table and extended his hand. "Nice to meet you. We've got plenty of food. Why not join us?"

MaryRose swung Missy around in a circle away from them. "Oh no, we couldn't. We're going up to my house for a quiet lunch with Dapple. Both of us have busy weeks ahead, and this is our only chance to visit. Maybe another time."

Randall cocked his head sideways and gave Missy a crooked grin. "At least come meet everyone before you go."

"Love to." Missy followed him toward the picnic tables and grill area on the dock. Andrea sloshed out of the lake dragging the young man with her. Introductions around the group took forever, and MaryRose's best friend charmed each of them, as she always did. But MaryRose had had enough of the family happiness. She nudged Missy's arm.

"Don't let us interrupt. We'll get out of your way now. Enjoy your day, everyone."

The disappointment etched on Randall's face almost convinced her to stay. But only almost.

Missy glared as they entered the house. "That was rude. You didn't give me time to meet everyone and talk a while before dragging me up here. What's up with that?"

She shrugged.

"What's going on?"

"I'm having a bad day. Papa Shane keeps harping on me to go back for the trial. I miss Nana, Mom, Dad, and Sean already. Nagging me about the trial doesn't help."

She swallowed. "This morning I was going to hang pictures and couldn't even take one out of the box."

"Can't believe I am about to say this. Faithless me. Have you prayed about how you feel?"

"Sure. For all the good it does. I think the words bounce off the ceiling." She plopped on the sofa.

"Girl, you got major anger brewing inside you. Keep holding it in, and it's going to erupt. I don't want to be in the way when that happens."

MaryRose clenched her jaw.

She glared back. "Okay then. I'll sit here and pout with you."

"Look, I'm sorry I'm such a pain in the butt today."

"It's all good. You've sat with me through enough of my funks over the years."

As MaryRose waved at Missy a wave of loneliness broadsided her. What a relief to finally be understood. Well, maybe not so much understood as accepted. Either way, the afternoon had both brightened her day and made the night lonelier.

She headed to the lake. All was quiet and peaceful now.

At the water's edge, she splashed her feet in the coolness. Missy had helped her transcribe by impromptu acting scenes out. She did a perfect rendition of Gramma Rose pacing around in her bedroom talking to herself about how ridiculous the whole dream and courtship was. It made for lots of laughter.

A hawk swooped lazy circles above MaryRose. And the mockingbird nesting in the dogwood beside her cabin perched atop the grill and sang to her. She'd named it Selah since it gave her daily musical interludes.

"No matter the weather, I wish I could sing through my day as you do, Selah."

She leaned back on her hands and gazed at the clear sky. Blue as Randall's eyes.

The intoxicating scent of his aftershave wafted down the hill from behind her. Oh goodness.

Randall cleared his throat. "Um, hi. Sorry to disturb you."

She straightened up. "No problem." She brushed her clothes and wiped her face. "I'll get out of your way."

"You're not in my way. I'm heading to the boathouse."

"Have a nice evening, Randall."

He turned to the boathouse but didn't move. Was there something else he wanted to say?

"MaryRose?"

Guess so. "Yes?"

"I—uh—never asked earlier when we saw you, how's the wound?"

She raised her foot and extended it in front of her. "The swelling's down, and it's almost scab-free. Bet I won't have as much scarring as you would expect."

79

A blush spread across his cheeks. It reminded her of the way Sean used to do when something she did got to him.

He ran his fingers through disheveled hair. "Should you have it in the water like that?"

"I think a few minutes won't hurt it." She flexed and extended the ankle a few times before placing it back in the water. How long would he stare at her legs?

Mumbling something he finally turned to the boathouse. Before he took two steps, the door to the apartment above the boathouse burst open. A young couple chased each other down the steps.

Randall paused as they called to him. He motioned to her. "MaryRose, come and meet my cousins."

He ambled back to her side and offered his hand. Once she stood, he seemed reluctant to let go. She pulled it away, hoping he hadn't felt the heat infusion between their palms.

"Guess I have more neighbors than I knew." She faced the approaching couple. The woman was fair-skinned and petite. The man resembled Randall—not quite as tall but the same wavy brown hair.

Randall touched her shoulder. "MaryRose Elliott, this is my cousin, Luke Matthews, and his wife, Rachel."

The couple spoke in unison. "Welcome to the neighborhood."

Randall glanced up the steps. "Where's Emma?" He turned to her. "She's their teenaged foster daughter."

Luke grasped Rachel's hand. "She spent the weekend with Rachel's mom and dad so we could enjoy our anniversary."

MaryRose swallowed the lump in her throat. "Congratulations. How long have you been married?"

"Five years." Luke drew Rachel close. "Excuse me. I don't mean to be rude but we have reservations and are already late."

"Don't let me keep you from your date. I'll see you around."

Rachel waved over her shoulder. "Pretty soon you'll get tired of us. We're teachers. Once school gets out, we hang around here all the time. Oh yeah, Randall, the rent check is already in place. Keep your eyes open."

Randall's laughter had a musical timbre to it. "The hunt begins."

He turned to MaryRose. "I used to babysit Luke and always picked on him relentlessly. He gets me back now by hiding the rent check each month. Once, a blue jay carried it away from the bird feeder. I stood there and watched my rent money fly away with the wind."

"What happens if you don't find it?"

"They won't let it be late. If I don't find it they give me hints." He glanced down, and his gaze held hers a moment. "Shall we sit? The boat can wait. We could bring those Adirondack chairs to the lake's edge so you don't have to sit on the hard ground."

"I'd like that."

He grabbed two of the low wooden chairs stacked on the deck and carried them to the shore.

She stretched her legs out and rested her head on the back of the chair. If he kept smiling at her like that she'd melt. As usual, his cologne tantalized her so much she'd swear her insides got goose bumps.

"Luke and Rachel foster a teenager when they've only been married five years?"

"Long story. But Emma is actually Rachel's niece. They got custody when Rachel's sister and brother-in-law lost parental rights. "

He picked up a rock and tossed it into the water. "I probably don't spend enough time down here."

"I'll probably spend too much time here. It's soothing."

He leaned back into his chair and closed his eyes. "You okay?"

"Just memories. Sometimes I handle them well. Today, not so much. Sean and I only made it to seven years."

"Then—Elliott—is his name?"

"I took my maiden name back after he died. Felt like I had to. 'Story of a Life.'"

"Harry Chapin. I always loved that song."

She hummed the melody a bit. "Me too."

"What happened to your husband?"

"He had a physical before he started working at the feed mill in Hertford. Routine blood work found a rare, hereditary blood disease. I've never been able to pronounce it—hemolytic-blah-blah-blah. It didn't hinder his work. But there wasn't much treatment available. When they tried with him, it didn't help."

Speaking about Sean without bursting into tears? What was wrong with her? Papa Shane said it was normal, but she wasn't sure. She figured she'd always feel broken remembering him.

"MaryRose?"

She jumped.

"You got quiet."

"Sorry. Sean died three months after our seventh anniversary. 'Story of a Life,' part one."

He inhaled deeply and let the breath out slow. "Children?"

"A beautiful baby girl. We named her Heather. Born with heart defects. She lived three hours and fifteen minutes." Mary-Rose bit her lip. "Story of a Life, Part Two."

She watched him rub his hands up and down his pant legs like trying to brush something out of the denim.

He shook his head. "I hate this. You try to be good, but it doesn't matter. How did you get through? I mean, at least I had Andrea when Jessica died."

"As cliché as it sounds, one day at a time."

"Yeah, I get it."

"I learned to rely upon God for everything, even the energy to put my foot on the floor in the morning and get out of bed.

He's faithful. He got me through the good and the bad and the terrible."

Randall studied a rock on the ground by his feet. He kicked it back and forth from one foot to the other. "I used to agree with that."

She had an irrational desire for him to stop kicking the rock and hold his hands. The hurt in his eyes made her want to help him. "We don't have to agree with it. It surely is difficult to do sometimes, but He expects us to believe. If we can trust Him to make the bad good, then we can trust Him with anything."

"And if we don't feel like trusting?"

"He waits. Sometimes we have to act ourselves into the feeling."

He rested his hands on the dock behind him and leaned back. "How exactly did you end up here?"

She tensed. "That would be part three of the story, and I'm not ready to talk about it yet. It's too soon, still too raw. I don't see God's hand in it."

He was silent a moment then pursed his lips and exhaled. "Or maybe you're not acting yourself into the feeling?"

She glared. "Excuse me?" He had just turned her words back on her. This situation was entirely different from his. Couldn't he see that? She grabbed her sandals and rose. Time to go.

His hands went up in surrender. "Hey, isn't that what you said to me? Maybe He's waiting for you right now." He rose and met her glare.

The problem was he spoke truth, and she knew it. Funny, her advice to him didn't seem so wise now. "I've taken too much of your time."

He shoved his hands into his pockets and grumbled. "I didn't mean to upset you. I'll leave. You don't have to."

"Yes, I do." Her head was jumbling images and words. She had to get away. She started up the walk to her house.

He followed close behind. "MaryRose?"

"I've got work to do."

Trying hard not to look back, she turned once more in his direction anyway. He stood on the path behind her. His chin dropped as he turned and walked off.

CHAPTER 9

*M*aryRose stepped away from her desk and stretched. A week sitting at her desk, while productive, had her quite cagey. She successfully sent three articles to Mr. Little and organized research for others. Hopefully, he would change his mind about Kitchen Cosmetics.

But if his attitude remained unwavering, she was prepared. Her budget was set and she could survive a few months if she lost the job. It would enable her at least enough time to find another job.

The only thing on her to-do list she hadn't accomplished sat in the kitchen daring her to sort through the photos it contained. Not today. No sorrow or hard memories would invade this sunny Saturday. Breakfast with Missy and shopping with Jonathon should keep her well distracted all day. She picked up her keys and purse and opened the door.

"Dapple, it's time to go."

In the VW, he circled the center of the seat three times before settling into a tight little ball with his blanket twisted around him. He peeked from underneath, and when she smiled at him, he thumped his tail.

The road to Chief Logan State Park was like every other road in the state. It wound up, down, and in between the mountains as if the trail guide had been a snake. Nothing shy of crashing into the guardrails would convince her they could actually prevent a car from disappearing off the side of a mountain. Yet people around there drove the roads without a care in the world. She held her breath every time a loaded coal truck sped around a curve. Not sure if it was more frightening to see them barreling towards her as she ascended or following behind as she went down.

At the state park, the two-lane blacktop weaved its way along the stream, curving with the water. Whitetail deer stopped eating long enough to glance at the car then returned to their meals. Two spotted fawns chased each other along the edge of the field. She slowed to watch.

A few feet ahead the road forked. Missy had said to take the right fork and follow the sign for the pool. The staff house was at the end of the road beyond the pool. As she pulled into a parking area beside the house, Missy burst out the back door and sprinted to the car.

"MaryRose, I'm so glad you're here!" She grabbed her before she got all the way out of the car. "How are you? How's work? Your foot? I've worried about you all week."

MaryRose laughed. "I'm fine. Wrote three articles this week. My foot's good as new. No need to worry."

"Glad you had a good week. Rehearsals stunk here; no one was in the mood. Bout drove me crazy. Then last night my agent and I had a big argument."

She kicked the dirt. "He's got several things in mind for me in California after the summer ends. So far, none of them thrill me. The best paying one involves nudity. I refuse to do that."

"It's good you hold to your values."

Missy glanced at a fawn on the edge of the drive then focused on her toe tracing circles in the gravel. "That's about the

86

only one I held onto. After my ex's abuse and the divorce, I walked away from God. But let's not talk about that."

"Gotcha. I'd as soon not talk about Mom, Dad, and Nana either."

"Good. Let's go have breakfast at the diner in Logan. The quaint town sits between the mountains, and has a river and train tracks that sort of divide it all up."

"Sounds charming."

Another seven miles of snaking roads and they pulled up in front of an old silver train car. The equally old wooden sign read Aracoma Diner.

"Don't let the look deceive you. Food's great here."

They chose a booth in the back. A harried waitress brought coffee. "My goodness, it's nice to see new faces in here of a morning."

Missy waved a dismissive hand. "Take your time; we're not in a rush."

The waitress froze. "Oh my gosh. You are Missy Greene. I went to New York and saw you on Broadway. Oh. My. Gosh. Can I have your autograph?"

She pulled her waitress pad out of her apron and placed it on the table in front of Missy who picked up the pen, looked at the waitress' name tag, "I'd be happy to, Alice." She wrote a little message on the back of the pad and handed it to the waitress.

Alice grabbed it and ran into the kitchen, yelling that nobody was going to believe she waited on Missy Greene.

MaryRose peeked over her menu at Missy. She'd never even considered the friend she used to get into trouble with had fans. So far the waitress remained in the kitchen squealing.

"Do you suppose she'll come back and take our order?"

Missy burst into laughter. "Who knows?"

"What did you write on her order pad?"

"I said to follow her dreams wherever they took her."

"That's a mite cliché, don't you think?"

"Yep. But I wasn't feeling creative. Alice seemed to like it. In the past few weeks I've learned a lot about West Virginians. They love their homes, their families, and they dream big. You'll not find a more beautiful place and people in our country."

"I was thinking about that this morning."

When Alice returned, her face was flushed. "I'm sorry. I got so excited I forgot to take your order. Thank you for your autograph. I can't get over you're here at this diner. What can I get for you? By the way, there's no charge."

Missy touched Alice's hand. "It's an honor to be here, and I will pay for our breakfasts too."

Once Alice calmed down, they placed their orders. It tickled MaryRose to watch Alice fawn over Missy.

The waitress placed two huge plates of blueberry pancakes in front of them. MaryRose had never eaten so many pancakes in one sitting. "How in the world will we walk out of here if we eat all of these?"

Missy slathered her pancakes with syrup and took her first bite.

"Yum. MaryRose Elliott, I know you can eat all of that and more and never gain a single pound."

In between bites Missy described the play and the cast.

"It's an historical musical about this Shawnee Princess named Aracoma. She rescued one of General Braddock's scouts from being executed by her father Chief Cornwall. They fell in love, but it does end badly for them. I tried to grow my hair for the role, but it was way too curly, so I bobbed it and wear a wig instead. I got you and Papa Shane tickets for opening night. It's in two weeks, can you come?"

"Wouldn't miss it. I might ask Randall—"

"Oh yes, tell me more about him."

MaryRose kicked her under the table. "Anywaaaay. I might ask Randall and his daughter if they want to come. Oh, and Trudy really wants one too. Can you get more tickets?"

"As many as you want. Now, Randall?"

"You're not going to let it go are you?"

"Nope."

"You saw him, what else can I say? I can hardly breathe around him. My tongue won't function. I haven't dated much, but the few times I did never affected me the way sitting on the dock and talking with him for twenty minutes did. I'm not ready for a relationship, though."

"Why?"

"Because—as you know, everyone I love gets taken. Maybe I should introduce him to my exotic best friend, the actress. No man has ever resisted her."

"Except for Randall. He couldn't take his eyes off you. Besides, we're talking about you. I'm not interested in dating anyone while I'm here. I'll be going back to New York or California soon enough. And the whole people-you-love-getting-taken thing is dumb. I'm still around. "

She ignored the comment. "I've never known you to be alone for long."

Missy nodded. "Guess both of us are kind of known for that."

"I was always with Sean."

"Really? What about the dreamy football jock? You dumped him hard and fast. Never did understand that one."

"It's simple. He wanted what I was unwilling to give. Thus ends this episode of jerks I have dated." She underscored her statement by trying to shove a forkful of pancakes into her mouth. She missed and they dropped dead center into her lap.

They burst out laughing.

MaryRose returned from Logan and tackled her writing. She was trying to put together character profiles of Patrick and

Rose for the novel she planned to write about them. But she kept being distracted when looking things up in a journal and getting sucked into the reading. Pushing that aside, she decided transcribing more into the computer files would work. No matter what she worked on it went about as well as mowing the lawn with scissors.

Maybe a light lunch before Jonathon arrived to take her shopping would lighten her mood. After chopping lettuce, carrots, tomatoes, and onions into a bowl, she topped the salad with violet flowers and a rosemary and vinegar dressing. Taking the salad onto the back porch, she sat down and leaned against the corner post. From there the view of the lake was perfect. But the cement floor was hard. A porch swing or glider might work out there. She'd look for one in town.

The honeysuckle bushes along the edge of the property line started blooming two days ago. The fragrance reminded her of summer and home and everything good.

Her reverie broke when Dapple's barking announced Jonathon's approach from the house on the hill. "Mind if I pull up a little porch and sit?"

"Help yourself."

As Jonathon sat and leaned against the other post, he patted his legs and Dapple ran across the yard and leaped into his lap. "This little guy may not be a guard dog, but he won't let anyone sneak up on you." Dapple rewarded the compliment with dog kisses on Jonathon's cheek.

He squirmed. "I'm thinking a chair would be more comfortable."

"I'm hoping to find a swing today."

"A swing?" He looked at the ceiling. "I know my brother's construction is strong enough, but is there really room?"

"It's worth a try." She took her last bite of salad and set the bowl down. "I'm enjoying the honeysuckle. What blooms next?"

He rested his hands behind his head and stretched long legs

out in front of him. "Well, there's mimosa and Paulownia grows all over the mountains. It's like nose heaven out here all summer."

She inhaled. "I bet so."

A butterfly flew across the porch and Dapple leaped after it, chasing it all around the yard. He jumped to catch it and landed in the middle of a puffball spewing brown dust all over.

"Oh Dapple, I was leaving that there. Now you ruined it."

"Why would you care about a puffball? I'm on Dapple's side, I too love stomping them." Jonathon brushed the dust off the puppy as he climbed back into his lap.

"They are nature's styptic powder. Collecting the powder is a bit tricky, but it lasts forever and quells bleeding more thoroughly than styptic. I always keep a little bottle of it in my first aid kit."

He stared at her. "You're a wealth of knowledge."

"Oh there is so much more to learn. Would you like something to eat? I can make a salad."

Chuckling, he rubbed circles on his stomach. "I came from lunch with Mom. Couldn't eat another bite."

The silence between them stretched lazily. She stood, grabbed Dapple and her dishes, and took them inside. When she stepped back onto the porch, Jonathon waited on the sidewalk.

"What are we shopping for, anyway?"

"My cupboards will look like Ma Hubbard's soon if I don't find the grocery store."

He stopped beside the Volkswagen and stared. "Still can't believe you came here in that old thing and all your stuff fit in it."

She patted the roof of the orange car affectionately. "This 'old thing' is a '73 Super Beetle, a classic. I had it tuned before I left North Carolina. It's in fine condition. Nana and Papa bought it for me when I graduated from high school. It was already a classic then."

Glancing inside, "It's in primo condition."

"Let me show you how great this car is!" She opened the passenger door for him and walked around to her side.

"I've never ridden in a bug before."

"Never?"

His answer was drowned out by the rumble of the muffler as the engine started. "What in the world?"

"Expanded muffler pipes. I did a little customizing when I added the stereo system. Sean wanted it to sound sporty so he had these tailpipes added. You should have heard the glass packs he added first. I about died when he came home with them. These are a compromise. I'm so used to them I think the whistle of the regular bugs sounds weird."

He looked sideways at her and raised his eyebrows. "Can't believe I didn't notice this last week."

"Me either." She stopped in the road.

"Umm, MaryRose, you're in the middle of the road."

"Are you going to tell me which way to the grocery store, or is my stomach supposed to find it?"

He wagged his finger. "Go to the end of the road and turn left onto Lakeview Drive. At the stop sign make a right. Food Corral is on the edge of town."

As she followed his directions, he pointed out landmarks. "Bobby Trumble's garage is over there on the right. He's about the nicest man I've ever known. The gas station's been in his family since before the lake was built. He kind of keeps track of everybody around here. Up ahead on the left you can see Faith Chapel Church on Maple Street. That's where Mom, Dad, and I go."

She looked toward the church. A quaint stone structure tucked back off the road surrounded by massive Sugar Maple trees. The stained glass windows were brilliant. She would love exploring the church. Behind the old chapel she could see a newer and larger stone structure. That must be the educational center.

"Your parents told me about the church last week. Do Andrea and Randall attend there also?"

"Used to. I don't think he's been in a church since Jessica's funeral."

She swallowed. Pain she related to. With God she was barely making it through. How did Randall face his grief without faith?

Jonathon pointed to the next intersection, "Make the next right."

"Has your family always lived here?"

"Pretty much. My family, the Cobbs and the Nolans, were landowners. They sold a lot of it to a land management company. They kept the home place where Randall lives and the little house where Mom and Dad live. We still own pretty much all of our side of Cobb Cove right down to the water."

"Lake Nolan is named after—"

"My mom's family."

"That name is real familiar. I'm not sure why. I can't place a finger on it, but seems like I've read or heard it before. I think that's why I decided to come here and find somewhere to live."

MaryRose slowed down to make the turn. "Maybe it will come to me. Jonathon, where do you live?"

"I have a small apartment on the other side of the lake. This nice couple from church turned their upstairs into an apartment after the kids moved away. It's perfect for me. There's the Food Corral on the left."

With a quick turn she was in front of a large store. "Looks like more than a grocery store."

Laughter, rich and strong, erupted from him. "It's an everything store."

"I love small towns. Mine was similar. Everything in Hertford was in the center of town on Main Street."

He nodded. "For years around here the mining companies owned the bank, the store, the houses, everything. Folks still talk about the Cabin Creek Wars and the Matewan Massacre. You should look them up."

"I will." She tossed her keys in her purse and turned toward the store entrance. "I like it here."

"Me too."

They stopped at the front doors. "Oh look. Porch swings. Do you think the ceiling would hold one?"

"Randall built it. It will hold anything. But if you want to buy one of those, we need to go back and get Randall's truck. Even with the seats folded down there's no way it will fit in the back of your car."

She crossed her arms. "Challenge accepted. Let's buy my food and my swing, and I'll show you how to pack a bug!"

"Ooh, she's spunky too. Tell you what. I have to go next door to the bank for a few minutes. I'll meet you back here, and we'll do our best to get the swing loaded."

"Got yourself a deal."

She wandered into the store and quickly purchased a few groceries, the swing, and the eyebolts the store clerk recommended for hanging it. After lowering the back seats of the car she studied the swing.

It would have to be taken apart. She opened the trunk and grabbed her little tool box. She unbolted the seat from the frame. As the seat landed on the pavement she looked up and saw Jonathon watching her.

He smirked. "The lady even has her own toolbox. Amazing."

Indignantly, she brushed her hands together. "I am not helpless I'll have you know. But, if you are a true southern gentleman you'll offer to help a lady in distress. They were out of the unassembled, boxed ones, so, I have to dismantle this one to make it fit inside the car."

He turned around, stood with his back to her, looked all around, and then faced her again. "Don't see a lady in distress anywhere. Just a stubborn one. West Virginia fought with the North, remember?"

His grin aggravated her, but admitting she needed help was the worst part. But four hands would do this task better than two. She grumbled.

"I give up. Will you help me?"

He bowed. "At your service, ma'am."

In short order they had the armrests unbolted and the swing folded. It loaded smoothly into the back of her car and they placed the grocery bags around it.

Jonathon brushed his hands on his jeans as he climbed into his seat. "I didn't believe you could do it. I'm duly impressed, MaryRose."

"I believe this is where I say I told you so, but I'll hold my tongue since I'm hoping for help hanging it on my porch."

"Good idea."

The evening air was still hot despite thunderstorms in the late afternoon breaking the humidity. MaryRose got the journal and a pillow and went out back. Time to try out the new swing.

~~~~

August 15, 1865

Harvesting. Canning. Sewing. It seems like that's all I do anymore. Gramma hardly gives me time to breathe, much less write or walk. I did get away last evening after supper and went to the river. I took my shoes off, raised my skirts, and waded in to my knees. How I wanted to swim. But there was some boys down river from me and I didn't want to do something wrong.

I don't reckon girls around here do that. I said something about swimming in the ocean to the two girls my age I met at church. I thought they was gonna pass out from shock right then. They said only the boys and loose girls swim around here. Guess I am a loose girl. Whatever that means.

I asked Gramma what it meant and she said it is a girl what goes around doing things with boys a lady would never do. Things only for married couples. Made me more confused. Does that mean its okay to swim after I get married? Stupid.

I think if you live near water you better know how to swim. I will teach my children. Don't much care whether theys boys or girls, I will teach them. Besides, why would you look at sparkling water on a hot day and not want to cool off?

Tonight after supper Gramma took me into the woods. She gave me a new kind of apron. It ties around my waist and has a bag attached. Inside the bag there are pouches. She showed me how to gather the wild flowers and plants we use for cooking and healing. I gather enough to fill a pouch and then go to the next plant and fill another pouch.

By the time we got home, my apron was heavy and all of the pouches were filled with something. Then we spread them all out on the table. Some we bundled and hung from the ceiling to dry. Others we put right in pots on the stove to cook the juices out. Then she got jars and we wrote on them what was going inside.

Let me see if I can remember. We had mint, late summer violets, yarrow, lemon balm, lemon grass, red root, sumac—she says its not the poison kind, sassafras root, senna, sage, puffballs, and swamp milkweed. I don't think my brain can hold all of this learning.

She had me opening the puffballs and storing the powder in a black jar. Says it is precious because it stops bleeding when applied to a wound. I always thought they was good for kicking and popping them open. But I about caught the house on fire. Some of the powder got in the fireplace and it blew up. Sparks flew all over the house. Now I know why she told me to be far away from the stove when I harvested them. At least I will remember that one.

So much more to write, but my eyes are not wantin to stay open. Grampa called and told me to out the lantern too.

Jesus, help me remember all Gramma is teaching me. I may be the last person in her family she can teach. Something tells me the people around here rely on her knowledge and one day maybe they will me too. Amen.

~~~~

MaryRose slammed the journal closed. It was one thing to read about Gramma Rose dealing with a child bitten by a rattlesnake as she was healing from her own, but to read about a puffball episode the same day she and Jonathon had a conversation about them? How many parallels between her life and Gramma Rose's would she find?

Leaving the journal on the swing, MaryRose raced out of the

yard down to the lake, Dapple close at her heels. Working her way around the inlet, she splashed in the shallow water at the edge where the bank was too steep for walking. She stomped the water and dared the rocks to trip her.

"Isn't it enough I'm alone here? I thought the journals would bring me peace. I hoped reading the romance of Rose and Patrick would bring solace. But no. Instead, it's like she lived my life before me. So how many of her family die and leave her behind? Tell me, Lord? How do you choose which people get to suffer the most? Why did you pick me?"

A wild rosebush snagged her cheek and scratched a path across her face. She grabbed it and ripped it from her face and hair, oblivious to the thorns still in her palm. As she rubbed the blood from her cheek, tears stung the scratch. "It's not easy trusting you right now, God. I'm trying. But whenever I think I've got it mastered and I understand this faith thing, something else happens."

She drooped to the ground and sat in the water. Calm ripples lapped against her legs. Tears traced down her face and dropped into her palms. "Lord, I wish I could go back—back to the hardware store and kiss Granddaddy one more time."

Eyes closed, she heard the song she'd always loved. It began as a soft hum then the words flowed out. The last verse came out in choked sobs. Drawing her knees under her chin and grasping them tight, she looked toward heaven and whispered, "I'd like a dream to follow, God."

CHAPTER 10

*M*aryRose wanted so badly to sneak into the back of the Sunday School classroom unnoticed. But who said you get what you want? The door creaked as she opened it and every person in the room looked up from their Bible and stared at her. It was as bad as being the new kid in school.

As her nerves increased and her stomach twisted, she considered running out, but, she'd promised God she would try. Jonathon jumped from his chair in the front of the room and welcomed her.

His smile calmed her nerves. "You got here in time to meet everyone before the lesson begins."

A tall man standing next to the podium extended his hand. "I'm Mark Wilson. You must be MaryRose."

She glanced around the room. Several people approached and welcomed her with comments about how they'd prayed for her after the snakebite. If only she could crawl under the table now.

Jonathon touched her shoulder and steered her to the chair beside his.

"Thank you." She sat quickly and tried to look small.

Before the teacher began the lesson the door opened again. He was obviously taken aback when Randall entered. Randall promptly took the empty chair on her other side and winked at her before facing the podium.

Everyone had told her Randall didn't go to church. Yet, here he sat beside her, the scent of his cologne gently inviting her to inhale more.

Jonathon leaned toward his brother. "Welcome. It's been a long time since we've seen you here."

He then looked back at her and smiled. "Would you join me for lunch after church?"

Oh goodness. Should she encourage him? She didn't feel any attraction to Jonathon, and definitely nothing compared to the breath stopping she experienced in Randall's presence. But Jonathon was the one asking her to lunch, not his brother. She looked between them and faced Jonathon. "I thought you didn't date?"

"It's not a date. On Sundays, we meet at the dock for a cook-out. All of us will be there."

"Everybody?"

"The whole family. It's a weekly thing for us during summer. That's what we were doing last week when you and Missy saw us. By the way, she can come too. It'll be fun."

"Missy's working, but I'll come. What time?"

"I'll be by around one."

Randall's jaw tightened and he crossed his arms over his chest. "Guess I'll see you there, then."

Did he not want her to come?

Mark cleared his throat. "Okay, y'all greetings are over. Open your Bibles to Matthew 6:14. We've been doing a study on forgiveness—"

She didn't hear the rest of his sentence. Her palms sweat and her eyes blurred. Heart pounding so loud she was sure Randall and Jonathon heard it.

Forgiveness.

She wanted to get away from the word. She didn't realize she'd been holding her breath until she let it out in one huge sigh.

Randall touched her hand and leaned toward her. "MaryRose?"

"I'm okay."

"Need to talk?"

Yes. No. Not to you. Can hardly think straight around you. "Maybe sometime."

"Anytime."

Open up. Share your pain. Allow Me to heal you. Forgiveness is where it starts.

She stared at him. "What did you say?"

"I said, anytime."

"No, after that. What did you say?"

"Umm, MaryRose, I didn't say anything else."

Her shoulders slumped. If Randall hadn't spoken then who? God?

Yes.

Oh great, now He chose to break His silence with her.

My house is a good place to do so. MaryRose, I love you with an everlasting love. Listen to the lesson.

She tried. But each mention of forgiveness and freedom made her feel more like Alice falling into the tunnel in Wonderland with all those people spinning around her. The words echoed and mocked. By the time Mark closed class with prayer, she couldn't stop the tears from flowing. How in the world would forgiving the drunk who caused her heartache actually make the pain stop? Stupid concept.

Jonathon passed her a tissue.

MaryRose dabbed her eyes and took a deep breath. As

"amen" was spoken around the room, she hoped a semblance of normalcy had returned to her eyes. No way could she face anyone. She slammed her Bible shut and stepped into the group leaving. Eyes downcast, she scooted out into the hallway and turned what she hoped was the direction of the sanctuary and walked right into Andrea.

"MaryRose! I didn't know you'd be here." A frown passed over her face and she touched her cheek. "You've been crying."

"I'm fine. The Sunday School class got to me a little bit." Little bit. Yeah, right. Guess she'd become quite the liar.

Before she could make a quick exit, Andrea looped her arm through hers.

"Well, you'll have to sit with Daddy and me during worship."

"Yes, please do." His soft words were like a breath behind her.

"Oh...I...no..."

Andrea pulled her forward. "It's all good. We'll sit in the back so no one has to know you've been crying."

If only that was all she had to worry about. How could she think straight about anything with Randall sitting beside her? She had to get a grip. She was as bad as a fifteen-year-old with a crush.

"I'd love to sit with you."

But not next to Randall. She took the aisle seat beside Andrea.

MaryRose sat at the lake's edge with her feet stretched into the cool water. Dapple stalked dragonflies up and down the shoreline. It had been a long time since she'd had a near-perfect day. The Cobb family treated her like one of them and her heart held a sense of belonging.

Giggles from the lake tugged at her heart. Rachel and Luke

were teaching Emma to swim. What a cute girl. Although they had said she was troubled, she sure was enjoying herself in the lake.

Before she could wallow in too much melancholy, the dripping adolescent ran up and dropped to the ground beside her.

"Luke and Rachel are going to do the swing. I don't like it. You look lonely. I hate being lonely. Can I sit here?"

"I'd love that."

"Good." She pointed to the tree with the V and swing hanging from a branch out over the water.

"You climb up the ladder and stand on the V. Then get on the swing. It looks fun, but when they let it go and fall into the water, it scares me."

"Oh, I think all of it looks great."

"Then you should do it."

She shook her head. "Not today." The first time she tried the swing would not be in front of Randall Cobb.

Emma looked into the lake where Andrea and her boyfriend, Kenneth, floated on rafts.

"That's Kenneth. I don't like him."

"Why not?" Andrea was obviously enamored with the young man, but he made MaryRose uneasy. Each time she caught him looking at her she felt naked. What did Emma see?

"He's always around. Andrea used to let me hang out with her. But now she's with him all the time."

Before MaryRose could reply, Emma stood and announced to whoever would hear, "I'm hungry. Good talking with you." She walked away.

Teenaged attention spans were a lot like toddlers. MaryRose looked toward the boathouse where the brothers argued over a boat repair. A hammer hit the deck, Randall swore, Jonathon picked the hammer up and handed it back to him. They worked together handing tools back and forth easily as if repairing a boat was a choreographed dance.

"I don't know about you, but I'm ready to eat." Randall brushed his hands on his jeans.

As they walked away from the boat, Jonathon approached her. "Think we got it running in time. Randall's temper was rising faster than his hunger."

She stood and brushed the wrinkles out of her cotton skirt and straightened the peasant blouse.

Jonathon nodded toward Randall standing by the grill. "He's got to do his whole grill cleaning routine before cooking. We've got time for a walk."

She looked at her skirt and bare feet. "I'm not really dressed for a hike. But I guess it will be okay if we walk around the edge of the lake."

She sensed Randall behind her as his cologne scent brought the familiar intoxicating fog into her mind. She faced him. His eyes drew her in, and the fog thickened. Too bad it wasn't Jonathon's grill ritual.

Jonathon tapped her shoulder. "MaryRose?"

She jumped. "What? I'm sorry—guess I got distracted." She slipped her feet into her sneakers and waved to Randall. "We'll be back soon."

When Jonathon grasped her hand and led her away, Randall's smile changed to a scowl. "I think we upset your brother."

"Him? Naw, he doesn't know what he wants right now. He'll figure it out."

Before she could ask what he meant, Jonathon changed the subject.

"I've heard bits and pieces, but am still not sure how of all the places in West Virginia you could choose you picked Lake Nolan."

She stepped over the rocks, leaning on him for balance. His strong hands steadied her. "It's Missy and my great-great Gramma's faults."

His eyes widened, and he cleared his throat. "Missy?"

"She's the lead in the summer plays at Mountain Theatre this season. I came with her when she auditioned and I fell in love with the mountains. And my great-great grandparents were from around here somewhere. Seemed a good time to trace my roots."

"Interesting. Missy is in the summer theatres? I love the shows. Try to see them every summer."

"Would you like to go opening night?"

"I'd love to."

"I planned to ask your whole family."

"What a great night out for us." He kicked a rock into the water. "Mom told me about your husband, baby, well, about your family. So much loss. That's rough."

She picked up a flat rock and skipped it across the water. "Even though I've never read anywhere in the Bible we're promised life would be fair, I do know He promises He won't forsake us. But, honestly, right now, in the middle of my losses, it's hard not to feel forsaken." She watched the rock skip several times.

"What about you? Your life in thirty seconds?"

"Mine won't take thirty seconds. I have a degree in divinity from UGA and I work for Randall at Sykes Construction. Never married."

"Not doing anything with your degree?"

"Not yet. I'd appreciate your prayers." He skipped a rock too and stared across the lake. "You have no family left?"

MaryRose clasped her hands together against her stomach. "No."

"That's rough."

She grabbed a handful of rocks and hurled them into the water. "You've no idea. Nobody does. My former pastor—who's also my step-grandfather and my husband's real grandfather—I know, complicated, says I still need closure. "

"What do you think?"

She walked ahead of him and kicked the water. "I try not to think about it. One minute I'm enjoying my new life and the next I want to break something. I'm not used to this feeling. I hate the drunk who killed my parents. I don't think I can ever forgive him. Isn't that closure?"

Jonathon caught up and turned her to face him. "Not really. Sounds more like PTSD to me. Bitterness inside will eat your heart like a poison."

"PTSD?"

"Post-Traumatic Stress Disorder. Your recent loss was a major trauma for you. You have symptoms of PTSD. Forgiving the drunk may be all it takes to make you feel better."

She shook her finger in his face. "All because one man got drunk? I shouldn't have gone to church today. It's easier to read my Bible in private and sing while I garden. I don't want him shown mercy."

There was a large rock by her feet. Stepping away from Jonathon she lifted it and threw it into the water.

"That rock hit the water sort of like Dad said you condition soil."

Was nothing secret? Heat spread up her neck and across her cheeks.

"He isn't a busybody. He was genuinely concerned about you and asked me to pray."

"Look, I know I can't hold this hate. It burns. I can't shake it either. After I finished my gardening tantrum I prayed and sang hymns. Calm settled in." She touched her chest where the ever-present burn dwelled. "But I know hatred is in here still. And it's messing with my writing, too."

"I'll keep you in my prayers."

"Thanks." The knot of tension in her shoulder unwound a little.

He offered his hand. "We should go back, but there's one more thing I want to talk about."

"Yes?"

"I'd like to get to know Missy better. What do you think? Is she available?"

The man rushed those words so fast she could barely understand them. MaryRose struggled not to laugh. "I think you'd have to ask her, not me?"

"Guess you're right." He turned toward home.

"Jonathon?" She stepped in stride beside him. "I'm glad we're friends, and for what it's worth, I think you and Missy could be good together." She stood on tiptoes and kissed his cheek.

A scream rent the air.

$\mathcal{B}$y the time Jonathon and MaryRose made it around the inlet Randall was coming out of the water with Rachel in his arms. She wasn't moving.

What in the world happened? Rachel was a good swimmer. MaryRose grabbed her skirt and held it above her knees so she could run faster but stubbed her toe on a rock rounding the last bend. She ignored the pain.

As they approached the dock an ambulance was backing down the driveway.

Luke knelt beside Rachel, hands shaking as he wiped blood from a wound on her head. Randall hovered over them. His breath was so rapid she feared he'd hyperventilate, but he wouldn't move out of the paramedics' way.

Jonathon tried to pull him back but Randall shoved his hand away. MaryRose stepped in front of Randall and he looked up. When their eyes locked, she said, "Randall, let them do their job."

He stepped back and let the medics by.

She touched his shoulder. "What happened?"

"She slipped on the dock and hit her head on the post. She's unconscious. There's so much blood. Blood—"

"Shhh, it will be okay." She squeezed his shoulder. "Everything will be okay."

"You don't know that." He shoved her hand away and glared at her. "I heard those words before and it wasn't okay. Nothing was after that."

He pounded his hands together. Pacing the deck he repeated, "Told me it would be okay. It wasn't okay. Never okay again."

MaryRose realized Randall was remembering another time, a different emergency.

"Randall, this is different."

"Why isn't she awake? It's all my fault."

"What—"

"You didn't see. Too busy kissing my brother to see anything. So why not leave us alone?" He stomped to the ambulance.

His words hit her as hard as any punch to her chest could. She backed away and turned toward her house.

Jonathon grabbed her hand. "Don't go. I'll talk to him."

"No. I'm a big girl. I can fight my own battles."

MaryRose straightened up and headed toward Randall. How dare he be so rude. How dare he treat her like a loose woman. When she got to his side, she met his glare with one of her own.

"You, sir, are a jerk."

She slapped him so hard her hand stung. The look of shock was worth every ounce of nerves shaking her whole body at the moment.

She stomped past him and marched to her house without looking back. Dropping to her porch swing, she let the weight of what had happened land on her. She was the outsider. She fooled herself into thinking she actually belonged with them. The man was nothing but her landlord.

She'd do well to remember that.

Dapple jumped at her legs and she picked him up cradling him in her arms.

Jonathon approached. "My brother was a jerk. But, I think your insight was right when you told him this was another time. He had to be remembering Jessica. Even so, he's probably needed a bit of sense slapped into him for a while."

"I shouldn't have. I was about as much of a jerk with Missy a few weeks ago when she was trying to help me. Grief messes with us, doesn't it?"

"That it does. I'm going to follow them to the hospital. I told them I'd clean the food up so the critters won't have a feast."

"I'll help." She placed Dapple inside and followed him back to the dock. They packed all the food back into coolers, turned off the grill, and rode up the hill in the Gator.

Unloading the coolers into the house was easy, but putting stuff away was far from it. Randall's kitchen was huge. She had no idea where to find food storage containers. By the time Jonathon joined her she had every drawer and cabinet door open.

"This is cleaning up?"

"This man has the craziest system I've ever seen in a kitchen." She pitched the dish towel toward him. "Thanks for the support."

He caught it before it hit him. His laughter boomed in the room. "Randall—a kitchen system? He puts things anywhere. Let me help you."

Once she located the correct containers, cleanup went smoothly. After she washed the last dish and let the sink drain, she leaned against the counter. "Thanks for the help. Let's pray before you go to the hospital."

They sat at the table, joined hands, and prayed. When they finished, he squeezed her hand. "It's nice to have a new friend."

"Would you like to come over tomorrow night for supper? I'll see if Missy is free."

He perked up. "That'd be great."

"Six-thirty?"

"Works for me."

Jonathon left and she began putting the containers in the fridge. Her stomach growled. No wonder, no one had a chance to eat anything. The family would probably be famished when they got home. Now, there's something she could fix.

She made a meatloaf out of the hamburger, boiled and mashed the potatoes, and chopped vegetables for a big salad.

While the food cooked, she explored a bit. There were pictures on the walls, tables, shelves—everywhere. A family history displayed. She swallowed a huge lump when she came to the pictures that no longer had Jessica in them. No smiles in an entire series of photos. The sadness in Randall's and Andrea's eyes broke her heart. Empty spots in pictures meant empty spots in lives. Her anger at him melted into compassion and empathy for their mutual pain. She walked from one photo to another placing her hands on them and praying for this man and his sweet daughter.

When the oven timer buzzed, she had difficulty pulling herself away from the photos. After setting the table and writing a note for them, she took a plate for herself and went home.

MaryRose stabbed at her supper. Hard to believe the man in the pictures was the same one she slapped.

The phone rang. Missy.

She swallowed her mouthful. "Hey. How was your day? Mine stunk."

"So cookout with hunky landlord wasn't so good?"

"He was a jerk. I slapped him."

Missy burst out laughing. "Uh-oh. Last man you called a jerk and slapped apologized for going to the beer party and became your husband two years later."

"That was different."

"Okay. Tell me why this one's a jerk."

"I'm not mad anymore. Actually, I'm pretty sure I owe him an apology." How could she stay furious at the sad man in those photos? Relaying the afternoon to Missy made her sure she had amends to make.

"One hunky man kisses you and his equally good-looking brother is obviously jealous about it and you can't see that?"

"Jonathon didn't kiss me. I gave him a friendly peck on the cheek. You hear the word *kiss* and that's all you focus on, isn't it? And, Randall is not jealous. He hardly knows me."

"Goodness me, those were the exact words you used with Sean. Can't help it if I'm a hopeless romantic."

MaryRose stood up and carried her dishes inside. "Helpless is more like it. Randall is my landlord. And it isn't me his brother is interested in. He asked me if you are available."

"Me? A divorced actress and a man with a divinity degree? Could be interesting, wouldn't it?"

"Stranger things have happened."

Silence.

MaryRose high-fived the air. It wasn't often she made Missy speechless.

"He also asked if you could get tickets for him for opening night. While you're at it, why not get enough for the whole Cobb family?"

"Even the landlord?" Missy's voice was barely audible. "How in the world do I look Jonathon in the eyes, knowing he likes me?"

"Yeah, even Randall. And you look at Jonathon the same way you do everyone else. It's not something I've ever known you to struggle with."

"Something tells me this is different." More silence. "I'll get the tickets. They'll be at the gate."

"Jonathon says he's been there many times."

Missy's sharp intake of breath sounded like a snake hiss through the phone. "Great. Another fan of the actress who did it for the past several years. I apparently have huge shoes to fill."

"I have every confidence you will."

"Hope you're right. Maybe Mr. Jerk will be back to Mr. Hunky Landlord by then!"

"I never called him that. You did. Are you free tomorrow night?"

"Why?"

"I invited Jonathon for supper and told him I'd invite you. You should have seen his eyes light up."

Silence.

"You're a big chicken."

"Yep. But I have rehearsal and photos tomorrow night anyway. So I can't come. Maybe next time."

"I'll hold you to that."

"Okay. Talk to you in a few days. Go ahead and make up with Hunky Landlord, too."

Missy hung up before she could respond.

Somewhere in the distance a dog barked. MaryRose opened her eyes but couldn't really move. Her knees were locked and the kink in her neck made moving her head almost impossible. She pushed herself upright and shrugged. Evidently lying down on the swing for a few minutes while Dapple was running around the yard had turned into sleeping for who knows how long. The soft pink in the sky and solitary star over the trees gave her an idea. The sun obviously went down a while ago since darkness approached.

Where was her dog, anyway?

"Dapple? Where are you, what was the bark about?'

The fence gate opened as Randall entered the yard. "Pretty sure it was me."

MaryRose reached up and brushed her hair back into the braid. She watched him cross the yard and willed her heart to stop pounding. It wouldn't comply. He stopped at the porch.

"Mind if we talk for a few minutes?"

"Sure. Pull up some porch."

He sat and leaned against the post. "You didn't have to cook for us. But I sure do appreciate it. Andrea and I hadn't even thought about eating until we walked into the house and smelled the delicious meatloaf. Thanks."

"You're welcome. How's Rachel?"

His eyes lit for a moment as he straightened up. "They're okay."

"They?"

"She's pregnant."

"That's wonderful."

"The doctor says the baby is fine, due in October. Rachel has a mild concussion and stitches, but she'll be up and about in a few days. This is exciting because she wasn't supposed to be able to get pregnant."

"What a wonderful blessing for them."

"Yep. But they'll have to move. The apartment above the boathouse has two tiny bedrooms."

"Sounds like a good problem to have."

"Yep."

Randall picked up a stick Dapple had left on the porch and began tapping it on his jeans. He reclined against the post again. He was a study in tension. Jaws set. Cheek muscle twitching. Brows furrowed. The vein in his neck popped the way Sean's had when he was stressed.

They spoke at the same time.

"MaryRose, I—"

"Randall, I'm—"

He raised his eyebrows. "Ladies first."

"I'm not sure I acted like much of a lady earlier. You had a crisis going on and I slapped you. Then I took your response to my action personally, when, in reality none of it was about me. I'm sorry I slapped you."

"I'm not."

"Why?"

"I deserved it. You called it correctly, I was being a jerk. Nothing warranted my attitude to you."

He stood and faced her. The intensity of his eyes touched her heart.

"I know it's been a long day and if this is presumptuous please tell me. But, how about we go watch the moon rise?"

"I'd like that."

He offered his hand. As their fingers interlocked, her heart fluttered. He squeezed her hand. Had he felt something too?

They walked to the end of the dock. He sat cross-legged while she dangled bare feet in the water. The sag of his shoulders and the weight of his exhale looked familiar.

How quickly current situations took her back to traumas and losses from the past. It felt almost as if they were happening right then. The silence stretched between them as the last waning light from the sun faded.

"It wasn't about you kissing my brother. I don't think it was really even about Rachel's fall. It started that way. But then all I could see was..." He stared across the inlet into the dark woods.

She whispered, "Jessica. You saw her, didn't you?"

"How'd you know?"

"Been there, done that. Still do."

"Seeing Rachel lying there, Luke's fear, the sirens, the hospital—brought it back like yesterday." He reached for her hand again. "I panicked. Felt like there was something I should do. Then you convinced me to get out of the EMT's ways. I was on the edge of rational thought. MaryRose, you calmed me." He looked down at her. "And that frightened me. Jessica was the only person who ever had the ability to calm me when I was losing it.

"I'm forty-one." His knee bounced up and down like a twitching eyelid. "Jessica died when I was thirty."

He reached over and grasped her hand. She wasn't sure it was as much a conscious move as an emotional reaction. But the effect it had disarmed.

"Life was good until Jessica began having trouble with shortness of breath. The doctors did all kinds of tests and found a heart murmur. They assured us it wasn't a problem. Told us she could live with it for years. But she didn't. Andrea begged us to go out and watch the moon. We took the boat out and anchored it outside the cove. A perfect night until she collapsed. Massive heart attack. Died in my lap. Nothing I could do."

They sat quietly for a while. He wiped his eyes and then cleared his throat. "I've never talked to anyone about that night."

She touched a tear trickling down his cheek. "Sometimes things have to wait awhile before we let them out."

He inhaled deeply. "Maybe. Today was the first time Andrea and I've been in church since the funeral. At the hospital, she told me she's glad we went. Then she said we need to let Jessica go. And MaryRose, all I could think about was you."

Warmth filled her chest. The rising moon shone in his eyes. Somehow, she felt sure if she could look into them right now she'd see pain and vulnerability.

"I don't know how to let go. Guess I thought I already had. All I could think of was maybe you'd know. Do you?"

"I open up to God. He removes the pain and frees my heart. I wish I could say it's a done deal now, but I'm still working on it. It starts with prayer."

"What kind of prayer?"

117

"It's not a kind of prayer. I ask Him and He helps the pain slowly go away. He still helps me. Yesterday He did."

His hand rested lightly on her jean-clad knee. "While you sang?"

"You heard?" At least in the dark, he couldn't see her blush.

Releasing her hand her grasped her chin and turned her toward him. "I liked it."

"Well, it was more like after I stopped singing I knew God was helping me again. But I have a long way to go. I was reminded at church. Jonathon helped me get a little perspective."

His shoulders tensed. "I see."

"I don't think you do. Jonathon and I are friends. His counsel to me today was the same I've been feeling and fighting. God's way of confirming what I knew already."

He shook his head. "MaryRose, I don't understand faith like yours, but I'd like to know the peace you have."

"I don't always have it." She chuckled. "I imagine my slap felt less than peaceful."

"True that. Will you pray with me?"

"Sure."

MaryRose faced him and crossed her legs. Their knees touched. She held her hands out and he placed his in them.

Time passed, or did it freeze? Connection. Peace. Calm. Even after they stopped praying, they remained. The silence was as powerful as the prayers.

Dapple barking in the house broke the quiet.

"I guess that's our cue. My puppy needs to go outside."

At her door, he embraced and kissed her. She watched him walk up the hill as Dapple raced around the yard. Then she went inside and lay on the sofa. Not sleeping.

CHAPTER 12

aryRose stared at the ceiling. The soft moonlight shadows morphed into sharp-edged designs. Kind of like her. One minute she slapped the man with a vengeance, and then a few hours later allowed him to give her a brain-rattling kiss.

She spent the whole night flip-flopping on the sofa.

As the rising sun brightened the horizon, she took the journal, walked onto her front stoop and sat. Yawning and stretching, she closed her eyes, raised her chin and soaked in the morning.

She opened the old book and brushed her hands across the page. If only she could take a walk and talk with Gramma Rose. Maybe the parallels between her life and Gramma Rose's weren't so bad.

~~~~

August 16, 1865

I caint write much this night. My hand is about to fall

right off. I been writing and thinking all day. Gramma pulled out a fancy leather book. Way fancier than mine. She writes her important stuff in it, and I have to use proper writing in her book. Guess I should do it in here too. We got up fore the sun and worked till bedtime. The house smells like a plant store, or doctor's office, or something.

I had to write down the instructions for everything. She says we will be doing this all week long. Then we have to gather more and do more. The tomatoes, peppers, beans, and all sorts of garden things are in too. I may not get outside anytime soon.

Much as I hate to do the wash, it may be the only chance I get to go down to the stream. I will offer to do that tomorrow I reckon. I don't guess I will be doing much writing in here this week either.

Dear Jesus, Help my attitude. I know this work is important. I know it will be like this when I am married. Help me grow up some more and not resent what I am supposed to do. Maybe you can help me make my responsibilities be my dreams. Amen.

~~~~

A book with the recipes? MaryRose hadn't seen one in the box. She slammed the journal shut and ran inside. How amazing it would be to have the original *Kitchen Cosmetics* book. She grabbed the box of journals and went through them one by one. The history of the Elliott family: five journals, one paper-thin solid-gold wedding ring, a cotton nightgown—yellowed now—

but beautiful all the same, and a simple ivory, satin wedding dress.

No leather journal containing information on herbs and recipes.

She slumped back on the floor.

"Hey MaryRose." Andrea called from the kitchen door. "Can I come in?"

"Sure."

"Whatcha doin'?" Andrea breezed in and joined her on the floor.

"I was looking for a recipe book Gramma Rose mentioned in her journal. No luck, though. It would have been like finding another treasure."

"I came down to say thanks."

"For?"

"Helping Daddy last night. He really needed to talk to someone. And after he spent time with you, he was different. He walked around the house whistling."

"Whistling?"

"Um-hm. You should slap him more often." She giggled and then rested her head on MaryRose's shoulder. "I've missed having a mom, especially the past few years. I know Daddy's been lonely too. It's like God brought you here for us."

Her heart pounded a rhythm she hadn't felt in years.

"It's hard to explain. My father is himself again, but different too, kinda scatterbrained. The other morning he misplaced his coffee. He wasn't paying attention to what he was doing because he kept looingk down here. When he finally found it he knocked it off the counter. Funny to watch. Gramma says he was that way when he courted Mommy. I think every child should get to see their parents when they have a crush."

A crush. Him too?

Andrea reached over and fingered the satin dress in Mary-Rose's lap. "Who's wedding dress?"

"It was my great-great Gramma's."

"It's beautiful. It would look so pretty on you, with your hair down like it is now. If you ever get married again, you have to wear this dress!"

Words became a big lump in her throat, and her cheeks warmed.

Andrea touched her face. "You're cute when you blush." She stood and brushed off her skirt. "I can't wait to spend more time with you this summer, but I have to go to work now." She kissed MaryRose's cheek then headed out the door.

MaryRose returned the dress and nightgown to the trunk and closed the lid. Then she put the journal away.

Sitting at the desk and reading the journals did nothing to get her mind off of Randall's kiss. She squeezed her eyes shut. If only she could shake off the errant thoughts.

"I have to write today." Transcribing the journals was one thing. It was a matter of copying word for word. Eventually the old journals could be safely stored, and she'd not need to open them as much.

Today she'd planned to start the story, but it proved more daunting than she'd imagined. Hours later she broke for tea. How had the day gone by so rapidly? She spent it pretty much stumped. Shouldn't writing the story be as easy as it had been when she was little sitting on Nana's lap listening to the family stories? Nana always managed to catch the personality of the people in her retelling. How'd she do it?

MaryRose read the details of Patrick's dream again, then pulled out the historical records and read the account stored forever in the county history. She could picture Patrick showing up at the house and imagine Rose's surprise. But that's as far as her imagination would go.

As she read the journals, the people came to life, like they talked to her. All except Patrick. Why was it so difficult to get inside Patrick's head as he prepared to meet his dream bride?

There was something missing. And somehow she knew the fault rested within her.

Something prevented her from hearing the man's voice. He would never get to follow his dream in the story she hoped to write until she figured out why her mind closed him out.

"Oh Lord, I sound like a crazy person. Help me."

She opened the county record and read the now familiar words:

April 22, 1865 Patrick Elliott dreamed about his future bride; where she lived, how he would introduce himself to her, what she would be wearing and how long they would court. The next day he dressed in the clothing he'd worn in his dream and rode his horse 63 miles to a farm he'd only seen in the dream. Upon his arrival at the large estate he introduced himself to the man of the house, Matthew Thomas, who invited the young man to stay for victuals. When Rose Thomas came to the dinner table her father introduced Patrick to her stating the man was there to court her. As happened in the dream, the two were married in Aracoma, West Virginia on November 6, 1865.

It was beyond MaryRose's comprehension what would make a man follow such a bizarre dream. She couldn't begin to get inside his head on this one. And without that she'd never do the scene any justice.

She powered down her computer. Time to make supper anyway. Until she could grasp the whole blind-faith thing, Patrick would have to sit on his horse and wait for her to get back to him.

Spaghetti, salad and garlic bread would make a fun supper. She looked up the hill. Why did Randall refuse her invitation to join them? Did he think she kissed any man the way she did him last night? She flung the dish towel in the sink. And she'd allowed herself to think last night had been the beginning of something special.

"Fine. I'll not let him kiss me again, that's for sure."

A knock at the door interrupted her tantrum. Thank heavens.

"Come in."

Jonathon came in and plopped on the wicker sofa. "How did writing go today?"

"Actually, I'm a bit stuck. Patrick had the dream about his future wife and I left him sitting on his horse in the middle of the road. I'm not sure what he's doing next. He hasn't told me."

Jonathon walked across the room and fingered the stack of papers on the desk. He raised his eyebrows. "The characters talk to you?"

"Well, yeah."

"How?"

"It's hard to explain to a *normal*."

"A normal?"

"An author I love calls people who are not writers, normals. I have the journals and the plot's all laid out in them. But when it comes to the story, I sort of think about the characters and what they will say or do. I get so involved it seems like they tell me their stories. Poor Patrick. I had to leave him on his horse until he tells me what comes next."

"Okay, then. May I help you set the table?" He crossed his arms and smiled. "Or do you want me to feed Patrick's horse? I mean if he's sitting there a while they may get hungry."

She tried to glare at him, but laughed instead. "Now you sound like me. Setting the table would be fine. There will be four of us."

"Four?"

"Luke and Rachel are coming. Missy has rehearsal tonight. I invited Randall but he got grumbly."

"Typical. Glad Rachel and Luke can come."

When they arrived at six-thirty, Rachel appeared to be well. Luke insisted she sit down as soon as they entered.

MaryRose hugged her. "Congratulations."

"Isn't it exciting?" Her hand protectively covered her stomach. Rachel's eyes filled as she rubbed circles over her abdomen. "I miscarried a year ago. We decided not to tell anyone until I made it past the first trimester this time. I'm surprised no one noticed. But our boathouse apartment is going to shrink rapidly. After Emma's summer camp ends, we have to look for a bigger place."

Luke joined the conversation. "I spoke with Aunt Ruth and Uncle Jeb last night and they told us to give it a little time. They might have a plan that will work well for everyone. It's what they do with family."

MaryRose didn't know them well but had seen enough to know this was a close-knit family. She saw Jeb as a watchdog to Ruth's mama bear.

Jonathon came out of the kitchen. "The table is set, and the oven timer is going off. I don't know about you all, but I'm ready to eat."

The spaghetti and garlic bread were a hit. After dinner they all went back into the living room so Rachel could recline on the sofa.

Luke leaned forward and looked at the old journal on the coffee table. He touched the leather gently. "This is amazing. I understand you're writing a book. What is it about?""

"It's a fictionalized version of my family history. I guess it's a historical romance. I'll give you the abbreviated version. It's about my great-great-grandmother's life. She moved from North Carolina to somewhere around here. She married a pastor named Patrick Elliott. My grandfather ended up back in North Carolina years later. That's why my family is from the coast instead of around here."

She curled her feet under her and stared at the floor. "It's a bittersweet love story."

"How does the book end?" Luke asked.

"You'll have to read it to find out." She teased. "Really, I guess for now, the story ends with the four of us sitting here talking about it."

"Ohhh, that's intriguing." Jonathon leaned forward in his seat.

Rachel yawned. "That name sounds familiar. I bet Mrs. Kelly at the library would remember it. And if not her, Vinnie Burns would. She's probably the oldest lady around, knows everything about Lake Nolan."

"If you can catch her on a day her mind is clear." Luke laughed. "Can I see what you've written so far?"

"I'm not ready to share." She pointed to Rachel curled up on the sofa about to drift off. "Besides, your wife needs her rest."

"You're right." Luke helped Rachel to the door, then stopped. "I'd be happy to help you with editing when you finish the book. Will you let me know when you do?"

"Absolutely."

Jonathon had helped MaryRose clean up before he left. Except for the teapot whistling on the stove the house was quiet. She poured steaming water into the fresh mint in her mug. Every ounce of her wanted to take the tea down to the lake and enjoy the moon. But she had promised herself something else tonight.

It was time to tackle the box of photos. She'd dragged it out of the closet into the center of the kitchen before putting the dishes away. Now she sat on the floor beside the box. Dapple climbed into her lap. As the lid opened, a wad of newspaper fell out and Dapple grabbed it and ran around the room.

A light tap sounded at the door. Andrea stood outside,

waving in the window. MaryRose motioned her in.

"Is it too late for me to stop in?"

"Not at all. There's a pot of mint tea on the counter if you want some. The honey's in the cabinet."

"No, thanks. Daddy and I had milkshakes. He makes the best. Actually, that's why I came down here."

"Because your dad makes the best milkshakes?"

"He pouted all night like the kid who wasn't invited to the party."

"He was invited. Turned me down."

"That's because he's got the crazy notion you like Jonathon. I told him it's obvious Jonathon is not the one you like. But he growled at me."

"I. But. Umm—"

Andrea burst into laughter. "You're as bad as him. I wonder if you look up the hill at the house as many times a day as he looks down here." She reached into the box and lifted the first picture out.

"Who's he? He's hot."

"Sean. My husband. On our honeymoon in Bermuda. It's my favorite picture of him."

"I can see why. He looked good in shorts and a muscle shirt."

"That he did."

MaryRose took the picture and touched Sean's cheek. She placed it aside as Andrea grabbed the next one.

"I'm sorry. Maybe you don't want me here. This is personal." She set it back down.

"Actually, I think it helps to have you here." MaryRose handed her a tatted wedding invitation. "Sean's mother made this for us when we got married."

Andrea traced the carving around the edge of the frame. "Bailey? But your last name is Elliott."

"I took my maiden name back after my parents died. It seemed the right thing to do."

"Oh."

"The next one is Nana and Papa Shane when they got married. They met because of me and Sean. He is Sean's Grampa."

"How'd your real Grampa die?"

"Mom's father died of a massive heart attack at the hardware store. He was there to buy me a new bicycle. Heather had the same genetic heart defect as Sean. He died because he loved me too much to leave me for a special treatment in Europe. And Mom, Dad, and Nana were on their way to meet me at the cemetery so I wouldn't be there alone on the anniversary of Sean's death. All my fault."

Andrea reached over and stroked MaryRose's hair. "I don't know much about much. But I do know enough to know things happen, and you can't kill yourself carrying unwarranted guilt. I used to say Mommy wouldn't have died if I hadn't wanted to go out on the boat that night. But, MaryRose, it wasn't my fault. And it wasn't yours."

"I know this in my heart, but sometimes it's too much. Makes me afraid to let anyone close again." She wiped her eyes and put the photos back into the box.

"I'll hang them up another time. Tonight was about tackling the ghosts. Thanks for helping me."

"No wonder you and Daddy make such a good pair."

A good pair? She pushed the box back toward the closet and stood.

"What do you mean?"

"Nothing. Really. I think maybe it's good you moved here. I better go up and check on Grumpy. Thanks for the talk." Andrea headed for the door and stopped shy of exiting.

"For what it's worth, I think my daddy is as good-looking as Sean was and will be a really good second husband for you."

She turned around, ponytail flipping behind her as she left.

MaryRose stared at the door. A long time.

aryRose placed her hands on the small of her back and arched, stretching as much as possible without falling backwards. Between that ache and her locked knees she was about to give up on the final flower bed. But the surviving yellow rosebush kept her going. If it could survive these weeds, so could she.

Pulling weeds was the most thankless job in the world. She'd spent many summer afternoons weeding Dad's garden. Even now, she could hear him as clear as if he stood right beside her. He'd cross his arms, raise his eyebrows and say, *MaryRose, you can whine all you want to, but this job will be done before you and Missy take that boat up the creek.*

She removed her cap and wiped her sleeve across her brow. "Okay, Dad, I can hear ya, but I still hate the task."

While she stood there, the gate squeaked. Jeb crossed the yard and placed a potted plant on the ground beside her. He eyeballed the flower bed. "Um-hm, world's most fulfilling job you're doing here."

"You're kidding, right?"

"No ma'am, weeding is a godly duty."

"I've never looked at it that way."

He bent and grabbed a few thistle weeds and ripped them from the soil. "Miss Ruth wanted me to bring you this evening primrose plant."

"Is it like a four o'clock?" She pushed the garden cart closer to the pile of discarded weeds and loaded them inside.

"Maybe. It's the dangdest flower I ever saw. Comes in pink or yellow. Think this one will be pink. The plant grows about three feet tall. The flowers open at sunset. Sure as shooting, you can step outside as the sun goes down and watch the buds open up wide."

He reached for another handful of redroot weed. She placed her hand over the plant blocking him from pulling it.

"Leave a few of them. They're good in salad."

"You eat weeds too?"

"Some."

"Landsakes, you are an interesting little lady. Not sure this yard has ever looked better."

"Wait till I finish. I plan to make it look even better when I fill the gaps in with herbs." She walked around the house looking for the perfect place to plant the primrose. She wanted it where she'd most likely see it each evening. She clapped her hands.

"I know where to plant this flower. If we put it over by the back porch. I can watch it open when I sit on my swing in the evening."

Jeb followed. "Well then, let's get it in the ground." After planting the flower he touched the small buds. "You'll have blooms by the end of the week, I think."

"Thank you, Jeb. Please thank Ruth for me too."

He tipped his hat. "I will, ma'am."

The gate squeaked again. "MaryRose, you here?" Randall called.

Oh great. Covered in dirt, wearing her worst cutoffs and a

T-shirt with the sleeves cut out. Why did the man always show up when she was dirty or otherwise not put together? Nana and Mom would say that's why a lady never goes out without her lipstick on. Yeah right.

"We're out back." She brushed her hands on her shorts and then tucked her hair back under the cap as he rounded the corner of the house. And there he was, looking straight from a men's clothing catalog, tanned, filling his T-shirt out better than a man should.

"Who's we?"

Jeb leaned the shovel against the house and clapped Randall's shoulder. "Your mom sent me over with one of her primrose plants. Now I better get home for lunch or she'll have my hide."

He made a quick exit, then turned back and waved. "I almost forgot. Miss Ruth wanted me to ask you what your great-great-gramma's last name was. She's been looking through all sorts of old family books to see if she might have something to help you out."

"Same as mine—Elliott."

"I'll tell her."

While Jeb spoke with her, Randall approached. Her knees wobbled when she caught the scent of his cologne.

"Hi, Randall."

"Hey, Pretty Lady."

That was it; her mouth stopped working. A softball sat in her throat.

"We finished the drywall ahead of schedule, so I gave everyone the rest of the day off. Do you have any plans?"

She lifted filthy hands and struck a pose. "Well, while I'm dressed for it I might go shopping for a formal."

His laugh echoed across the lake.

"What do you have in mind?"

"Well, I was thinking—"

"Do you make a habit of that?"

"Uh-oh. She's pretty *and* smart." He stepped onto the porch and sat on the swing. "Want to walk around the lake?"

"I'd love to. I have to clean up and have lunch first."

"I can be back in a half hour."

Thirty minutes to shower, change, eat, and get ready for a walk with him? The man had no idea what he was asking. "Perfect." She lied.

"Okay then." He stood and jumped off the porch.

She ran inside and took what Dad called a 'turbo' shower, dressed in baggy shorts and a T-shirt, clipped her hair in a bun and inhaled a sandwich. She was placing the last dish in the sink as he knocked on the door.

MaryRose stepped out the door and got lost in blue topaz. That's what Ruth meant about those blue eyes and the siren's call.

"Ready?"

"Lead on, sir."

He took her hand and wove his fingers with hers. The strength in his grip comforted, but the flutter in her heart, not so much. He rewarded her with a sideways grin.

"I'd rather walk alongside if it's okay with you?"

"Yeah." She was way out of practice, but it felt like he was flirting—and she liked it.

They headed toward a well-worn path in the woods. "This trail circles the lake. Takes all day to hike the entire thing, if you're a fast walker. I'm not. We'll do part of it today."

"What about snakes?"

He shuddered. "I try not to think about them."

"If I didn't know better, I'd think you're afraid of them."

"Can't stand them."

"But you didn't think twice about chasing them away from me and Dapple."

"Sometimes we do what we have to. Doesn't mean we're not afraid. I'd be okay if I lived the rest of my life and never saw another snake. Of course, I live in the wrong place for that. Aren't you afraid of them now?"

She stepped over a log. "Just more cautious. There's not much I'm afraid of." Except facing her grief.

"That's a shame." He squeezed her hand. "Men like to rescue women in distress."

"I'll be sure to let you know if I'm ever in distress."

Randall grinned. "Sounds like a plan." He pointed to a narrow asphalt road ahead of them. "There's the trail."

She stopped short at the edge of the trail and almost pulled him off his feet when she reached down and picked a handful of honeysuckle. She pulled a small drawstring bag from her pocket and unrolled it.

"And that is for?"

"Collecting. Nana taught me to always take my bag with me. Woods and fields are ripe with treasures."

She walked beyond the honeysuckle and grabbed a handful of the mint. Before stuffing it into the bag, she held it up to his nose.

"Okay, so—what do I smell?"

"Spearmint."

"Nice."

"Come on over sometime, and I'll give you fresh mint tea."

He grabbed her hand again as they stepped back onto the trail. "I might take you up on that."

She studied the foliage. "There is so much here. I need a bigger bag. I could spend all day collecting."

"I see plants and weeds."

"Nana used to say weeds don't exist. I think there are some. But right here I see wild violets, sour grass and lemon balm. The makings of a great salad—"

"Violets in salad?"

"And this mint in my bag also makes a great hair rinse. Cleanses it of residues."

"Residues? You speak Greek to me." He shook his head.

"Tell you what, I won't spend our whole walk doing this. Let me gather those plants over there. Another morning I can explore on my own and collect whatever I want. I'll even make lunch for you. Does Thursday work?"

"Lunch. That's something I understand. You have a deal."

She stepped off the trail again and pulled violets, sour grass, and lemon balm. The man's tolerance for her weed picking might run out. As she closed the bag and clipped it onto her belt loop, Randall burst into laughter.

"Did I agree to eat weeds for lunch?"

"I guess you did. Dad always said he expected Mom to feed him sawdust and wood chips someday."

"If you ever decide to try it, I can certainly get a bunch for you."

She shook her head. His presence muddied her thinking. Better get moving. She returned to the trail. "I'm all yours now." Oops, that didn't sound right.

His raised one eyebrow and glanced sideways at her. "How about we take a walk?"

They came to a wooden deck overlooking the entire lake. "This is huge. You can really walk it in a day?"

He nodded. "I said if you walk fast. It's a long day. West Virginia has many lakes, all of them manmade. This one is, in my opinion, the most beautiful. Someday maybe I'll take you for a drive along the old road where the creek feeds into this lake. It's a peaceful place."

Randall guided her to a community park and showed her the band shell he built. "West Virginia Day is coming up on June 21. That's a state holiday celebrating our statehood. It's a fun day here. I hope you'll join us." He glanced at his watch. "Andrea will be home by the time we get back. I forgot to leave her a note. We should probably head back and finish this walk another day."

Lunch. A walk around the entire lake. A drive along the creek. West Virginia Day. Did he realize he had now made plans for four more times to see her? Her heart fluttered. She shook her head. He was right. She had to get home and do a little writing before making supper.

"You'll let me know if you see any more snakes, right?"

"You think I will?" A chill covered her.

"The den is gone. I promise."

"My real grandfather talked to a cotton mouth once."

"Talked to a snake?"

She nodded. "I was helping him pick strawberries. Our property was alongside a black-water creek. I reached in to get one of the biggest berries I'd seen all day. He grabbed my hand and told me not to move. Then he had me slowly stand up and back away. He told me to go to the house. I could tell he meant business.

"As I walked away, I heard him talk to the snake. He said, "Mr. Water Moccasin, I know you live around here too. But I don't take kindly to you bein' so close to my granddaughter. Now I'm getting my pistol and if you are still here when I get back I aim to shoot you. If you go on and leave, then we'll be fine.""

Randall's eyes widened. "What happened?"

"The snake was gone when he got back, so, he finished picking the strawberries."

"MaryRose Elliott, you have a most interesting family."

"You don't know the half of it. I'll have to share what I'm finding out about Gramma Rose. She became a true mountain woman."

"There's something nagging at the back of my mind about someone named Rose something. Oh dagnabbit, I can't remember? I'll have to ask Mom."

They rounded the final turn toward home. Their excursion ended too soon.

"Randall, this has been delightful."

"Yes, it has." He bowed and lowered an imaginary hat.

"It'd be nice to bike this trail every day. Is there anywhere around here I could buy a bicycle?"

"Sure is. Let's see, this week is shot with Kenneth's graduation on Wednesday. Weed lunch Thursday." He winked. "I could take you after work on Friday if you wish?"

Hmm, number five? She smiled. "I'd like that."

Oh how she wanted to kiss him again, but she'd not be so bold.

He squeezed her hand, kissed the top of her head, and walked away.

MaryRose threw the covers back. Weed lunch with Randall today. She'd barely slept. She was about as excited as she'd been before her first prom with Sean. Honestly, she'd hardly been able to focus all week, anticipating this date. And, yes, she had to admit she was having a lunch date with her landlord.

She got a mug of coffee and stepped out onto the back porch so Dapple could run his circles around the yard. He'd be drenched from the dew by the time he came back inside. But hopefully, he'd be worn out too so she could get an early start gathering weeds for lunch.

After her last sip of coffee, she called Dapple inside, then grabbed her backpack and headed to the woods.

No trail today. The best herbs grew undisturbed. Nana would probably tell her she lived in a veritable Garden of Eden. Memories flooded. Nana turning leaves over and showing her new ways to identify them or breaking tender stems and offering them for her to smell and taste. She placed a mint leaf in her mouth and chewed. For the moment there was no anger in her heart, only peace. Almost as if Ma and Nana were with her.

"Thank you, Father."

I will never leave you nor forsake you.

She stopped, raised her hands toward heaven and closed her eyes. God hadn't spoken to her for a while. Or she hadn't been listening. She should get away like this more often.

After placing one final bunch of sage in the backpack, she zipped it closed and rounded the curve toward the inlet. Was this how Gramma Rose felt on the days she ventured to the river alone? Or especially when she rode to the place where their cabin was being built? No wonder she'd been content to settle here. MaryRose hoped to live in these mountains forever.

At home, she turned on the radio and began washing herbs. She divided the mint and placed some in a pitcher of hot water to steep. The rest she bunched and hung upside down in the window to dry. After chopping the lemon balm, she placed it into the salad bowl with lettuce, peppers, tomatoes, onions, and radishes. She snipped violets off their stems and dropped them into the salad. She sprinkled chopped sour grass over the salad and put the rest into a small glass carafe.

Then she mixed rosemary, lemon juice, lemon balm, and a bit of vinegar in the carafe for salad dressing.

Aah. The kitchen smelled like Nana's. And she still had time for a shower before tackling the biscuit recipe on the counter. Tackling? With all she knew about herbs and cooking, a simple recipe with six ingredients had her worried. How Nana would laugh at her.

Ruth's biscuit recipe had been tucked underneath the sugar bowl since the night she brought it home. Common sense told her the first time to try was not when Ruth's son came for lunch, but it also made no sense to let a biscuit recipe get the best of her. She gathered the ingredients, mixed them, and rolled the dough out on the counter three times before it looked right. Without an old peanut butter jar lid, she settled for the rim of a one-third-cup measure. She cut the biscuits, placed them in the oven, and got the counter clean before he knocked at the door.

"Come on in."

"Hey, Pretty Lady." His smile lit the room as he studied the herbs hanging all over the kitchen. "There's an eclectic blend of aromas in here. Do I smell biscuits too?"

She nodded. "Your mom's recipe. Hope I did it right."

He walked to the stove and counted the pots. "Soup?"

"Hardly." She handed him soap and a hand towel. "Most of them are for cosmetic purposes."

Randall scrubbed the sawdust off his hands. "You're kidding?"

"I'm serious."

"Sawdust and wood chips for dinner are sounding more realistic all of the time."

MaryRose opened the oven, removed the cookie sheet and set it on a rack to cool. She scooped one of the biscuits, pulled it apart and showed it to him.

"How'd I do?"

He took one half and shoved it into his mouth and chewed. His eyes bulged. "Mmm, thasss really hotttt and really goood."

She giggled. "I didn't mean for you to eat it yet. Wanted you to look at it. Here, this tea will cool your mouth. We're ready to eat."

She reached across the table and grasped his hand. "My family always held hands when we said grace. Do you mind?"

"Not at all."

Him at her table, holding hands, and blessing the food was more natural than she'd have imagined. The prayer ended too soon.

The salad was a hit. She loved the surprised look when he

saw the variety of plants in it. His face puckered when he took the first bite. He chewed then smiled.

"Good stuff."

Randall ate all of his salad and finished off four biscuits he'd slathered with apple butter. As he popped the last bite of biscuit into his mouth, he picked up the jar and looked at it.

"What is this again?"

"Apple butter."

"Never had it before but it's delicious. Tell you what, you can serve me weeds with biscuits and apple butter anytime you want." He wiped his mouth, crumpled the napkin, then stood and carried his dishes to the sink. "I guess I better get back to work."

"I should too. I sort of played all morning."

"MaryRose, thanks again. I look forward to taking you bike shopping Friday."

Then he planted a soft kiss on her lips.

All she wanted was more.

CHAPTER 14

*M*emorial Day weekend ushered in the first heat wave of the summer. MaryRose stretched out on the grass along the shore dipping her toes into the water. She thought summer in the mountains might be more comfortable than a coastal one, but forecasters called for temps in the nineties all week long.

Dapple stopped running in the water's edge to look up the hill behind MaryRose. He barked once, then raced behind her, greeting Andrea who scooped him up and snuggled him close. "Good morning sunshine! Catch any rattlesnakes today?"

"That's not even funny." MaryRose rubbed the scar on her ankle.

Andrea sat beside her and placed Dapple back on the ground. The dog ran happy circles around them. "You're right. Sorry. Do you have any plans today?"

"Other than going bike shopping with your father this evening, no. Was Kenneth's graduation nice?"

"It was fine. There were a lot of graduates in the stadium. Guess mine would have been that way if I hadn't gotten early admission into vet school which meant I skipped graduation.

Anyway, Kenneth's headed to Myrtle Beach for a week. And I shouldn't say this but it feels like while he's away, I'll be able to breathe easier." Andrea picked up a pebble and tossed it into the water.

MaryRose watched her out of the corner of her eye. The girl's brow was etched in a frown. She kept digging up little stones and absently tossing them into the water. MaryRose picked up a rock and handed it to her. "Sometimes you need to throw a bigger one."

"Good idea, girlfriend." She stood and whipped it into the cove, then offered her hand to MaryRose. "Would you like to go to the diving rocks with me?"

"That means a swimsuit. I don't have one I care for anyone else to see me wear. Besides, aren't the diving rocks dangerous?"

"They are, but the freedom you feel flying through the air is worth it. Let's do it another day. I'll take you bikini shopping this morning."

MaryRose looked for a wink, but it never came. "I don't do bikinis."

Andrea elbowed her. "Me neither. You'd look good in one."

She nudged back. "Not as good as you."

"I don't need to wear anything that gives Ken more encouragement than he already has. I swear he's like an octopus sometimes with more hands than I can handle. If I promise no bikinis, will you let me take you shopping? It'll be fun. Afterwards, if you don't want to do the rocks, we can drop off the swing here."

"Now dropping off the rope swing sounds like fun. You've never shopped with me. I hate trying clothes on. Swimsuits are the worst. This could take all day, and I'll be a total grouch by the time your dad picks me up."

Andrea draped her arm across her shoulder. "However, you're shopping with West Virginia's shopping queen. Let's go!"

She dragged MaryRose up the path from the lake.

How had she allowed this young lady to talk her into this? True, she lived on a lake and planned to swim as often as possible—but someone else tagging along with her while she shopped for swimwear? She must be daft.

Andrea's jaw was set. Might as well get this over with. Maybe they'd have fun after all. MaryRose scooted Dapple into the house then slipped into her sandals and grabbed her purse. On the way up the hill, she ran her fingers around her braid to be sure most of the curls were tamed.

As they entered the house, Randall's familiar cologne lingered in the air. Mmm.

He stood in the doorway, smiling at them. "It's my two favorite girls."

"Daddy, what are you doing home?" Andrea ran to his side and kissed his cheek.

"Got the whole way to the resort site and realized the thumb drive was still on my desk." He looked at MaryRose, "Hey, Pretty Lady."

"Morning, Randall."

Andrea grabbed the keys from the hook on the wall. "We're going swimsuit shopping."

His eyebrows rose. "Oh yeah?"

Heat spread up her neck and across her cheeks. With her tongue stuck to the roof of her mouth, MaryRose stood speechless.

Andrea giggled.

Randall rubbed at a scuff on his hardhat. "I, um, better get those blueprints. Have fun shopping. I'll see you after work, MaryRose." He cleared his throat as he left the room.

Once he was out of sight, she could breathe again. "Are you ready, Andrea?"

"Yep." Andrea touched MaryRose's cheek. "You're blushing. That's cute."

143

Randall parked his Jeep behind the VW and walked around to the passenger side. MaryRose met him at the vehicle and waited for him to open the door. Who'd have thought jeans and a polo shirt could look so good? His brown hair was wind tousled and his crooked grin triggered the now familiar heart pound.

"Andrea tells me you were queens of shopping in Beckley today." He closed the door.

Did Andrea also tell him about how many swimsuits she tried on before finding even one she was willing to wear in public? She prayed he wouldn't keep this flow of conversation because thinking of him seeing her in the black one-piece gave her pause.

He backed the car out and headed up Lake Drive. "The store we're heading to is nothing like Beckley's shopping district. Lake Nolan has one big hardware store. The owner is Walter Trumble, Trudy's husband. He uses the cliché 'if you can't find it in his store you don't need it.' The thing is, he's right."

They parked in front of the post office and walked down Main Street, which looked like it ended at the lake's edge. Storefronts were old but charming. People walking around town were smiling and friendly. Everyone they met shook Randall's hand or called out to him.

He stopped in front of a small diner as he bent to tie his shoe. "What was your hometown like, MaryRose?"

"Similar actually. Smaller though. Dad liked clichés too. His favorite was if you closed your eyes when you drove through town you'd miss it." Her heart cinched. "The day a McDonald's came to town was a huge thing. We had arrived. Most free time focused on fishing or going to the sound or the ocean."

"What made you choose here of all places?"

"Always wanted to see where my Gramma Rose lived. It made sense."

"And her name was Rose—Elliott?"

She nodded.

"Mom pulled out old family paperwork. Her mother's family was the Nolans. She was looking for something specific, but I don't think she found it. I've heard stories of an old mountain lady, named Rose E., who lived somewhere around our place before the creek was dammed and the reservoir built. They say she was a kind old lady and helped everyone. Why, even when the Hatfields and McCoys warred with each other, they would go to her, and she'd treat them all simultaneously. Never took to any fighting on her mountain."

"Hatfield and McCoy?" Her chest burned. "Oh my goodness, I read something about them in the journal. Could my gramma be your Rose E? She wrote about treating two of them after a fight, and my great-great-grampa got real mad at her. Told her to stay clear of those two families."

Randall walked her about half a block down the street and pointed to a large brick building on the corner across the street. "On the second floor of the building is our little public library. You might be able to find stuff about your family there." He shook his head. "I can't believe I may be walking down the street with a relative of the famous Rose E."

"Where's the name Rose E come from?"

"They've called her that as long as anyone around here remembers. But they say it like it's one name—Rosie."

She started to cross the street toward the library. Who cared about buying a bike?

Randall chuckled. "You'll have to wait. They don't have Friday hours. It is open Saturday mornings, and every weekday afternoon between three and seven. The librarian's mother, Vinnie May Banks, is a sweet old lady who loves to talk about the mountain people around here. If anyone knows about Rose E, it would be her. But you have to catch her on an alert day."

"Luke and Rachel mentioned her. Does she have Alzheimer's?"

"Dementia."

MaryRose wanted to skip. There was someone around here who might have firsthand information about Gramma Rose. Randall's laughter interrupted her thoughts. "What?"

"You look cute." He kicked an invisible rock on the sidewalk. "By the way, I'm glad your search brought you to my cottage."

The blush spreading across his cheeks was most likely matched by the one she felt on her own.

He grasped her hand and laced his fingers between hers. Whether she planned on it or not, it appeared romance might be in the works.

"How about we make quick work of this bike shopping and then stop in at Sarah's for cherry pie?"

"Mmm. Goodest Pie."

"What?"

"When I was little, I wouldn't eat cherry pie. Not sure why. But one day Nana convinced me to try one bite. She promised me if I didn't like it she'd buy me a bag of silver bells to make up for it. How could I turn her down? So, I took a bite and told her it was the 'goodest pie' I'd ever tried. It's been goodest pie ever since."

"Then you have to try Sarah's. It's the goodest pie around." As he held the door to the hardware store for her he cocked his head. "Silver Bells?"

"Hershey's Kisses look like silver bells."

There was a small selection of bikes in the front of the store. Randall started pulling them out and wheeling them around the room, one at a time. "I like the blue one. What about you?"

She froze. Her heart fluttered and she couldn't catch her breath. Fog settled around the bike. Waves of nausea attacked. A spinning room sent her wobbling backward into a shelf knocking down a rack of balls. She tripped over the balls as she raced out the door.

At the street, she came close to darting in front of a car. Randall came up behind her and wrapped strong arms around her. He held her while she shook.

She slipped from his grasp and slumped onto the sidewalk. Her grandfather. Bike shopping. Heart attack. Never saw him again. Except in the casket.

"'I like the blue one, what about you?' That's what my grandfather said. And I told him okay. He went in and never came out. My fault. Don't want a blue bike."

Randall sat beside her. "It's okay, MaryRose. We can get a bike another day. I'll find a neon orange one if you want, or spray paint it any color you want."

He tilted her chin so she could look at him. "Something tells me we need the pie now."

She nodded and took a few deep, cleansing breaths. It'd been a long time since she'd had a panic attack. After all these years a blue bike still affected her. And Randall saw. But he also calmed her.

"I'm so embarrassed." She stared at the asphalt.

He offered his hand to help her stand, then looped her arm through his.

"Don't look now, but everyone in town is wondering who the pretty lady with me is. I'm quite the catch, you know." He winked.

"Maybe I'm not trying to catch you." She tried to release his arm, but he held tight.

"I'm not letting go yet. Don't want you to fall or have the chance to slap me again." He stopped in front of Sarah's Diner. The bell on the door jingled as he opened it.

A plump woman in an apron spoke from behind the counter. "Well, I'll be. Randall Cobb in here on a Friday night with a lady holdin' onto his arm. Don't that beat all?"

He pulled out a chair for MaryRose. "Miss Sarah, this is MaryRose Elliott. She's renting my cottage."

Sarah wiped her hands on her apron and hustled to their table. "Hon, it is so nice to meet you. What can I get for you?"

"Randall tells me your cherry pie is the best."

He nodded. "Sarah, we'd like two slices and two big glasses of milk."

"Sure thing. Be right back."

MaryRose looked out the window at the sun lowering over the lake. "How did you know I'd want milk with mine?"

His eyes sparkled and his smile brought her out of the sadness.

"What else would you drink with goodest pie?"

This man knew exactly what to say to calm her anxiety and make her heart beat faster at the same time. Thankfully, before she could ponder too much, Sarah walked up with pies and milk.

"I heated them too. MaryRose, it is surely nice to meet you. I hope you will come in and visit more often."

"I'm sure I will." She took a bite of the pie and moaned. "This is the goodest."

Randall handed her a napkin. "Monday is the official season opening of Lake Nolan. We usually have an extra family cook-out. Please say you'll join us."

"I will. As long as I'm not intruding."

"That's silly. I think everyone already considers you family."

She finished the pie and the last sip of milk.

"I bet one day you'll be ready to tell me about your grandfather."

She stared at the table.

"One day."

"MaryRose, can I come in? I'm getting drenched out here."
Andrea stood at the screen door as the blowing rain pelted her
back.

MaryRose looked up from the herbs she was tying.
"Come in."

"Okay." As she stepped inside the screen door banged behind
her. She frowned. "Daddy was supposed to fix that."

"What's broken?"

Andrea stomped her feet on the floor mat, then kicked her
sandals off. "The door. He was supposed to fix it before anyone
moved in."

"Tell him to leave it as it is." She crossed the room, opened it,
and let it bounce closed. "I like it. Reminds me of Nana. Sometimes I can almost hear her calling me to get out of the
confounded creek again before a water moccasin grabbed me."

She filled two glasses with mint tea and dropped a couple of
ice cubes inside. "Have some."

Andrea picked up the mint and held it to her nose. She
glanced at the bundles hanging over the kitchen window. "I've
never known anyone who saved weeds."

"This is spearmint. It may grow like a weed, but it has many
uses."

"Like?"

"After the bundle dries, I grind it up and use it in tea, or bath
bags, or hair rinses. Many uses."

"Bath bags?" Andrea sipped her tea and changed the subject.
"I hope it stops raining soon. I was supposed to go swimming
with Jamie, my best friend. I guess now she'll come over to
watch movies and talk about boys."

"You mean like Kenneth?"

Andrea ran a small gold heart back and forth on the chain.
"Yeah. We've been together since high school. He played football
for West Virginia University too. Everybody thinks I'm the
luckiest girl because he chose me. But, I don't always feel it.

They don't know the other side of him like I do—but—oh, never mind. We all have good and bad days."

"What are we never minding?"

Andrea dismissed the question with a flip of her hand. "Nothing. What is a bath bag?"

"I'll get some." She went to the bathroom. There was something about the way Andrea played with her necklace. What was she not saying? MaryRose grabbed a jar from the medicine cabinet and went back to the kitchen.

She dumped several small muslin bags on the counter. "They're filled with herbs. You put the bag in the tub as it fills, then you soak in it."

Andrea giggled. "I brew myself?"

"More like a slow steep. See the labels? Different herbs have different qualities. Pick the one you need—like this lavender and chamomile one for relaxing before bed."

"I think I might try this one tonight."

"Take as many as you want. I like the rosemary-marjoram one better for calming. I'll make a jar of bags for you once all my herbs dry."

"Thanks." Andrea peeked outside. "Looks like the rain is stopping. I should make a break for the house before Jamie gets here. Is it alright if I come down early Monday morning, before the cookout?"

"Sure."

"I have a surprise for you. Oh, and I can't wait to see Daddy's eyes when he sees the swimsuit we bought."

CHAPTER 15

*M*aryRose sipped the last cup of coffee as the swing gently creaked back and forth. This morning she was relaxed, not weighted by sad things. She rose before sunrise and walked along the shore, then watched the sun rise over the water. The brilliant golden light over the lake invited her to newness.

She'd been sitting on the swing with Dapple since returning from their walk.

A hummingbird flitted to the feeder Trudy had delivered and set up on a shepherd's hook in the flower bed. It sat there drinking until Dapple saw it and barked like a ferocious beast. Not to be defeated by a little bird looking like a bug, he leaped off her lap and raced around the house.

Within moments he hurried back to the porch and growled toward the driveway.

"What do you hear, buddy?"

A purple ATV pulled up beside the fence. Andrea's long braid tumbled across her shoulder as she removed her helmet. She opened the gate and picked Dapple up as she headed to the porch.

"Morning."

MaryRose brushed her hands together. "A purple ATV. Really?"

"What can I say? My daddy loves me! Are you ready for a ride?"

"Where are we going?"

"To Mommy's grave. It's so pretty up there on the mountain. I'd like it if you came along."

"Where exactly is your mother buried?"

"In a cemetery on Estep's Mountain. All of her family is up there, as far back as the Revolutionary War. You'll love it. It's the most peaceful place I know."

"And why not drive?"

"We are." She opened a box on the back of the vehicle and removed another helmet. "It's good your hair is braided. Ponies don't work well."

MaryRose stared at the vehicle. It didn't ease her nerves to see a pistol attached to a bracket on top of the box. "A gun?"

"Yes. We don't go up into the mountains unprepared for rattlers. Or bears. I have a carry permit, and I'm a great shot."

MaryRose shook her head and backed toward the house. "I'll stay here after all."

"You've never ridden one of these have you?"

"Nope."

Andrea leaped onto the seat. "Come on. You'll love it. I'll drive first."

"First? I'm pretty sure you'll be doing all of the driving."

"Do you have a gun?"

"No. Why?"

"Because you should. Daddy can teach you how to shoot."

"Didn't say I can't shoot. I used to compete on a 4-H rifle team. Just don't own a gun."

Andrea cocked her head and smiled. "Well, you are full of surprises. Hop on!"

MaryRose had barely straddled the seat when Andrea laughed loud, revved the engine and took off.

Gravel shot behind them as they skidded onto Lake Nolan Drive. They'd gone a few miles when Andrea turned onto a dirt road that looked more like a utility cutout. It went straight up the mountain. She stopped on a level area and pointed to the clearing. "I love it up here. We're not at the top yet, but this is where the diving rocks are."

MaryRose looked through the clearing and gasped. "Breathtaking. You dive from up here?"

"Mostly. We go over the edge there. The trail cuts back down the mountain to the rocks. I think it's a little higher than high diving platforms in the Olympics." She turned the vehicle left and pointed to a tiny trail. "The cemetery is up there."

It looked like it went straight up. Yet, Andrea took off and sped up the incline without a care. How they made it up without flipping backward baffled MaryRose. At the crest, Andrea pulled beside an old, rusted cast iron picket fence. A grove of trees surrounded the area that looked like it continued into the forest forever. The hillside was dotted with old and new iron fences. They wove in odd angles and divided the cemetery into little individual plots.

A gentle breeze teased MaryRose's neck. The trees swayed in a uniform wave. No wonder Andrea found peace here. The air was thick with it. This was holy ground.

She followed quietly as Andrea approached an area marked with a simple sign bearing the word, *Estep*. She opened the gate and walked to a black marble gravestone. She knelt beside it, kissed her fingers then placed them on the stone.

"Hey, Mommy."

MaryRose stayed outside the area. Best to let Andrea be alone. She sat on one of the benches to wait but Andrea motioned her in.

"Come here." She patted the ground beside her. "Sit with me. I want you to meet Mommy."

A knot, big and hot, burned MaryRose's throat. Andrea's reverence and respect for her mother touched her. She knelt.

"I'd be honored to meet your mother."

"Mommy, this is MaryRose Elliott. I bet you already know she rented the cottage. Did you help God pick her out? It sure feels like it. I like her. And, Mommy, Daddy does too. He's smiling again."

Chills raced up MaryRose's spine. She longed to hug Andrea but knew it would destroy the moment. Instead, she reached over and ran her hand down Andrea's braid.

Andrea smiled.

"See, Mommy? It's okay isn't it?" She faced MaryRose. "I know Mommy's in heaven. I also know most girls my age don't still use Mommy but I was only ten when she died. I still like to come here and talk to her. I bet you know what I mean."

MaryRose nodded.

They sat for a while. No words. A few trucks approached and people began drifting through the main gate. They carried flowers and little American flags.

Andrea stretched her legs out in front of her.

"It will get busy here soon. That's why I come early." She stood and brushed her jeans off. "And so you know, I meant what I said about Daddy liking you. I'm glad he does too. Now if we hurry, we can probably get on the rope-swing before everyone shows up. I know you've been itching to try."

"How did you know?"

"I've seen you watching me and Ken on it. It's a blast."

They put their helmets back on and took off. Literally. Andrea zoomed down the mountain. The only consolation was holding on tight and praying they wouldn't crash almost stopped her from thinking about Andrea saying Randall liked her.

MaryRose stood in a crotch of the tree and prepared for another flight into the water. The first few times she released too late and ended up doing a belly flop. After the third one, she figured out the timing. As she leaped into the air and swung out over the water, she squealed. The moment of release, her heart fluttered, and she free-fell into the water. She swam to the bank and walked out.

Andrea yelled from the tree. "I told you so."

"I love it."

Andrea swung out and released. MaryRose climbed up once more and caught the rope as it swung back to her. Before she swung out, she saw Randall steering the boat into the cove. She waved at him before flying into the water.

By the time she walked out of the water, Randall and Jonathon had the boat docked. She grabbed her towel and dried off, then wrapped a little skirt around her waist. Her heart beat the now-familiar 'Randall rhythm.'

He stepped off the boat and walked toward her. When his gaze traveled from her head to her toes and then stared deeply into her eyes, she about fell over.

He coughed softly.

"I see the swimsuit shopping was a success. Nice."

She had no words.

Andrea grabbed his hand and pulled him away from her. "Daddy, you guys took long enough. We're getting all pruned up in the water waiting for you to get back and start cooking. Catch anything?"

"Nothing. Fishing was a bomb. I have burgers and dogs on standby. Give me fifteen minutes, and we'll be ready to eat."

He stared at, no, ogled, MaryRose. At least that's what Missy would call it. Her cheeks instantly warmed.

Jonathon elbowed him in the ribs. "Close your mouth and

stop staring, buddy. You're not a teenager anymore. Let's start cooking before we have a mutiny on our hands."

Andrea giggled and led MaryRose away from the dock. "We'll get out of your way while you cook." She dragged two chairs to the water's edge and plopped in one.

"See, I told you he likes you. It's fun watching my daddy fall in love."

The only other man who'd ever made her pulse race was Sean. The only other man who'd ever invaded her dreams and blown her away with one kiss was Sean. After seven years, Randall was rapidly replacing Sean in her mind's eye during waking moments. Falling in love? Probably.

"Aw, look, he's bringing your food to you. I'm outta here." Andrea stood and winked. "This is great."

Randall balanced a plate in each hand and carried a soda under each arm. He handed her a plate heaped with food. "This seat taken?"

"It is now."

"Good." He sat and chugged his soda. "Did Jonathon tell you his news?"

"Yes, we spoke earlier in the week."

"It's great to see him going back for his Master's. He's meant to be a pastor. But, man, we've been working together since high school. I'll miss him."

He traced a lazy pattern on the arm of her chair. "West Virginia Weslyan isn't too far away, and he'll be home on weekends. But it will still be weird." He took a huge bite of burger and washed it down with soda.

"MaryRose?"

"Yes?"

"Andrea likes you."

"She said you do too." Oh goodness, she'd better capture her thoughts before they spilled out in words.

"She's right. I do."

Uh-oh. "Did I say that out loud?"

He winked. "Um-hm. I wanted to thank you for helping her. I know she needs a woman in her life." He shook his head and kicked the ground. "I meant—"

"I like her too. She's sweet." She reached over and flicked a tomato seed from his arm. Chill bumps covered his arm. "Are you cold?"

"Far from it."

He leaned toward her. His lips were soft and warm against hers. Why in the world did he have chills? She was suddenly quite warm.

"MaryRose Elliott why is your brain so scattered this morning? There's work to be done and you have been somewhere else all day."

The words rang as clear and fresh as if Nana had spoken to her rather than surfaced from a long ago memory of Sean kissing her for the first time. She was supposed to have been hanging plants to dry but had daydreamed most of the day.

Just like this week.

Five days since Randall's kiss. And it still made her dizzy thinking about it. Five days she couldn't get her article written, journals transposed, or herbs processed.

But Randall hadn't been down to the dock all week. Maybe it was a one-sided kiss. Not good, but she would accept that. She moved here to find her roots not a relationship anyway. She had to forget the kiss.

Yeah, right.

Andrea knocked once, then walked in. "Aah! Wild flowers and herbs. MaryRose, if solace had a scent this would be it."

Good timing since she'd been sitting at her desk staring out the window for most of the morning. "If I'd known you were coming I'd have made tea. Can I get you anything?"

"Not really. I need to talk."

"Sure." MaryRose motioned toward the loveseat. "Is this about Kenneth?"

"How did you know?"

"I saw you walking with him the other afternoon. I'd have expected you to be tickled he was home, but you looked sad."

They plopped onto the love seat. Ten years of age separated them, a wealth of sorrow united them, and need for each other connected them.

"What's up, Andrea?"

She twirled her hair. "Can I ask you a question?"

"Anything."

"What does love feel like?"

On second thought, maybe not anything. She took a deep breath. "It's feeling like you can't finish a breath without thinking of him. And not being able to speak a word around him. It's electricity if he holds your hand, more if he kisses you. Feeling as if you were only half a person before you met him and you'll never be complete without him. And—"

"Is that how you felt about Sean?"

"Yes."

"Can you ever feel that way again?"

"I think so."

"You and Sean were together a long time?"

"We grew up together, best buddies all our lives. We started dating in high school and never looked back."

Andrea twirled her hair and then took a deep breath. "When did it go from friendship to love?"

"When all of those things became a part my identity."

"Can I ask you a *really* personal question?" She stood up and paced.

Might as well. "Sure."

"Were you and Sean virgins when you got married?"

She gulped.

"Yes."

The tension in Andrea's shoulders eased a bit. She must have been struggling with that question for a while.

Andrea stared at her feet. "Wasn't it hard? I mean, nowadays most people figure sex is part of dating."

"It wasn't easy. Being in love only makes it more difficult. We are created to be connected, Andrea. But only after marriage. Not many of my classmates waited for anything, but it's worth the wait. Mom taught me how to focus on what's right."

"How?"

"She told me to remember Jesus joined us on every date, went everywhere we went. At first, it seemed like fuddy-duddy talk, but when Sean and I got closer, I realized she was right. When I found myself in a compromising situation and I could see Jesus sitting there with me, it gave new meaning to the saying 'What would Jesus do?'"

"Oh." Andrea's eyes welled up.

"You miss your mom don't you?" MaryRose grasped her hands.

"I do, but that's not why I'm crying."

They sat quietly for a few minutes as silent sobs shook Andrea's shoulders.

"Andrea, can I share a few Bible verses with you?"

"Yes."

"I'm not great with my word for word memorization. But I'll write these down and you can look them up. Proverbs 4: 23-27 talks about how important it is we be careful of what we think because our thoughts run our life. Then there is Hebrews 13:4. Mom made me remember this one. My version of it, simply stated, is marriage is to be honored by everyone and the marriage bed kept pure. Meaning, if I am not married it is not okay."

Andrea stared at her.

"It's like whoever wrote those words knew me. I don't know

159

if Ken will accept them. Not sure anything will make him stop pressuring me. He says if I truly loved him I wouldn't hold this back from him."

"Andrea, no matter how much you love him, if you're not married when you go to bed with him, the marriage bed isn't pure."

Andrea crossed her arms and hugged herself. "He says it will solidify our love."

"Love is not cement. He's lying to you. If he loved you, he wouldn't even ask. The most important thing to him would be wanting what you want."

"I hadn't thought of it that way."

"It's the truth. Is he a believer?"

"He believes in God, but he won't go to church and won't talk about God."

"Think about this verse too. Second Corinthians 6:14 says: 'You are not the same as those who do not believe. So do not join yourselves to them. Good and bad do not belong together. Light and darkness do not belong together.'"

Andrea wiped her eyes. "My head is spinning."

"Andrea, true love waits. Can you wait for true love?"

"I think so, but I don't know if he can."

"Then it isn't true love. Nobody says it's easy. Think about people like Uncle Jonathon. He hasn't even met his future wife yet."

"Or you and Dad."

A lump the size of one of Dapple's tennis balls stopped in her throat. "Well...uh...we both had love. But Jonathon is twenty-six and still waiting."

Andrea hugged her. "Thanks. I needed to hear those things. I have to talk to Ken. Can you write those verses down for me?"

"Yes. I'll be praying for you."

"Thanks again. I feel much better now."

After she left, MaryRose sat back down at her desk and noticed the date on her little calendar.

June first. Five months ago the police came to the graveyard to tell her about the accident.

Nothing about the day went well after Andrea left. MaryRose's editor called and scheduled a meeting for Monday morning. He told her things would be changing. Oh joy.

This was Missy's opening weekend and Papa Shane should arrive any minute. She'd spent the last half hour chasing Dapple around the inlet. She'd been stupid enough to think he would come right back. When he didn't, she ran after him in flip-flops. Her toes found every rock between the house and the edge of the cove, and the lovely pedicure she'd given herself was scuffed.

She dressed in a teal skirt, peasant blouse and cotton flats. No way would she let those ugly toes show. Thanks to the race through the woods and the humidity in the air, her hair was an untamed mat of curls and fuzz. She twisted it into a bun and clipped it up.

When someone knocked on the kitchen door, she presumed it was Papa Shane. She called, "I'm so glad you're here. Come on in."

"Now, that's the kind of welcome a man likes to hear. But I better not come in."

It wasn't Papa Shane. Randall stood at the back door, covered in mud. Not just covered in it. He looked like he'd been mining it.

She bit back a giggle. "I know I told you to go casual, but this is a bit extreme, don't you think?"

"We had a bit of trouble at work today. A pipe our schematics didn't show burst. I came home for my sump pump

161

and to tell you I don't think I'll be able to make it tonight. Maybe you can take me sometime later this summer."

Her heart felt like it would sink into her stomach. She hadn't realized how much she was looking forward to this night until she knew he wasn't coming. He looked disappointed too. She shrugged and tried to look less upset than she was.

"Sure we can go another time."

"Have fun, Pretty Lady. I'll talk to you later."

Before she could close the door, Papa Shane pulled into her driveway. She rushed to the car and into his hug.

"I have missed you so much. How was the drive? Did you have any trouble finding me? How long will you stay?"

"Hold on, Lassie. Give a man a moment to catch his breath. The drive was fine. No trouble finding ya once I asked about the Cobb's place. Seems everyone 'round here knows all about the red-headed lass, living in this cottage, who almost died from the snakebite. I don't remember ya tellin' me ya almost died."

"You know how stories get blown out of proportion."

Randall cleared his throat. She forgot he was still there. "Papa, this mud man is my landlord, Randall Cobb."

Randall nodded. "I'd offer my hand but figure you'd rather I keep my dirt to myself. It's nice to meet you, sir. I have to work tonight but hope to meet you all for dessert."

"That's a shame, it is. Ya lose when ya miss a Missy Greene performance."

He turned back to MaryRose. "Are ya ready to go?"

"Randall's daughter, Andrea, should be here any minute. She's riding with us."

"Well, then maybe we have enough time for me to give ya the surprise I have."

"Papa, you've given me too much already."

"It's shushing ya better be doing. This isn't really from me. I found a box your nana had tucked away in the attic, mostly junk, but there was one thing I think ya might have use for."

He reached into the back seat and picked up a box. "I meant to give this to ya later, but I canna be waiting. Be careful. It's fairly old."

Tears pooled in his eyes as she took the box.

Randall still stood behind her.

The smell of old leather and dust overwhelmed her as she lifted the lid. Nestled in a bed of cotton fabric was another journal. But it wasn't like the others. This one was smaller and made of soft leather. She lifted it out and unfolded the cloth it was swaddled in.

"The recipes." All of the recipes Gramma Rose wrote as her gramma taught her to be a medicine woman. "Oh, Papa, oh."

Then she unfolded the yellowed linen. The apron. She handed the recipe book to papa Shane and held the apron up. "Look at all of the pockets. Gramma Rose gathered herbs in this. She hugged the apron to her cheek. "You have no idea how important this is to me."

Papa Shane laughed. "I think I do, milady. Now go put those treasures away. I'll talk with Mr. Cobb."

She headed inside. There was something fatherly in Papa's voice as he said he'd be talking with 'Mr. Cobb.' How she'd love to hear that conversation.

CHAPTER 16

No wonder MaryRose always woke before sunrise. The blinding light coming through the window was harsh. She'd choose a slow sunrise over the lake instead of light piercing her retina any day. She must have slept in quite late. She squinted enough to see the clock.

Eight thirty. Nana would have said she'd wasted half the day already.

MaryRose stretched and slipped into her robe. She'd stayed up way too late last night reading every recipe in the book. Many of them she recognized—had been using them all her life. Others were new ones she couldn't wait to try.

Dapple slithered out from under the afghan and gave her sleepy puppy kisses.

"Guess I kept you up last night too. Thanks for keeping me company."

He cocked his head and watched her speak. "You should have seen Missy. She was a perfect Indian princess. I'm pretty sure Jonathon is smitten with her. And she with him. Randall got there in time for dessert. I tell you he looked much nicer without the mud, but even if he was muddy I could get used to having him around all the time."

Thank heavens Dapple was the only one who heard her say that.

"Now, let's get you outside and fed, then I can spend more time on the journals. It will keep my mind off the conversation about the trial Papa Shane will insist on having when he calls to let me know he made it home."

Dapple leaped off the bed and ran happy circles around the room. She let him outside then started her coffee.

Once she had a nice mugful she went out to the porch. The humidity was already rising and she could almost feel her hair curl. Would be a good morning to do research in the library. Maybe she'd get lucky and Vinnie would be there.

Dapple raced from the front of the house to the gate as Andrea approached. "Morning. He was eating those white flowers along the fence. Will it hurt him?"

MaryRose clicked her tongue. "The chamomile again. He has an affinity for it. I'll be lucky if I get enough to make your hair rinse and my tea. Come on in. Coffee's ready. This is early for you on a Saturday."

"I volunteer at Doc' Jackson's office today. Ken's picking me up soon and taking me to breakfast on the way to work. We're taking the boat out tonight."

"Busy day." MaryRose picked one of the flowers and placed it in Andrea's hair.

"Actually, I'm not scheduled to volunteer today, but Doc's doing an orthopedic surgery I want to see."

"Surgery on a Saturday?"

"Yeah, it's rather an emergency. He canceled appointments to do it."

Andrea picked a flower out of Dapple's mouth as they walked inside. "Pretty."

"Do you have time for tea or coffee before Ken gets here?"

"Coffee would be nice."

"How are things?"

"Kenneth got the management job at the new bank in Huntingdon. He leaves the end of July."

"How do you feel about that?"

Andrea shrugged. "I've been with him a long time. It's hard to imagine not having him around."

"I see." She poured the coffee. "The cream and sugar are on the counter. Summer goes fast, and before you know it your last year of vet school will start. A busy year."

Andrea sipped her coffee and looked at the herb jars on the counter. "Don't I know it?"

"Nobody'd ever guess you plan to be a veterinarian. You look more like a model."

Andrea laughed. "Me? A model? That's silly. I like to eat way too much."

"Why don't you have any pets?"

Andrea twirled her hair around her finger. "Mommy had allergies. I used to ride horses but didn't have one of my own. After she died, I couldn't ask Daddy for a pet. It would have felt like I was glad she was gone or something. My apartment in Morgantown doesn't allow them. One day I'll have lots of pets." Andrea placed the flower she'd taken from Dapple in her hair. "What's this one for, anyway?"

"We haven't covered it yet?"

"Nope. We did facials the other day remember?" Andrea's eyes crinkled as she giggled. "I had to stop Daddy the other night. I mixed honey and yogurt for the face mask and put it back into the yogurt container. He was about to eat it."

"Would have tasted rather good."

Her laughter grew. "You don't know my daddy well enough yet. Girl stuff is hard for him. He gets all goofy. He can't talk, and he blushes. When I told him it was a face mask, he grumbled something about 'women things' and got mad when I laughed."

MaryRose could see the whole scene right down to his grumble. She adjusted the flower in Andrea's hair. "This chamomile makes a mild, relaxing tea. It's also a great rinse for blonde hair. Steep the flowers, strain the liquid, and use it as a rinse right away. You can also cook it with marigold flowers, orange and lemon peel, and apple cider vinegar. With either one, after shampooing, massage the liquid into your hair and rinse with cool or tepid water."

"This is so cool."

"Here's the really funny thing. It also makes a yummy salad dressing."

"Oh yeah, I can see me going into the kitchen and asking Daddy to give me the salad dressing so I can wash my hair. Talk about making him goofy."

An image of another day, another time popped into Mary-Rose' mind—Sean turning to her with a jar of her hair rinse, furious he had put it on his salad. Probably more furious that he liked it.

"When Sean and I first got married, I had to label my things so he would know food from cosmetics." She brushed her hands on her jeans, "I think I have some of the last batch I made before I moved here. You want to try it?"

"I'd love to."

Kenneth arrived while MaryRose was in the bathroom pouring some chamomile rinse into a small container. Andrea ran out to greet him. Through the window, MaryRose watched him scoop her into his arms. He kissed her possessively and patted her on the bottom. Andre pressed her hands on his chest and pushed him back.

"Ken, I've asked you not to do that."

"Why? Are you afraid she'll see? I bet she doesn't mind.

Someone with her looks has probably been around. You know what they say about widows." He chuckled.

"Actually I don't know what they say about widows. MaryRose is a lady. Why do you talk like that?"

"She may be a lady, but she is *hot* and your dad's hangin' around her a lot. He's been alone a long time. So has she...you do the math." He laughed.

MaryRose clenched the jar of hair rinse. If Kenneth had been in front of her she'd have knocked him out by now.

Andrea stomped away from him. "Stop it. I don't like this conversation. She's a lovely lady and not an object of your desires. I think I'll drive myself to Doc's today."

"Ah, Babe, I didn't mean nothin' by it. You know I love you." He rubbed her shoulders.

Andrea shrugged his hand away. "Sometimes I wonder."

"I'm sorry. I'll stop." He pulled her to him and kissed her cheek. "Better?"

"A little." She gave him a weak smile.

He touched the flowers in her hair, "I like that."

MaryRose took a deep breath. And another then planted a fake smile on her face as she headed outside. The man was trouble.

"Andrea, here is the hair rinse. It should be in the fridge to stay fresh. Label it clearly so Randall won't drink it."

Kenneth eyed her. The way he looked at her, she might as well not have had any clothes on. When their eyes met, the darkness in his caused her to pause.

He stepped close to her. "So, what have you been teaching my girl today?"

"Hair rinses." She backed away.

"Nice."

Andrea checked her watch. "Come on, Ken, I need to go. Thanks, MaryRose." She headed up the hill.

Kenneth mumbled something like, "Widows. Yum." Then he winked at her.

"Excuse me?"

"If you ever get too lonely—well, I guess that won't happen—you got Randall hanging around all the time." He leaned in and inhaled. "You do smell tasty."

She slapped him, and he fell backwards, laughing.

"Oh, I'm sorry. My hand must have slipped." She glared at him.

"If I didn't know better, I'd swear you were her real mommy." He rubbed his cheek, "Got a mean slap too."

"You need to leave now. I'll be expecting an apology."

"Truth hurts, huh?" He got up and brushed the dirt off his clothes. "You got spirit. I like that."

After he left, she saw the young Rose-of-Sharon bush she'd brought from Momma's garden. Crushed. She dropped to the ground and stared at the crumbled plant. She held the broken pieces of the plant to her heart and rocked back and forth. One small section remained firmly rooted in the ground. Like her—nothing left but one little root of faith. The difference was, with TLC the shrub would recover. She wasn't sure about herself.

MaryRose trimmed the broken branches. She stuck a small wooden dowel in the ground and tied the fragile main stem to it, mounded soil around the trunk, and added plant food. The one leftover blossom looked like it might open in a few days. At least something would recover quickly.

A regular whirlwind spun around in her head. Family, journals, Randall, kisses, Andrea, Ken, the plant, death…it was like a rapid-fire movie trailer. A movie she had no interest in watching.

She needed to get away. The peace and quiet of a library always calmed her anxiety.

As she drove into town most of her thoughts settled. Kenneth's behavior kept injecting into her calm, though. He might have been the most popular boy in high school and college, but he was trouble. She knew his type. Had dated his type.

She shouldn't have ignored his actions on Memorial Day. They played volleyball in the water. She had a blast until Ken joined her team. The first time he brushed against her, she ignored it. Each successive time, he was more forward. When he intentionally fell against her, he actually said, "Sorry, I slipped."

Yeah, right.

She'd stormed out of the water, telling everyone she didn't want to play anymore. She should have spoken up but chose to avoid trouble. After today, she wouldn't keep silent.

MaryRose entered the library and inhaled the familiar scent associated with bookstores and libraries. The entire upstairs of this old house had been opened into one huge room filled with books from floor to ceiling. Old, cushy chairs dotted the floors. At one end of the room an old circular stairway led up to a loft lined with more books. She could stay for a week.

A woman about Nana's age looked up from the main desk. "Can I help you find something?"

"I hope so." She extended her hand. "I'm MaryRose Elliott. My great-great-grandmother, Rose Elliott used to live around here. I'm hoping you might have local historical records with information about her."

"You said Elliott?"

She nodded.

"Oh my word, you wouldn't be talking about Rose E., would you?"

"I recently learned Gramma Rose is likely the same as Rose E. Did you know her?"

"Oh no, no, no. I just know of her." She peered at me over the top of her glasses and clicked her lips. "Aren't you about the purtiest thing, too? I'm Sandra Kelly, by the way."

She began thumbing through files and boxes. The shelves behind her desk were piled high, but something told MaryRose she knew exactly where everything was in those stacks.

"I think the best place to start is with the microfilm. I know there was a big shindig for her hundredth birthday. That would have been in—"

"1948. And she died in 1953."

"If we have it, it's in the microfilms we still have." She walked from behind the counter and pointed toward a small room to the right of the stairway. "There's the microfilm room. Do you know how to work the machine?"

"Yes, ma'am."

"Then you go on in and holler if you need anything."

"Mrs. Kelly? I was told there is a lady in town who comes here a lot and she might have known Gramma Rose. I think her name is Vinnie?"

"Land sakes, I shoulda thought of her. Vinnie Burns is like a mother to me. She knows about everything about everybody most days. But dementia plays with her memories on others. When she comes in, you never know in which era she exists. She's a feisty old lady. Every bit of ninety-five-years-old and still lives in her little cabin outside of town. She might come in while you're here. If not, shall I give her your number?"

"I'd appreciate that. Thank you." MaryRose wrote the number on a sticky note then entered the microfilm room.

Rose Esther Elliott's obituary. MaryRose touched the screen. The woman she never knew, but shared a name with smiled at her. She had no idea how old Rose was when the picture was taken, but even in old age, she was beautiful. The freckles across the bridge of her nose looked like MaryRose's.

It said she died peacefully in her home. Didn't say who found her or how long she was there. Oh, how sad she was alone. The screen blurred. She wiped her eyes.

Mrs. Kelly came in.

"I wanted to tell you. I do remember a few things. When she got real old, people around here wanted her to go to a nursing home, but she refused. Said she'd not leave the home her Patrick built for her until her Lord took her home. That's when the Nolan Women's League set up a schedule. Every single day one of them went to check on Rose E. to make sure she was okay. Vinnie was the one who found her in her bed. She went to sleep and never woke up."

The lump in MaryRose's throat burned.

"So she wasn't there for days?"

"Oh no, honey, we take care of each other around here."

"Is the Women's League still operating?"

She shook her head. "It shut down years ago. But, I'll get you and Vinnie in touch."

MaryRose turned back to the microfilm machine and brought up the article about Gramma Rose's hundredth birthday celebration. It didn't really say much except how the church put together a party for her. Whoever was in charge of social events and obituaries must not have had much column allowance. She hit the print button and printed both articles.

At the front counter, she showed the papers to Mrs. Kelly. "What do I owe for these?"

Sandra dismissed the question with a wave of her hand. "Aw, that's silly. No charge for a couple of papers."

MaryRose's mood was substantially better as she walked onto Main Street. She had a true connection to Lake Nolan. Gramma Rose had lived somewhere around. The drive home passed quickly as she pondered where Patrick had built the cabin.

Reality slammed into her as she entered the kitchen and saw the note Papa Shane had left on the table with the trial details. She had to make a decision. "Come on Dapple, we're going to the lake. I have to think."

When she'd said goodbye to Papa after the play he told her they still needed to talk about the trial. He'd left early morning to go back, but he promised they'd talk soon. A meeting with her editor and a phone call from Papa about the trial—both loomed.

She had to convince Papa Shane her reasons to avoid the trial were valid.

Are they?

Great. Now God decides to talk to her heart again.

I never stopped.

She sat at the edge of the dock and kicked the water. She hadn't remembered what today was until she got home. June 15. In a breath she was ten years old again.

Gramps had told her to wait in the car while he got her bike. She waited a long time. Then a policeman rushed into the store. And an ambulance came. And the store owner came to the car and opened the door.

"Oh, honey, you have to come with me now. Your mama will be here to get you soon."

She fought to stay in the car. "Gramps told me to stay here and wait for hi—"

Then she saw them wheeling him out on a gurney. She jumped out of the car and ran to his side. The lady pulled her off of him. Someone screamed real loud. It was her.

Gramps was gone before they got him to the hospital.

MaryRose cleared her throat. It still felt like her fault. She chose to go to the store for her bike. She had to have a blue one. Of course, the doctors said it would have happened no matter what.

They were right.

She kicked the water again. "Oh, yeah? What about Ma, Pa, and Nana? If I hadn't insisted on going to Sean's grave they wouldn't have been on the road. I could have stayed home. I should have told them to stay home and let me go alone. I could even have gone to the grave another day. Is that why You turned away from me? When I want something someone has to die?"

For it is given to every man once to die.

"What?"

Everything has a season. A time to be born. A time to die. I will never leave or forsake you. Come to me when you are weary and heavy burdened and I will give you rest.

"But I don't understand."

The secret things belong to the Lord.

"Will I ever know why?"

Everything has a season. A time to laugh. A time to cry.

At some level she knew it wasn't really her fault but she couldn't always convince herself. Sitting there thinking of Andrea and Randall, she was afraid to care too much. She didn't want to lose anyone else. But Andrea needed her help, even if she didn't know it.

While the setting sun cast red sparkles on the water Dapple curled up beside her. She looked toward the opening of the inlet. Kenneth and Andrea were out on the lake somewhere. She bowed her head. "Lord, I don't know what to do. One minute I argue with you and the next I run to you. I'm fickle. But I am concerned about Andrea and I think I need to talk to Randall. Please give me Your words for him. Teach Ken to respect Andrea and understand when she says no she means it. Or better yet, get him out of her life."

Randall cleared his throat behind her. "Who?"

What was it about this family? They all sneaked up behind her. "How long have you been here?"

"Just got here. I thought you were talking to me, heard my name. Didn't mean to eavesdrop." He sat on the deck beside her.

Dapple grumbled as he shifted position to give Randall room.

She clasped her hands. Here was the opportunity. "I was praying for you and Andrea."

Sliding his feet out of his flip-flops and splashing them in the water, he cocked his head sideways and looked at her. "Well, thank you. And who needs to respect and understand when someone says no?"

"Kenneth."

His shoulders tensed. "Is there something I'm missing?"

"Actually, yes. They went out on the boat alone."

He relaxed. "He handles the boat well. I told them they could go."

The man wasn't going to make this easy. "Randall, it's not the boat I'm worried about. They went out on it alone." Did he understand yet?

He shook his head. "And?"

She took a deep breath. Although they were fast becoming more than friends, she wasn't sure what boundaries she might break by mentioning this to him. If it was her daughter she'd want to know.

"How long have they been together?"

"I don't know. Since high school."

"Next question. How long were you and Jessica together before you had to establish boundaries? Or...maybe you didn't make boundaries."

His jaw dropped. He stared at her.

She didn't know her hands were wringing until he took them into his.

"What's going on?"

"It's not my business, but I think you need to know."

There was no way she could do this with his strong hands caressing hers. She pulled free and clasped them in her lap.

"How long were you together before the boundaries?"

"Uh, I guess a year or so before we had to sort of watch it. I mean, when we started dating, she was a freshman. I was a sophomore. Guess it took a while before pressures got to me. And, well, she was the one who pulled back. I didn't want to. But I respected her and followed her lead—kicking and screaming."

"Now, let me ask again. How long have Ken and Andrea been together?"

"I told you, I guess about—" He froze. "What's up?"

"I'm not sure he shows her the respect you showed Jessica. He doesn't show it to me."

"You?"

She faced him "This is not about me. I'm not afraid of him, but he has been less than a gentleman with me."

"What did the boy do?"

"I've seen her push his hands away only to have him do it again. She and I had a long talk the other week. It may have helped for a while. But I think he's pushing again."

"I'll set him straight."

"Pray first. Talk to her next."

"Can we sit here until they get back?"

"Sure."

He placed his arm around her shoulders and pulled her close.

"So we don't appear like we're spying." He winked.

Before she could calm her heartbeat or think of a smart reply, an approaching boat distracted them.

"Thanks for staying with me." He kissed her cheek.

"That's nice."

"Yes, it is."

Andrea waved as Kenneth steered the boat toward the boathouse. Kenneth glared.

MaryRose leaned toward Randall and whispered, "He's upset."

"Looks like it."

It took the couple a long time to exit the boathouse. When they finally did, Kenneth had his arm around Andrea's waist and guided her directly to his car. As she climbed into the passenger side she called back to them, "We're meeting Jamie and Mitch for coffee. I promise I won't be too late getting back."

Randall looked down at her. "She is twenty-one. Don't figure I can demand she stay home. Thanks for telling me and for sitting with me."

"Anytime." Seriously, she'd sit with him. Liked it a lot. If the boat hadn't returned so soon would there have been another of those kisses? She bit her lip. This wasn't about a kiss. It was good they came back early. By the look on Kenneth's face, Andrea had won this battle.

"I really do thank you."

With his free hand, he tilted her chin up, bent and kissed her. There was a boatload of promise in his kiss.

"Thank you too. It's been a long time since I rested against a strong man."

"I know what you mean."

She nudged him. "About resting against a strong man?" Probably killed the moment, but she needed to, or she'd end up kissing him again.

His laughter boomed.

"You set yourself up." She stood and stretched. "I have to get back to my writing now and you need to be there when she gets home."

"You're probably right. " He picked Dapple up and handed him to her. "Hey, this Friday, June 21, is West Virginia Day. Would you accompany me to the festivities?"

"What day?"

"The day we celebrate when West Virginia became a state. It's almost as big a deal as July Fourth. We have a mini-regatta here on the lake. There's food and fun and a dance and fireworks. Join me?"

"I'd love to." He walked her home and stood between her and the screen door. His eyes bore into her soul. He brushed a curl from her face.

Silence.

"MaryRose—I—um—oh darn."

She raised her eyebrows. For once, she had breath.

Until he kissed her.

"You're the most beautiful woman I've ever met."

He kissed her again. Deeper. So much for having breath. A spark ignited in the depths of her soul. A tremor she felt go through his body suggested he felt the same.

He pulled himself away and headed up the hill.

"Goodnight, Randall."

"Night, Pretty Lady."

It appeared they might have to make boundaries of their own.

CHAPTER 17

*R*andall smiled at MaryRose as he started the boat. The look in his eyes reached right down into her heart and whispered something that felt a lot like forever. They'd been doing lake tours all morning. Even with a boat full of strangers enjoying the free ride they might have been the only two people in the world.

He reached across the wheel and touched her cheek. "You've got more freckles than a few weeks ago."

"Nana told me every freckle was where an angel kissed me."

"You've been keeping the angels busy this week then."

She leaned against him and he placed his arm around her shoulder as if it belonged there. Maybe it did.

"After this group unloads, we'll pick up Andrea and Kenneth at the marina. She wants to go to the diving rocks."

Once the last person disembarked, Andrea jumped onto the boat and hugged her.

"Ready to dive?"

"Not sure."

Kenneth sidled up and nudged her. "You'll love it. And of

course if you have a problem, Mr. Cobb will surely be happy to jump in and rescue you."

She tensed. This brazen young man needed to be brought down a few notches.

Randall cleared his throat, placed his arm around her shoulder, and pulled her tight against him, then sped up.

The boat lurched. Kenneth fell backward and landed on his butt. She stifled her laugh in Randall's shoulder.

"Sorry, Kenneth. I slipped."

The young man's eyes widened. He obviously recognized the phrase.

Randall whispered to her, "I'm going to have a talk with him."

They stopped beside the cliffs and tossed the anchor in. Several boats dotted the lake. MaryRose looked up at the cliffs and saw people leap, run, or dive off the edge. It did look like fun!

Randall pointed to old, rickety steps going up the slope. "That's the way up."

"The steps look more dangerous than the jump."

Andrea removed her cover-up and grabbed MaryRose's hand. She dragged her to the side rail. "Come on. You told me you dove off the platforms at NC State. This isn't much higher. I'll race you to the shore."

MaryRose rubbed her hands together. This was one adventure she'd not miss. It looked like a blast. She touched Randall's shoulder. "You care to join us?"

He raised his hands in surrender. "Not me. I don't cliff dive."

"Suit yourself." She turned back to Andrea. "Let's go!"

They dove into the water. Andrea was a good swimmer, but MaryRose was faster. She reached the steps ahead of Andrea, climbed out of the water, and stood with arms crossed. By the time Andrea joined her, she was tapping her foot impatiently.

"You're fast." Andrea hopped next to her on the step. "But I'm the mountaineer. I bet I can beat you up these steps."

Andrea raced up the rickety steps. MaryRose didn't attempt to keep up. This was way different from swimming fast. The old wood steps might give way any moment and send everyone bouncing down the rocks.

When she made it to the top, there stood Andrea, her arms crossed and toes tapping.

"Touché!"

They walked to the edge and MaryRose looked over.

"Oh my."

Andrea grabbed her hand. "The first time is the most difficult. I think it works best if you just go. The longer you take to ponder and plan, the more freaked out you get." She lifted their hands high and waved at Randall and Kenneth.

"On three?"

MaryRose ignored shaking legs and nodded.

"One, two, three."

They leaped into the air.

MaryRose stretched into a long swan dive and glanced sideways to see Andrea doing the same. It looked like they synchronized it. Oh, the freedom. She raised her eyes skyward and arched her back. The moment before closing her hands over her head and aiming for the water, she experienced weightlessness. All too soon she flew into the water, diving deep and turning upward. She burst through the surface and cheered.

Andrea surfaced a few feet away.

"Oh goodness, I could stay here all day."

Andrea chuckled. "Nope. A few times up those steps your legs tell you it's enough. Too bad they don't have chairlifts here like they do at ski slopes."

"What a great idea."

They opted for one more dive, promised to come another day, and then swam back to the boat. As she climbed into the boat, Randall wrapped her in a towel. If only the rest of her life was as uncomplicated as this moment.

Randall docked at the marina, and Kenneth jumped off to secure the lines. Andrea joined him, and the two ran up the hill hand in hand. Randall's brow creased. "I've been watching the boy more closely. You're right about him. He wouldn't talk to me while you two were diving. The thing is he reminds me of someone I used to know."

She stopped folding towels. "Who?"

"Me. Before Jessica slapped my face and made me pull over to let her out of the car. She walked home from one of our dates. Told me she'd not get back in the car with me again until I learned how to be a gentleman."

"What did you do?"

"Became a gentleman." He held the gate for her to exit the boat onto the dock. "Haven't you noticed that about me?" His wink tickled her.

"Yes, sir, I have."

After she stepped onto the marina deck, he motioned the people waiting to board for another tour. He sideways glanced at her. "Wish I hadn't volunteered to do these lake tours. You look way too pretty in your swimsuit and skirt for me to have you walk away."

Randall's eyes took on the deeper blue she'd seen before he kissed her. He leaned over the rail and kissed her forehead. "I'll be back shortly. Be prepared for me to monopolize your time and fill your dance ticket this evening."

"I shall hold you to that." She twirled once, headed up the deck, then stopped and waved. His smile, oh, his smile. At the end of the marina, she scanned the crowd for Jonathon and Missy. She couldn't wait to see how their first date was going.

CHAPTER 18

$\mathcal{M}$aryRose sat on the front stoop, looking for shooting stars. She'd already seen three. If she'd seen them earlier tonight she would've wished for the night to never end.

While she wasn't a fan of country music or country line dancing, she had to admit line dancing around the big pavilion was fun. When Randall pulled her into his arms and twirled her around as the band sang their version of the Lonestar song "Amazed," she could have melted. If she closed her eyes, she could imagine him still holding her.

The fireworks over the lake were incredible. And his goodnight kiss was, well, more dangerous than rock diving.

She smacked another mosquito off her arm. "I'm getting eaten alive out here. It's time to go inside."

But there was no way she'd be sleeping anytime soon. She made chamomile tea, plopped on the sofa, and then opened a journal. Within moments she was back in post-Civil War West Virginia.

~~~~

September 5, 1865

I borrowed Grampa's horse today and went for a ride. I wanted to see the house. So he told me how to get there. I cannot believe it. The walls are up and the roof is on. The door was open so I went in. It has wood floors already. And there is glass leaning against it for the windows. I am gonna have a window in my kitchen and in my bedroom. Oh my, will I ever stop blushing when I think about my bedroom?

It is hot tonight after all.

Gramma hung my wedding dress and my wedding night-dress on the hook in my room. I had to hang the wedding dress in front. I can't look at the nightgown without getting so jittery I drop my brush.
It's real hot tonight. I need water.

Gramma asked me if I like the gowns. I told her yes and thank you. She winked at Grampa when I told her which one I hung in front. Like they have a big fun secret.

The water didn't cool me down none.

I think about Patrick all of the time. I wonder how he is, where he is, and when he will finish up and come back here to settle. I hope he will be back a little while for us to walk together more before we get married.

Goodness, it seems like no matter what I write about it leads back to my wedding. What is wrong with me?

We got a letter from Mama and Pa this week. They will

come in after the harvest is over. Pa's gonna see to setting our fences and animals up. He says they should have built our barn before our house. Why? We don't have any animals anyway.

I am right glad they built the house first. Mama says she will bring what I need to set up my new house. It will be wonderful good to see them. Course they have to go back before the first snow. I sure hope Patrick gets back so we can have the wedding before they leave.

I bet James has grown a mile this summer. He probably looks like a man. I hope he's been helping Pa instead of sneaking over to Mary's house all the time. Sides, I ~~aint~~ am not there to cover for him ~~no~~ anymore. Pa's gonna be making sure he turns into a man real soon.

Tomorrow, Gramma is showing me how to take all the plants we gathered and dry some, then make poultices, or salves, teas, and well, I guess about everything. She told me she wants me to be sure and put everything in the special book so I will always have it.

She made me a mite afeared when she said that. Cuz she hugged me and told me that she wasn't allas gonna be around. She said I needed to know this stuff, my family and all of the people around here would count on it. She looked up to the sky and smiled real sweet like. It hurt my heart, the whole talk we had.

Jesus, please keep my family well. Amen.

~~~~

September 10, 1865

I got a letter from Patrick yesterday. I read it so many
times the folds in it plum near tore it apart. He says he
will be coming back the beginnin' of next month. He gets
done this month then has to tend to his affairs in Hertford. His cousin who was running the family farm is
buying it from Patrick. Patrick don't want to sell the land
yet but figures he must. After Patrick sees to things there
and packs his wagon up, he heads here.

Then he will help them finish our house. He says he is
gonna work on a special wedding present for me. One I
caint see til after we get to our house on the wedding
night. Land sakes, I dropped the letter right then and it
almost fell into the river to be washed away. I wonder,
does every bride have these wonderful and scared to
death feelings about getting married? How will I act like
a lady when I will be nervous as a field mouse cornered
by a cat?

I know my skin has tanned in the sun this summer and
my face is sprinkled with so many more freckles. Will
Patrick mind that? So much for my fair complexion. And
my red hair has blonde in it too. Almost looks like I
striped it. Maybe I worry too much. Gramma says I have
a beauty she never seen before, but she is my gramma.
And, much as it scares me I do want my husband to
want me.
Oh my, it is warm in here. I best close my book and sleep.
On top of all the other work tomorrow Gramma will
give me more grammar lessons as I write in her book.

Jesus, help me right now. I have a hard time picturing my

future, and a hard time letting go of my past. But I caint be okay with now until then, can I? Amen.

~~~~

September 30, 1865

I haven't written for a while. I do miss my book when I cannot get to it. But Gramma has me working hard. We have been dividing all we've harvested so far into those for her and those for me. I never dreamed I would start my house with a full winter's supply for my pantry. She says I worked for it too.

She says I am talking and writing better now. Land sakes, it is hard work to talk proper. Nobody else around here does. But she says a preacher's wife must be different. I guess I thought I was already different enough.

I was so proud of me yesterday. Gramma was over at the Estep's place birthing Sally's baby and John Atkins came over. Abigail had a stomach thing, well, he called it that, but I know he meant a woman pain. I mixed up cinnamon ginger tea for him to take to her. Told him she'll be good as gold tomorrow. When Gramma got home I told her all about it, about what I mixed up, and her smile lit up the whole kitchen. Maybe I am learning.

I wonder if Patrick will be pleased with his wife, with the things I learned and can do now. And soon as I start wondering I get all warm in the face. Did Momma wonder like this? All Gramma will tell me is it is nothing we talk about, but to be sure and trust God because God has a special present for a man and wife.

Just wish I knew. Gotta sleep now.

Jesus, Thank you for Gramma and Grampa. Thank you for all I have learned. Keep my Patrick safe. And bring Momma and Papa and James here soon. I miss them. Help me be who you want me to be. Amen.

~~~~

October 25, 1865

Oh my goodness, so much has happened. Patrick came back two days ago. He rode his horse up to the house and I about died. His beard makes him look so much older, but the sparkle in his eye melted my heart all over again. He got off his horse and walked straight to me. He took both of my hands in his and then he bent down and kissed my lips. In front of Gramma and Grampa he did that.

My knees got so weak I near fell over. Then he said the sweetest words. He said, "Rose, your letters have worked magic and you now hold my heart. We must be wed soon or I will suffer greatly."

Then I was right bold. I stood on my toes and kissed him back. He chuckled a bit then whispered, "Watch out or your Pa will grab his gun and make us marry right here and now."

I thought that wouldn't be so bad. Then it hit me what he said. Sure enough, a wagon was coming up the road. It was Pa's wagon. I pulled my hands out of his, held up my skirt and ran up the road to my Momma. I couldn't believe it. Not only had Patrick come back, he went and brought my family with him. Momma grabbed hold of me and hugged me like she woud never let me go. I didn't want her to either.

We had us a fine feast, a fine time. Patrick has gone and moved into our home now. He's gonna finish the work on it right fast. Momma and Papa are sleeping in Papa's old bedroom, and James has to sleep on the floor in my room. They will stay till after the wedding.

Oh, the wedding. I will be married just shy of two weeks. Momma and Gramma been fussing and fussing over packing things for me for my new house. The wagon was about all loaded with stuff from home for my new home. Sometimes I get so excited about the wedding I plum near explode. Then other times I get so scared I wanna hide in the barn.

Mostly I'm excited. I guess I will git awful busy the next two weeks.

Jesus, help me in all the ways. They's so much, help me. Thank you for getting everybody here. Amen.

~~~~

November 6, 1865

Tomorrow I get married.

Jesus, Make me be a good wife. Amen.

~~~~

November 8, 1865

Gramma was right. Marriage is real good. God's special present is too.

Thank you, God, Amen.

~~~~

MaryRose wiped a happy tear from her cheek. After her wedding night when she was only eighteen, would she have written more words about it than Gramma Rose? MaryRose enjoyed imagining the newlywed Rose Elliott sitting with her journal open unsure what to write, probably blushing as she did so. "You know, Gramma Rose, I think saying marriage is real good about covered it."

But wouldn't it have been fun if Gramma Rose had written a little bit more?

CHAPTER 19

*M*aryRose rolled over and hit the snooze button on the alarm clock. The noise continued. As the fog of the sweet dream cleared she realized it was her phone. There was only one person who would call before sunrise.

"Morning, Papa Shane."

He chuckled.

She propped up against the headboard. "How are you?"

"Had me a fine trip. Was good to see Missy succeeding in her craft and you happy in your new home. Been thinkin' about ya ever since I returned home. It's pleased I am to have met your new family. They are fine people."

New family? She liked that. "I read in the journals last night and got to Gramma Rose's wedding. It made me cry happy tears."

"That's a good thing. Lass, I have to get me day started, but I need ta ask have ya baked any cookies lately?"

"Umm, no. That's an odd question."

"It won't be when ya get to needin' your cookie jar." He snickered.

She plodded to the kitchen. The cookie jar lid was askew.

How had she not noticed that? She lifted it and peeked inside. No words. The jar was filled with money. The phone she held between her head and shoulder slid free and hit the floor.

Digging her hands into the cookie jar she pulled out twenties, fifties, and a generous amount of hundred-dollar bills. After retrieving the phone she put it on speaker and set it on the counter.

"That's a lot of money. Where on earth did it come from? You can't afford to give me this much."

"Tis your nana's money. She always told me to be sure you were cared for if anythin' ever happened to her."

"But—"

"Tis time for ya to find your dream, not follow someone else's, even if the someone is your ma or nana."

"But—"

"No, there is no arguin' with me, Lassie. I want ya to call the boss of yours this mornin', soon as he is in his office, and tell him ya don't need his magazine. Ya have enough money in your cookie jar to carry ya through for a while. And soon ya will be receiving a check for the rest of your family's estate. My dear, ya don't have to be working ever again. Surely, ya don't have to be working somewhere ya don't want."

"If I quit, I'll let Ma and Nana down."

"You'll be a letting them down if ya stop following your own dream. Write your story."

He sighed so loud into the phone he could have been standing right beside her.

"What's wrong, Papa?"

"There's more, ya know. Take the money out of the jar. I think you'll be a baking cookies soon as we hang up. I know ya bake when things weigh down your heart."

He wasn't going to let up about the trial.

"I know ya are still dealin' with your parents' deaths. Both of us are. Ya refused to talk about it while I was there, but, I'll be expecting ya here for the trial next week."

MaryRose pinched the bridge of her nose. The taste of bile hit her mouth before the gag. Acid burned her throat.

"MaryRose? Get a drink of water. I'll be a waitin' here."

Water wasn't going to stop this panic attack. Her brain was dancing circles around her skull. The house shrunk and the air was sucked right out the window. She swallowed another gag as she reached for a glass from the cabinet.

Shaking hands filled the glass and promptly dropped it on the marble counter shattering it. As she tried to clean up the mess a large piece of the glass cut her palm. She flinched then pulled a chair toward her and dropped into it.

That was it. The dam burst. The broken glass surrounding her became her tormentor, daring her to move from this turmoil. Grabbing a tea towel from the counter, she wrapped it around her palm.

"MaryRose? Ya still there?"

Miraculously the water had not reached her phone yet. She moved it to a dry spot on the counter.

"I'm here. I dropped the glass and it broke."

"Did ya hurt yourself?"

"Got a little cut. It'll be fine."

"Do ya feel better now?"

"No. I can't do this. Why are you asking me to? I can't face him. I'm doing okay here." She twisted and squeezed the hem of her nightgown into a knot. She couldn't stop. "Let him rot in hell."

She froze. She swore to Papa Shane. What he must think of her.

"Ya don't be meanin' that now, do ya?" Nothing in his voice sounded the slightest bit shocked over her swearing.

"I hate him. I don't care what happens to him."

Silence.

"MaryRose, do ya remember the year your Mama lost all but one of her Rose-of-Sharon plants?"

Of all things for him to bring up. She glanced toward the front door and pushed away the anger of having seen hers on the ground, "Yes."

"She was upset because it was the last of her grandmother's shrubs."

"I know."

"And what did she do? She nurtured and cared for it and finally one small section of the plant began to grow again."

She didn't like where he was going.

"Do ya remember why the plant got so bad?"

"Something to do with the root."

"The root system had a spot in it and it poisoned the whole plant. She saved one part of the plant by getting rid of the bitter root. How is your plant growin' there?"

"Beautiful, flourishing. Well, it was. The other day a smart-mouthed young man landed in it after I slapped him. Andrea's boyfriend was rude and fresh with me. "

"Ya slapped him. Ya just swore at me. See what I mean? You're growing and flourishing down there, but, sweet child, ya have a bitter root growin' in your soul. It will slowly kill ya if it can. Ya need to come here and face this. The Lord and me will be with ya."

"I can't do it."

"Ya can, and ya will. I'll be seeing' to it." His breath puffed and she'd bet his jaw was set. "I'll be back to get ya if I have to. Sleep on it tonight and pray too. I'll call after work tomorrow. Night, child." He hung up.

"I can't do it. Lord, you know I can't do it. Everyone expects too much of me."

She paced the length of the dock. As she'd been doing for the past hour or more. She couldn't sleep and hoped sitting on the dock would help. Stupid thought. The longer she stayed there the more agitated she got.

Anxiety turned her into a frantic-pacing-crazy lady. Her heart raced. Her fists clenched so tight her nails dug into her palms. She opened her fingers, stretched them apart, and took a deep breath, only to clench again. Her jaw had been clamped shut pretty much all evening. The tension had created a killer headache. She could almost hear it mocking the ginger tea steeping in her mug.

MaryRose stopped pacing long enough to stare out over the black hole of the lake. Clouds blocked the moon and stars making everything look as dark as her mood.

"I can't do it."

Someone approached from her cottage. Who would be down here so late? Of all people, Trudy walked toward her.

"I heard you talking to yourself. Child, what on earth is it that has you up and telling the darkness you can't do something?"

"Trudy, what are you doing here?"

"The Lord woke me and sent me here. I guess He thinks maybe you need me."

"Nobody can help me. I can't do it."

"Come here." Trudy quickly cleared the steps between them and wrapped her in a hug. "You know the Lord wants you to do this—whatever *it* is—or you wouldn't be battling so hard. I bet it's the ugly trial that's got you so all-fired upset."

"You don't understand. Nobody does. God wouldn't ask me to do this."

Trudy smoothed down her hair. "Why, sure He would. He's in the business of askin' us to do things we think we can't. But this is more about you. He doesn't want you tormented like this; wants the anger out of your soul."

"That's what Papa Shane said."

"He's a wise man."

"But you don't get it." She tried to pull free, but Trudy held tight.

"I remember a time I fought God."

"You?"

She nodded.

MaryRose calmed a little as Trudy sat at the picnic table and motioned for her to sit also.

"When my sister Alice died."

She shuddered.

"Alice, the wild one, the rebel. She got herself in all sorts of trouble in high school. When she met Jimmy Dotson she settled down. He was a mighty man of God and led her back to faith.

"The summer before their oldest boy started high school, the whole family went on a mission trip. They went with a group to a Cree reservation in Canada, building a church, doing the Lord's work. What happened didn't make any sense."

She patted MaryRose's leg.

"There's a large addiction problem there. Alice was working the soup kitchen when the local gang came in. They held up the workers and took her hostage. They robbed several stores using her as a shield, and when they felt safe, they shot her and left her by the side of the road. All because they needed drugs and booze."

MaryRose caught her breath, and then her shoulders shook. An invisible hand pressed her chest, preventing air from going in or out. She was strangling.

Trudy grasped her chin and looked her in the eyes. "Breathe with me. In. Out. In. Out."

Slowly MaryRose began to breathe normally.

Trudy traced invisible things on the tabletop.

"I know the anger you're feeling. Took me a long time to work through it. Want to talk?"

"Alcohol, it's always alcohol." She spoke through clenched teeth and pounded a bass drum beat into her thighs.

"No, it's sin. Alcohol may be the avenue, but it's always sin. The unforgiveness you harbor inside of you is sin too." Trudy grasped MaryRose's hands.

"The trial starts next Tuesday. You know how I feel about him."

"Hate about makes you sick, doesn't it?"

"Yes."

"Has your faith ever been this weak?"

"Never."

"MaryRose, that's why you have to go. You have to see the empty despair in his eyes."

"No, I don't." She pulled her hands from Trudy's and turned toward the lake.

"Yes, you do. You have to look at him and let the Lord talk to your heart. Then you have to find forgiveness."

"Never." She shook her head so hard her hair slapped her face.

Trudy pointed to her towel-bandaged hand. "What happened here?"

"I broke a glass."

"Is this how your mother taught you to treat a wound?"

"No."

She placed her open palm across MaryRose's heart. "There's a wound inside you, and you have a dish towel wrapped around it. It's not going to heal. The infection will spread. I think you know you can't live like this. Holding this hate will kill your tender heart. And you'll never move forward and love again until this is behind you."

"Maybe I don't want to love again."

"You already do." Trudy's voice was barely audible.

She twisted to face Trudy. The woman was right.

"But I can't do this."

"Can't? Or won't? It seems easier to be angry than to let it go, but you know it isn't. Listen to the Holy Spirit talking to you right now. He brought me here because He loves you.

"Now, I'll walk you to your house, clean the cut proper, and go help Walter open the store. I'll be back next Monday morning about ten to pick you up. We're takin' us a road trip. I'm going with you to North Carolina so you can be there Tuesday."

"I can't ask you to do that."

"You didn't ask. Always did want to stick my feet in the ocean anyways. Now let's get you cleaned up, and you call Papa Shane and tell him to have a room ready for us."

"I don't really have a choice, do I? Either I go with you or Papa Shane comes and gets me. None of this means I'll forgive the man or I will stop hating."

"God will take care of what's going on in your heart."

"If it happens, it will be because He did it, that's for sure."

"No one else could do it, child."

They walked to the cottage in silence. Trudy cleaned and bandaged her hand then hugged her again. "Call Papa Shane then get yourself through this day. I'll see you Monday morning bright and early." She kissed the top of her head and left.

CHAPTER 20

*I*f another cricket chirped or cicada chattered outside her window, MaryRose was going to scream. Their nighttime chorus joined by owls, tree frogs, bull frogs—and who knew what else—had kept her awake most of the night. But the sirens and screeching cars in her dreams stirred up memories of the most horrid moments of her life.

Tossing and turning all night left her tangled in a mass of covers and nightgown. She tried to kick free and stand, but one toe was still caught in the lace on the sheet which caused her to tumble to the floor with a thud. Dapple peeked out from under the comforter and growled.

Sobs racked her. Her hands trembled so hard she couldn't grab the sideboard and pull to stand. When she finally stood, she walked on shaky legs into the kitchen. Water splashed out of her glass as soon as she poured it. It looked like the way Grampa Elliot's hands used to tremble with palsy.

The kitchen still smelled like chocolate chip cookies. Making three batches before bed had not calmed her enough to allow sleep. It would take a lot of coffee to get her alert this morning. She was showered and dressed before it finished brewing. The walls closed in. She had to get out of the house. How in the world could she make it through the week knowing what was ahead?

Praying was a joke. Her prayers went up and bounced off the ceiling. What difference did it make? Nothing in her wanted to try again. Despair wrapped tentacles around her heart draining the last of her fight.

She was empty. Sitting at the kitchen table with her head down, she cried herself dry. Light tapping at the door interrupted. Randall. With daisies. His frame filled the doorway as much as his presence filled her heart. Trudy was right. She motioned him in.

Randall crossed the room and enveloped her in his arms. The intensity in his eyes as he looked into hers she felt in her soul. Maybe she didn't have to go. There had to be a way to turn her back on the killer and that part of her life. Couldn't she do it without going to the trial?

She leaned into his chest. "Who told you?"

"Trudy and Mom are best friends. They talked last night. Mom called me a little while ago and told me to get down here and check on you before work."

She pulled out of his arms. "I'm not going. I'm not strong enough."

He cupped her face in his hands.

"You are the strongest woman I know." He tapped the tip of her nose. "You have more faith right there than anyone I've ever met. I know it's floundered some, but it's still there. You think you're not strong enough, but remember you're not alone. Trudy and Papa Shane will be with you. And we'll all be praying. And, as you've reminded me, Jesus is going with you."

"I don't know anymore. Maybe I was wrong." She shook her head and tried to step away. He wouldn't let her.

"Shh, MaryRose. Doubt doesn't fit you. We'll get you through this week."

No one really understood what this was doing to her. Even with Randall standing there holding her, she felt alone.

"Come closer, please." He pulled her tighter into his embrace. She breathed his scent. It struck her that, more than anything, he smelled like home. The warmth in her chest grew into a lump at the base of her throat. She didn't know if she wanted to sing or cry.

"You've got all week to get ready. See if Missy will come and stay a few days. I know Jonathon would love having her a little closer than the park."

"That's a great idea."

"Are you free tonight?"

"Yes."

"How about dinner? I can pick you up around six?"

"I may not be the greatest company if I can't find my way out of this funk."

He leaned down and kissed her soundly. "You're always the greatest company."

As he left, the screen door banged behind him. He looked at it, then her. "You still don't want me to fix that?"

"Nope."

"Women." He mumbled.

She dropped into the chair by the phone and dialed Missy.

"Wh-what in the world?" Missy's voice was thick from sleep. "Some people like to sleep in the morning, you know? What time is it anyway?"

"It's already eight. The day's wasting."

"Maybe for the crazy people. But those of us who are sane don't see a reason to be up this early on their Monday off. Hang on." Covers rustled, and Missy mumbled something more about ungodly hours. "Okay, I think I got the paste out of my mouth and the glue from my eyes. Spill it."

"Want to go on a date?"

"You're not my type."

"Ha-ha. Randall asked me out. Want to double?"

"That's a no on several levels. You really are rusty at this dating thing aren't you?"

"What do you mean?"

"The man asked *you* out. He didn't ask if you wanted to double. If Jonathon and I show up, it will probably ruin his plans. Besides, I also have a date tonight. Jonathon's taking me to a fancy place on the other side of the lake. I have to get all dressed up for it."

"I guess I am out of the dating loop and more than a little nervous about a real one."

"Tell me about it. I'm scared half to death."

"You, scared of dating? Since when?"

"Since I started falling in love."

Her too? "Ditto."

"It's different with me. I was married to an abuser. I'm a divorced woman, and Jonathon is going to be a pastor. I'm an actress, for Pete's sake. And you and I both know I'm not the most faith-filled woman these days. It scares me how Jonathon treats me like a treasure."

"You should be treated like that. Why not take things as they come. If you fall in love, then so be it. Give God a chance to work this." She heard her words and wasn't even sure she believed them anymore.

"I don't remember how to talk to God, believe Him, trust Him."

She stood at the sink watching the lake. Unlike her roiling emotions, the water was serene this morning.

"I'm having a rough week, could use some time with you.

Why not come over here after your date? Hang out for a few days. We could swim and take long bike rides like we used to."

"That sounds great. MaryRose, you know me and nature have a love/hate relationship. I chased three raccoons out of my garbage last night and saw a rattlesnake under my little porch last week. I could use a break from this whole roughing it thing."

"Roughing it in a cabin?"

"Keep in mind; I've been a city girl for the past eight years. Do you have a key hidden somewhere so I can get in if you're not home yet or already sleeping?"

"I'll be up. Always have a hard time going to sleep after I see Randall."

Missy chuckled. "I get it."

MaryRose poured another cup of coffee, opened the journal but pushed it aside. Thanks to Nana's stories, she knew what happened next and didn't want to read about sad things today. Maybe she could write more in the novel. If only she could capture what Patrick must have felt as he stood on the porch waiting for someone to answer the door. Before she could get into his point of view, Andrea was at the door.

"I know it's early and I probably should have called first. I found something the other day and I have to show it to you. Are you up for another trip to the cemetery?"

"I guess so. What's up?"

Andrea covered her mouth with her finger and grinned. "I have to show you. You're already in jeans. Come on."

She fed Dapple and then followed Andrea to the purple machine. Andrea tossed her a helmet and climbed on the back. "You drive this time."

"No way. Not up that trail."

"Aw, come on, where's your sense of adventure?"

"I tell you what, I'll drive until we get to the steep part and then you can take over. Think I even remember how to get there."

"You got a deal."

MaryRose climbed on and fastened her helmet as Andrea got on behind her. MaryRose revved the engine and took off. It had been a few years since she drove an ATV, but it didn't take long to remember the joy of the ride. Andrea even whooped as she took a few of the curves fast enough to skid on the gravel. She stopped at the overlook.

Standing there watching the fog rise from the valley was breathtaking. Almost looked like a reverse snow storm. The beauty of these mountains never ceased to amaze her.

Andrea bounced into the driver's position and revved the engine. "Come on, MaryRose. What I want to show you is even more incredible."

The girl's enthusiasm was contagious. MaryRose hopped onto the seat behind her.

"Okay, let's go."

"You're a big chicken."

MaryRose's response was covered by the gunning engine and Andrea's whoops as they lurched up the incline at a speed dangerous on flat ground, much less up the side of a mountain. When they pulled into the parking area at the cemetery Mary-Rose's wobbly legs barely held her up.

"You win. I'll drive next time. Slower."

Andrea laughed. "Wait till you ride with Daddy. He's a speed demon." She grabbed her hand and dragged her through the entrance. They wove through the fenced areas to one in the back. The iron was rusted and the gate hung forever frozen partially open. A small nameplate was attached to the gate.

MaryRose bent to look at it and stopped cold. She scratched at the rust on the nameplate. Sure enough, it was what it looked like. She traced the letters and stared.

THOMAS ~ ELLIOTT.

Andrea stood at the far edge of the plot, pointing out an old-looking section. "They're over here."

MaryRose tiptoed as fast as she could between the stones. Her ancestors right here? She really did belong here. As she walked into the area she examined stones so old the carving was beyond recognition. Then she saw one she knew. "Alice Mary Thomas." Over time the weather had effaced the date away. The stone beside it read "Arthur Milton Thomas."

She dropped to the ground and sat between the headstones and traced the letters. "Gramma Rose's grandparents, the ones she stayed with before marrying Patrick."

"Come over here." Andrea whispered. She was sitting on the ground beside three graves under an old dogwood tree.

MaryRose examined a few other stones before joining Andrea. Her heart thumped so hard she thought it might beat right out of her chest. One step. Another step. How could it take so long to walk a few feet? Stopping in front of Andrea, she leaned down and looked at the next headstone.

A simple marker with simple words. Her heart soared.

Patrick Michael Elliott.
Husband. Father, Preacher—Loved and Missed

Her great-great-grandfather buried right here, so close to her. When she started looking for places in the mountains to move, how could she have guess she'd end up in the exact location of her family home?

I did.

God?

I Am.

Chills chased up her spine. She looked at the next stone. The dates had worn away, but the letters were still clear.

Rose Esther Elliott

Known to us as Rose E.
Beloved Healer, Faithful Wife, Mother, Grandmother, Friend

MaryRose dropped to the ground and sat beside the head-stone. Leaning against it and hugging it, she didn't try to stop the tears. For the first time in months she was connected to family.

Andrea sat down beside her and lightly touched her shoulder.

"MaryRose, look at the one beside Gramma Rose's. I pulled the grass away before I came to get you."

Beside Gramma's headstone was a flat one barely visible except for the grass that had obviously been removed.

MaryRose Eliott
April 26, 1849
Four hours in our arms. Forever in our hearts.

Her hands covered her mouth. She knew they had lost their second child. She even knew the baby was a girl. But no one ever told her she shared a name with the baby that didn't live. Reaching over and touching the stone, it hit her: Gramma Rose knew how it felt to hold a precious daughter for only a few hours.

"I never knew."

Andrea brushed the hair out of her face. "What?"

"That I had the same name as their baby girl." After brushing more grass away from the stone and tossing the weeds away, she touched the gravestone again. "Do you mind if we stay a while?"

"Not at all. Or we could borrow Daddy's truck and bring equipment up one day and really do it justice."

"I'd like that. How did you find it?" She pulled weeds from around the gravestones.

"When I came up to visit Mommy, I saw those daisies along the fence and went to pick a few for her grave. I'd never been in this section before, so while I picked the daisies, I looked around. When I realized what I was seeing, I forgot all about the daisies and came down to get you. Now I'll pick some for Mommy and Gramma Rose."

"And MaryRose."

"Yeah."

They worked around the plot until their stomachs growled louder than the cicadas chirped. At least the gravestones were no longer covered in ivy and periwinkles, and a bundle of daisies lay across each one. MaryRose brushed her hair out of her face.

"I guess we better go. I still have many things to accomplish today and I have to be done in time for supper. Oh, and Missy is coming over later tonight to stay for a few days."

"Daddy is all excited and nervous about the date."

"You know?"

"He made sure I was cool with it. I helped him figure out where to take you."

MaryRose's curiosity piqued. "Should I dress up?"

"Definitely. It's a nice place." Andrea winked, tossed her the helmet, climbed on the four-wheeler, and revved it up.

CHAPTER 21

*M*aryRose twisted her hair into a loose bun and clipped it with the silver butterfly barrette Nana gave her for graduation. She fluffed her gypsy skirt, and then smoothed the cotton peasant top. The neck scooped lower than she remembered. She tied the closure on the top a bit tighter to cover a little more. After applying light makeup, putting on her green Austrian-crystal necklace and earrings, she slid into her leather sandals, and then dropped back on the edge of the bed.

Oh goodness, she hadn't been on a date for a couple of years. A horrible date. The son of a friend of a lady at church. He was supposedly well-mannered, well-off, and quite the perfect catch. Ha. He was attractive enough but quite arrogant and was pretty sure she'd be honored to allow his hands free roam of her body. When she slapped him, he pinned her against the front door and insisted he go inside with her.

MaryRose grinned.

The knee she soundly delivered to his groin impeded him long enough for her to scoot inside her house and lock the door. She hadn't been on a date since. Hopefully, Randall was more of a gentleman because she didn't want to be disappointed.

There was barely time to tuck Dapple into his crate and close the bedroom door before Randall called in the back door. "Hey MaryRose, are you ready?"

She dabbed a bit of Lacey Pearls cologne on her neck and wrist.

"Coming."

He stood at the door. Phew. The man made khakis and an oxford shirt look good. Real good.

"Hey."

"Hey, Pretty Lady. I have reservations at this quaint little place I know."

"Oh, should I have dressed up more?"

"You look perfect." He winked. "I think we'll walk."

"Walk where?"

Randall took her hand and led her to the dock. Party lights hung from one side of the dock to the other. Soft music played from the boom box on the picnic table. A small table with two chairs, candles, and place settings for two was set up on the end of the dock.

"I felt like eating in tonight. Our food should be here soon. Can I interest you in sparkling cider while we wait?"

"I—um—wow. I would love some. This is amazing."

"Glad you like it. Sarah's delivery boy is bringing our meal. I have no idea what's coming. I asked for her special."

"I don't know what to say."

He handed her a glass and placed his arm around her shoulder. They stared out over the water.

"Not sure what they call it nowadays, but when I last dated we called it going together. So, MaryRose, say you'll go with me."

"I will."

He took her glass and placed it on the dock with his. Then he swung her around in a pirouette and pulled her into his arms. His husky voice tickled her ear. "MaryRose look up."

When his lips claimed hers, his kiss was like no other. She melted into his embrace as her passion matched his. He pulled away when the delivery truck from Sarah's beeped as the driver parked beside the boathouse.

As they stood on the dock, the young man removed all of the containers and served dinner for them. Once the table was set he walked to them and bowed.

"For your dining pleasure tonight we have beef Stroganoff on noodles, rolls, fresh green beans, salad, applesauce, and sweet tea. Dessert is Sarah's cherry pie; however I was instructed to call it goodest pie. When you are finished, you may place everything in the bin I left on the driveway. I will be back to pick it up later tonight."

Before they really had a chance to respond, the young man turned and left.

Dinner was delicious. They talked about everything and nothing. They watched the sun set over the lake. As the red and purple turned to indigo, they finished their dessert.

Randall stood and offered his arm. "Might I have this dance?"

"Yes."

He twirled her into his arms and glided her in circles on the dock. Her feet barely touched the ground. He held her close, and as they slowed to a stop he kissed her again. And again.

He stepped back and blew his breath out. "Mmm. I'm not sure I trust myself with you, MaryRose. I think I better clean up from dinner now."

She stood on tip-toes and kissed him once more. And once more. He was right, but it wasn't only him who needed to get a little bit of control.

"This was the most perfect date I've ever been on. I should get back. Missy will be here soon."

"I'll walk you home, then come back and clean up."

Randall placed his arm around her waist as they headed home.

"I'll miss you next week."

"Ugh, reality is always there isn't it. I still don't want to go."

"I know, but I think you need to. Don't you?"

MaryRose kicked at the ground. Everyone else thought she needed to. "I guess I'll find out. Keep me in your prayers next week, please."

"Of course."

He bent and kissed her one more time. Even a soft little kiss drove her crazy.

The first thing she noticed when she stepped inside the kitchen was the blinking light on her phone. She sat in the chair by the phone table and listened to a message from Missy.

"I hate to do this. But they scheduled a couple of charity performances this week. I can't come over. Please forgive me. Call me when you get in from your date."

She hit delete and shrugged. She brewed mint tea, grabbed the journals and curled up on the sofa. Dapple snuggled across her feet like a living afghan. She reached down and scratched his neck, then began reading.

~~~~

January 24,1866 ILUP

I caint believe I have not written in here since my wedding. But I spose it is OK too. We had Thanksgiving at Gramma and Grampa's house. Momma and Papa stayed here until then. They left right after. Everybody told them the mountain pass could close any day. I miss Momma.

Me and Patrick had a quiet Christmas here. The first

snow came Christmas Eve while we were at church. It was such a pretty, quiet ride home. He gave me a new pen and ink and another journal. I made him a new warm shirt and wrist warmers for when he is out on his home visits. Patrick shot a turkey for our meal.

He preached a real good sermon on Christmas Eve. I do love to hear him preach. But I caint bear to be around him when he's a writing his words. He paces enough to wear a body out. Then he speaks and speaks it over and over. He kicks and groans when he messes up. I learned I am better off taking my horse for a ride when he writes.

My horse. She's a pretty roan mare. Momma and Papa brought her to me from home. I named her October. I think she will foal in the spring too. Patrick's stallion made sure of that.

Oh yes. I never wrote about my wedding gift. Patrick remembered how much I liked the bed at that place in Aracoma. He made us a bed almost exactly like it. The quilt Gramma made looks so pretty on it. I do love having my husband. Will I ever stop getting warm like this when I think of him? I hope not.

The past three mornings I woke up feeling real bad. Barely got to the outhouse before I got sick. Then cooking up the bacon about made me get sick again. I aint never been one to get sick. Funny thing is I always feel better by dinner. I gotta watch out too. I maybe been making too many Johnny cakes for Patrick. My dress feels a bit tight when I button it. I have to remember to ask Gramma for more of her peppermint for bad stomachs.

I did something what would make people shamed of me yesterday. I got tired of the snow in my pantaloons. I took a pair of Patrick's pants and put them on when I was in the barn feeding the chickens, milking Mabel, and mucking the stalls. I bout died when Patrick came in and found me like that.

His face got all red. Then he frowned. Then he smiled, scooped me in his arms and told me he liked it. He told me to keep those pants and mend them to fit me better. Then he winked at me and said I better not ever wear them around the church people. I got the feeling he liked me in them. It sure was easier to work in the snow with them than with skirts and petticoats.
I better stop now. Patrick is ready for bed. Me too.

Jesus, Thank you for my Patrick. Help me to not keep getting sick. Keep Patrick safe and strong. And be with all the rest of my family during this long winter. Amen.

~~~~

February 1, 1866 ILUP

Gramma would not give me any of her belly mint tea. She said it was no good for a woman with child to be drinking stuff like that. I fell out of my rocking chair. With child? Me? I figured it up and I reckon she may be right. How will I tell Patrick? What will he say? They's no way we are ready to have a baby. How could God think we are? Why we are still learning how to be with each other.

I am scared. But I have to tell him before he picks up my

book to read. Sometimes he does that. That is why I
write the four letters in the corners. They mean I love U
Patrick. It's my secret code to him. Not anymore I guess.
Maybe I will cook his favorite pot roast tonight and tell
him while he is all happy from supper.

Jesus, help us. You made this baby, so you have a plan.
Help us trust your plan. Amen.

~~~~

February 2, 1866

I am married to the best man God ever made. We was
sitting at the table, he was on third helping when I told
him we needed to talk about stuff. Then I told him about
the baby. Oh goodness, he jumped up from his chair and
knocked his coffee all over his plate getting to me. He
scooped me off my chair and swung me in circles until
we both got so dizzy we fell down. We sat on the floor
and laughed till we cried.

I caint believe I am having a baby. How can I be a
Momma? I hardly know how to be a wife yet.

Jesus, help me, please. And thank you for long winter
nights. Marriage is real good. Amen.

~~~~

MaryRose chuckled at the things Gramma Rose left between
the lines. Cute. It even made her blush a bit too. Where did
Gramma Rose keep the journal? In a drawer of the dresser or
maybe in a special box Patrick made for it. Despite being old

and yellow, even brittle, the pages held together firmly with strong stitching. The name Rose was burned into the cover of the old book. Had Patrick done that or Rose's father? How many times had she held the closed journal to her chest the way MaryRose was doing right then?

Then it hit her. Between Missy not coming this week and her free time since she resigned the magazine job, she'd have plenty of time to read the journals. This would be a great week to go to the library and do more research. Maybe Vinnie would be there. Bright and early tomorrow she'd go to the library. Another day this week, she could borrow Andrea's four-wheeler and go back to her family's plot at the cemetery.

MaryRose arrived at the library when it opened at nine Wednesday morning. Sandra Kelly motioned her to the front desk. "MaryRose, how nice to see you again. Vinnie hasn't been in for days, but you picked the best day to be here. Today is Wonderful Wednesday Women, and she almost always stops in."

"Wonderful what?"

Sandra clicked her dentures. "It's a group of ladies who gather here Wednesday mornings. They talk about books they've read—"Sandra leaned forward and whispered—"and gossip. They know everything about everybody and make my Wednesdays a joy. I don't think there's a one of them younger than eighty. Vinnie will most likely be here."

"I wouldn't want to bother them."

"Honey, they don't let anyone bother them. They already know Randall Cobb has a pretty little thing renting his cottage. They might stop coming here on Wednesdays if I don't intro-duce you."

"Oh."

"Now you go on and do whatever you planned to do. I'm

fixing to get the reading room ready for them. I'll be sure to come and get you when they all get here."

MaryRose walked to a desk in a cubby. After taking her notepad and Gramma's journal out of her tote, she leaned back in the chair and watched a lone sailboat on the water.

Before she opened the journal, she sensed someone standing behind her.

Sandra stood beside a little old little woman who looked as if she might fall over. The woman clung to Sandra's elbow and pointed at MaryRose.

"Lawdy me, it's Rose E come back to us as a young woman."

"No, Vinnie, this is her great-great-granddaughter, Mary-Rose Elliott."

Silence stretched between them as Vinnie stared at Mary-Rose and tears filled her eyes.

Sandra finally spoke. "MaryRose Elliott, please meet Vinnie Burns."

Vinnie stepped forward, reached out and touched the top of her head, then her cheek. "You're the spitting image of Rose E. I cain't believe the good Lord brought you here to see me."

MaryRose wiped a tear on her cheek. "You knew my gramma?"

She nodded. Then she fluttered her hand at Sandra. "Now you go on and git. Tell the other ladies I got something more important to do this morning and I'll talk to them later."

Sandra brought a chair in and sat it next to MaryRose. Vinnie sat down and placed her hands in her lap.

"Now let me get a look at you." She squinted as she stared into MaryRose's face.

"I cannot believe I am sitting with someone who knew Gramma Rose. I had no idea this would happen."

"Well, child, it's a shock to me to walk in here of a Wednesday and see a younger version of the dear lady in my library. Everybody loved her. I'll be the envy of the town when people hear you wanted to talk to me. 'Course, I am the oldest one in town too."

She kept patting MaryRose's leg and shaking her head.

"I was twenty-eight when they had the hundredth birthday celebration for her over there in Patrick's Holler. That's what it was called then. Don't reckon it's anything nowadays. Lordy, I'm almost as old as she was."

Vinnie stopped talking and stared out the window across the lake. Her face was expressionless. Her breathing slowed but her hand still patted MaryRose's leg. Then as suddenly as she'd started staring she looked back at MaryRose.

"I can't get over it. I am sitting here with her great-great-grand young'un. You look just like her with your auburn hair and those green eyes. My word, I'd recognize your eyes anywhere. They say she was the purtiest young lady anywhere around here."

She reached over and touched the tear running down Mary-Rose's cheek. "Listen to me going on and on when all you want is something you can read about your Gramma Rose, as you call her."

MaryRose held up hand. "Oh no! Please don't stop. I was hoping you'd tell me everything you can remember about her. Two days ago, all I hoped for was to read something about her; and here I sit talking to someone who knew her."

Vinnie looked around the room and shrugged. "Tell you what. I could use a cup of Sarah's decaf coffee. I like my coffee high test, but the doctor says I can't drink it now. Decaf is like scared water to me, but it's what I can have. Don't know, but I think once you get as old as me, it makes no nevermind what you eat or drink or do. The Lord's a gonna call me home when He's ready."

Her eyes went blank. When her shoulders twitched, she snapped out of it like before.

"My dear, I am sorry. How you must think I am a daft old

woman. Sometimes I think this brain of mine needs to stop and reset a bit. Let's us go get our coffee."

Vinnie Burns was a spry little woman. She might be almost a hundred years old, but her eyes lit up—most of the time. She grasped MaryRose's arm as they crossed the street and walked down the block to Sarah's. The jingling bell on the door grabbed everyone's attention. A few heads nodded and Sarah left the table she was wiping and walked straight to them.

"Well, I'll be. MaryRose and Vinnie Burns, the newest and the oldest citizens of our town, come walking in here arm in arm. Why not take the table by the window? You're looking spunky this morning, Vinnie. How in the world did you and MaryRose come to meet?"

Vinnie grinned. "Sandra Kelly brought me to her. It was like seeing Rose E. standing before me. I ain't heard her name mentioned for years. I told her if she'd come over here and have coffee with me, we could talk awhile."

"And how would you know anything about our Rose E.?" Sarah poured coffee and placed a sticky bun in front of them. "My treat. Anyone who gets Vinnie Burns out of the library before lunchtime deserves this."

"Don't sass me, young lady." Vinnie winked. "That's decaf slur, right?"

"Only the best slur around."

The women's banter was easy and fun. MaryRose could see there was a bond between them. It made her wonder, but today's mission was finding out about Gramma Rose, not Vinnie and Sarah. She sipped the coffee. Really wasn't bad for decaf.

"Thanks for the sticky bun, Sarah. To answer your question, Rose Elliott was my great-great-gramma."

"You're kin to Rose E.? Why about everyone around here knew her or at least about her." Sarah propped her hands on her hips. "I'm plain daft. Look at you. How could anyone not see the resemblance? I wish I didn't have to work, or I'd sit down and listen to the stories too."

Vinnie brushed her silver hair from her eyes and readjusted her glasses. "First time I met your Gramma Rose, we'd just moved to the area. I was eighteen. Hiking all by myself over on Nolan's Mountain and got about scared to death by a big black momma bear. She ran away from me, but not before giving me a growl that sent shivers to my toes. I turned and ran so fast I didn't know which way I was going. I came out into a clearing and ran smack into clean white sheets hanging on a clothesline. Then I tripped over a rock and cut my knee something awful.

"I bled all over those clean sheets. This lady with hair as red as poison ivy in the fall and only a little bit of gray came out of the house. She took one look at my knee and grabbed one of them clean sheets. She placed it on my knee and went for water. Then she washed it off and grabbed, of all things, a puffball mushroom. She broke it right open and put the powder on my knee. It quit bleeding straight away.

"Then she told me she was Rose E. and if I would come in she'd make me tea and I could drink it while she sent her hired hand to get my parents."

MaryRose thought she might burst wide open with joy, hearing a real first-hand account about Gramma Rose. It was hard to picture the old lady across from her as a teenager except for the sparkle in her eyes.

"Thank you for telling me your story. I could listen all day."

"You catch me on my good days, and I'll tell you more stories. Then maybe one day you will let me read those journals."

"Absolutely."

MaryRose left the diner and took a long walk around the streets of Lake Nolan. She must have smiled at everyone she met. Main Street ended at the lakefront. Watching the children on the playground and the boats coming in and out of the docks, she could almost convince herself everything was right with the world.

Almost.

The need to be with family hit her like a punch to her chest. She rushed to her car and sped almost as fast as a coal truck around the curves home. If her VW could make it she would be at the cemetery soon.

CHAPTER 22

*M*aryRose steered up the mountain. Her trusty VW scooted up the mountain almost as easily as Andrea's purple machine. After parking in the lot, and hiking to the top of the cemetery, she stood at the cast iron fence thankful for this sanctuary.

The rusted gate squeaked as she pushed it more open and stepped inside the family plot. A hawk called from above. Watching it soar in and out of her view through the opening in the forest canopy brought comfort. The breeze blew the scent of new honeysuckle around her and brilliant sunlight shining through the trees created sparkling, leafy shadows on the ground.

This was the perfect afternoon to sit with Gramma Rose.

The daisies she and Andrea placed there on Monday had wilted, but she'd leave them for the time being. One day soon, she'd come up and plant perennials along the fence.

Today, she wanted to think and listen.

She leaned against Gramma's tombstone and watched the ancient oak trees wave in the wind. A few of those old trees had to have been there when Gramma buried her baby girl. And her

225

husband. MaryRose brushed moss away and looked at the dates. Eleven years. Only a few years more than she'd had with Sean.

Her heart hitched. Gramma Rose had been a widow at twenty-seven. How had she dealt with being alone all the rest of her life? Of all the things MaryRose was unsure about, one she knew for sure was she didn't want to be alone.

Randall's blue eyes lit her memory. She traced Gramma's name.

"It's okay I like him, isn't it? It doesn't feel unfaithful to Sean. It's more like he'd want this. But does he? Does God? Oh goodness, I've fallen in love again really fast."

The hawk called again. The wind whipped her ponytail, and a butterfly landed on one of the daisies. Nature communicated all was well. She could almost push thoughts of the trial away.

Almost.

"Oh Lord. Must I do this? Everything about going home hurts. Besides, it's not home anymore. It's a place I used to live. Nothing's for me there except a vacant house. I don't want to do this."

Be still.

"I am. I am sitting here on the ground being still."

Be still and know I am God.

"I don't doubt that for a second."

For I know the plans I have for you. I am the Lord, your God. I work all things together for the good of those who love Me. Do you love me?

"You know I do."

I am your shade on your right hand. I will guide you in the sun scorched land and lead you to the peaceful waters. Trust me. Follow me. Forgive as I forgave you.

"I'll try."

I am faithful.

MaryRose hugged the gravestone. How she longed for Gramma Rose to hug her back. She sat there an hour, or it could have been four. Time really didn't matter. As the shadows shifted, afternoon bathed her in sunlight. A chipmunk skittered across the ground and stopped beside her. It watched her until she took a deep cleansing breath then it scurried away.

MaryRose knew she would get through the next few days and tackle next week head on. Had to. She pulled the journal out of her tote bag. Nana had told her enough stories about Gramma Rose that MaryRose knew what would happen next. Still, she wanted to read the next pages while here with Gramma Rose. Her heart already felt heavy. She fingered the pressed, dried daisy that served as a makeshift bookmark, and then opened the page.

~~~~

March 10, 1866 ILUP

I am worried about Gramma. She has me so busy writing all her medicines and plants down. If she don't slow down I will fill up this little book before she is done. I wish I knew what the rush is. I asked her and she told me it was time to do it and once my baby comes I won't have no time to do this. Maybe she is right, but I think she is losing weight. And her silver hair looks limp when she takes it out of the bun.

I'm not getting so sick in the mornings now. But I have an awful soreness in my bosoms. Gramma says the body has to get ready to feed the baby once it arrives. I say ouch.

Jesus, thank you for my Patrick, my family, this baby growing inside me. Help me learn everything I need to know. And take care of Gramma. Amen.

~~~~

April 12, 1866 ILUP

My Patrick is twenty-four years old today. I made a
picnic and rode into Aracoma on his horse, October. He
was in the church working on building new pews when I
got there. I think his face lit up brighter than the
sunshine when he saw me. We went down to the river
and had us a grand meal. I love springtime. There are
flowers everywhere and the air smells like lilac and
crabapple blossoms. I picked a bunch of blossoms and
took them home.

Then all afternoon I spent making an extract of the
flowers to put in my bath. I filled the tub with buckets of
water I heated and soaked until the water got cold. I bet
Patrick will like me smelling like flowers tonight instead
of barnyard.

Jesus, thank you for Patrick's birthday. Amen.

~~~~

April 23, 1866 ILUP

A year ago I got this journal. Oh my goodness so much
has happened to me in a year. Who would have thought?
But, Jesus, I guess you knew. The coyotes have been
singing at night recently. Gramma says that means a
change is coming. I saw a black bear and her two cubs on
the edge of the creek yesterday morning. They were a bit
too close to my house for comfort. I asked Patrick if we
could get us a big dog. He said, he'd rather teach me how

to shoot. I laughed. Then I proved to him I am a better shot than he is.

Jesus, I felt the baby move. Oh goodness, when I first felt it, I didn't figure it was nothing. Then I felt it again. I told Patrick. He placed his head on my stomach and sang an old Irish lullaby, "Hushabye Hush," to the baby. I liked that.

Thank you Jesus, Amen.

~~~~

May 12, 1866 ILUP

Gramma is sick. I know it now. She doesn't have the energy to do any of her gardening. She asked me to plant enough at my house for them too. I don't know what to do, to see her sitting on the porch all day, barely moving, sometimes struggling to breathe is tough. So every afternoon, I ride over and sit with her and sing to her. Then she has me get the book and write more things down before she falls asleep.

Jesus, please make Gramma well. Amen.

~~~~

June 1, 1866 ILUP

Grampa hooked up the carriage today. We took Gramma to the doctor. He says there is nothing he can do for her. It's like something is eating her up from the inside out. I cried and cried. Then he looked at me and said the baby is growing fine. He thinks it will be here by September.

Gramma held my hand the whole ride back home. She told me she has to teach me about birthing. I shook my head and told her she was going to help me birth the baby. I guess we both know that won't happen. I caint bear to say bye to Gramma. Don't rightly know how I will live without her help.

Jesus, can you please see your way to heal her? Amen.

~~~~

June 30, 1866 ILUP

Patrick and me moved in with Gramma and Grampa for a while. He takes me to our house every morning so I can tend the garden and the animals. Then he goes to town. He picks me up at lunch and takes me back to Gramma's. I tell him I could ride my horse over, but he won't hear it. Says I shouldn't be riding this close to the time for the baby. I say it's not that close. But I shouldn't argue too much with my husband.

Gramma sleeps so much. She can still walk around and we do sit on the porch most of the afternoons. I am doing all the cooking and gathering. She teaches me as much as she can between her naps.

Yesterday she had me take her bun down. She had me wash her hair, and then cut it. It was so long, the bun so pretty. But she made me cut it all off. Each snip of the scissors cut a piece of my heart away. I gathered the hair up and wrapped it in a towel to take home and save.

She has short hair now, almost like a man. And Grampa did the sweetest thing. He came in from the lumber mill and told her she looked as cute as the day he met her fishing in the river with her brothers.

I cried more.

Jesus, is it okay for me to be mad at you? Cause I am. I ask and ask for You to make her better and You ignore me. Why? Haven't I always done what You wanted me to do? Can't You do this one thing for me? Please make Gramma get well. If You don't, I am not sure I will be able to forgive You. This disease is her murderer, and You can stop it sure as shooting. Why won't You? Amen.

~~~~

July 3, 1866 ILUP

Patrick and the church men are up on Estep's Mountain digging the grave. There's nothing more to write.

~~~~

MaryRose didn't wipe the tears away. She needed to feel this sorrow, this connection to Gramma Rose. Grief over a loss she didn't experience but was surely feeling right then. She couldn't focus on any singular thought. She read on.

~~~~

July 4, 1866 ILUP

I never felt pain like this before. How can sadness burn like a fire in my throat and chest? How can I walk around my house and want to scream? How can I go to the stream and not find enough rocks to throw in? How can a woman be this angry at God? And how did Gramma know this is what I'd feel?

She took my hand two nights ago before Patrick and I went to bed. I caint hardly write this, but I have to remember it. She told me I was the joy of her old life; I brought happiness to her heart. Then she said, "My sweet Rose, I can see the anger behind your loving eyes. We all have a time. Mine's come. Don't be mad at God and the world for too long.

I am ready to see my Jesus. And Him and me, well, we'll keep watch over you all the days of your life. He's going to catch your tears in his bottle. And remember to keep the kindness in your heart all your days, no matter what life brings to you. Forgive God for this pain in the same way he forgave you your sin. I love you, sweet Rose."

I am mad.

I am sad.

I am alone.

~~~~

July 5, 1866

Gramma was buried this morning. I caint think straight.
I keep expecting her to walk in the house and fuss at me
for wasting the sunshine and not doing the gardening.
But I don't reckon that will happen. Patrick said beautiful
words about her. And people came from all over. There
were even a few Indians there. More people than I knew
even lived around here loved my Gramma.

They brought so much food and Grampa made us take
most of it home. My smokehouse and root cellar are
already full before harvest even starts. I'll be canning
until this baby comes. Patrick made a brand new cabinet
for all of Gramma's herbs and medicines.

But I caint do anything. He holds me at night while I cry.
And he doesn't complain when his britches aren't
washed. I have to get better. But how?

Jesus, I don't even want to ask you to help me because
you didn't answer my biggest prayer ever. You could have
made her well. But you didn't. I don't like this mad inside
my heart. But I caint let it go neither. You are gonna have
to take it from me. Amen.

~~~~

Gramma Rose had spoken for both of them when she
penned those words.

MaryRose couldn't, wouldn't forgive. She didn't have a clue
how to let go of the pain, the anger, the hate. It burned in her
like acid, but she couldn't get it out. Like Gramma Rose had
written, God would have to do a mighty work to get the hate
out of her.

Was it possible everyone was right when they'd said going to the trial really was the only way she would get past this?

Yes, child.

She closed the journal and looked up. The hawk called. The chipmunk came from under a log and eyed her.

"Then so be it. Tomorrow I'll go, God, but You have to do the rest."

MaryRose closed the car trunk. She brushed nonexistent wrinkles out of her skirt, tucked unruly curls back into the French braid, and then looked at Randall and Trudy.

"I guess that's it."

Trudy patted her shoulder. "I'll get myself all situated in my seat. Take your time saying your goodbyes." She closed the door, then opened the novel she had tucked into her handbag.

Randall grasped MaryRose's hand and pulled her into his embrace. His strength enveloped her. His scent filled her senses as he kissed the top of her head.

"I wish I could go with you, but we've got crucial deadlines on the resort project. I'll pray you through this week. And you will call me each night, right?"

She nodded.

He tilted her chin up. If only she could dive into his eyes and stay there. This man hadn't said it yet, but eyes didn't lie. He was as much in love with her as she with him. So why did that make her happy and sad?

Because she still feared God would take Randall away too.

He kissed her forehead, then her nose. "MaryRose, this will be a good week for you. When you get back, we can focus on always. Now, drive safe and let me know when you get there."

His mouth claimed hers in a passionate kiss. Her heart was

about to beat out of her chest. When he pulled back, she could hardly breathe.

"Come back to me soon, MaryRose."

He opened her door, touched the tip of her nose with his finger, and after she got in, tapped the roof of the car twice.

Trudy closed her book and said, "Um-hm."

CHAPTER 23

*M*aryRose walked along the creek where she and Missy used to swim. The morning sun had burned most of the fog away, except for a low film on top of the water. It moved with her like her own personal stalker.

Remnants of the tree fort Dad had built hung like discarded toys from the old branches. On this tree she and Missy had dreamed of the future. Missy dreamed of acting and she dreamed of Sean, before he even liked her. How many hours had she spent at the creek? Yet the land on which she'd grown up was a stranger to her. She didn't belong there anymore.

Her impulse was to get back into her car and drive home to West Virginia. But she was stuck there, waiting for a trial she didn't want to attend.

She leaned against a tree and looked at the sky.

"I don't get it, God. Why do You take everyone I love from me? What did I do wrong the day when Grampa died? If I'd known he would die, I'd have never asked for a bike for my birthday."

She walked from the creek past the old house, then up the hill to the family cemetery.

"I've spent a lot of time around graves recently." She sat down between Mom and Dad's graves and rested her hands on the cold headstone. Rocking back and forth provided a soothing rhythm—something she sorely needed these days.

"I miss you all. It feels like this is all some kind of cruel joke." Anger burrowed in her gut like mud turtles did in the fall. "I'm not laughing, God."

Darkness, tangible and heavy, spread into her heart. The loving Spirit within her cringed, but it was easier to cave to the dark than fight it.

"I hate him, God. I'll never forgive him. I know you want me to, but I can't. He took all I had left, for what? Booze? My family was more than a fix."

Her soul shriveled from the hatred flowing through her like poison in her blood. Sweat rolled down her neck, and her shoulders trembled. She had to get away.

Running. No direction. The dust from the country roads she'd run barefoot on as a child choked her. She stopped in front of the empty tavern. Its red door hung by sagging hinges. So why could she hear laughter? She picked up a stick and hit the building with a thud. Then she took aim at a window. When it shattered, she had a moment of relief. The stick became her personal battering ram as she whacked and smashed again and again until she could no longer raise her arm.

A rock flew past her and thumped on the wood siding. "Want me to be gettin' a bat for ya?"

She whirled around stepping into Papa Shane's hug.

"It won't matter how many times ya hit, the darkness will not be satisfied. No matter how much ya run, the darkness will follow ya. Ya can shatter every window of every house in Hertford, and the pieces of your heart will still choke in the darkness."

She pulled from his arms. "What would you suggest I do? I didn't ask for this. Didn't want to come."

"There's a nasty poison in your heart a tryin' to kill ya."

"If there is any poison in my heart, God put it there when He allowed the man to kill my family."

"I see."

She shoved him backward. "You see what? You don't see anything. Nobody does. Where is God right now? Everybody says I have such great faith. I don't. I ask Him to calm me and nothing happens. I ask Him to make me feel better and He ignores me. I don't want this darkness in me, but it's part of me now." She turned from him and retched.

He held her hair out of her face while she threw up. When the nausea passed he handed her his bandana. "Stop trying to do it on your own. Give it away."

She wiped her face and held opened hands towards him. "Here then, you can have it. I don't want it."

"I'd be taking it if I could, MaryRose. But this one's between you and the Lord. He has plans for you, but He canna be helping one who won't let Him help." His shoulders slumped. "I have to go back and pray, and ya have to get ready."

"I'm not going."

His brows furrowed. "MaryRose Elliott, stop your tantrum and get back to the house. Breakfast is waiting. Trudy is waiting. And ya be in need of a shower before we go."

He thought she was having a tantrum?

You are, child.

She froze. God's Voice. Always saying what she didn't want to hear. What she needed to hear. A moment of calm warmed her. Then she shook her head and let the darkness back in.

I'll be waiting.

MaryRose sat in the back of the courtroom watching through a shroud of anger and hurt. When Mr. Taylor entered the courtroom she tensed. Trudy rested her hand on MaryRose's leg and squeezed gently.

She scowled at him. How could he sit there dressed in a suit, looking harmless? He stared down at the floor. Didn't he see her pain?

"He ruined my life."

Trudy kissed the top of her head. "Ruined his own, too."

MaryRose glared at the man. Why wouldn't he look at her and see her pain?

See his.

Who cares about his pain?

I do.

"You would."

"What was that?" Trudy leaned close.

"Nothing."

Court began. He waived his right to a jury and pled guilty. The judge gave a long dissertation on the meaning of the plea and the sentence. The specifics the judge laid out mattered not to her. Mr. Taylor at least had his life. Her family didn't.

Then the judge did something she wasn't expecting. He asked Mr. Taylor if he had anything to say. MaryRose froze. Nobody told her he would be allowed to speak. She gagged.

As he stood his eyes locked with hers. And she saw sorrow, remorse, pain. How could that be?

"Ms. Elliott, I have no right to speak to you, but the judge says I can. I'm sorry. I live every day filled with hatred of myself."

He was well-spoken.

"I have no excuse. My wife left—took my kids—tired of my long work hours, I guess. It was the first time in my life I ever got drunk. I'm a Christian and don't drink." He looked at the floor. "I'm sure that's hard to believe."

"But I wanted to numb the pain. My life was falling apart. I went to a bar. I should have run to my Savior, but I ran to a

bottle. Sometimes pain makes us do things we would never do."
He paused.

Like swearing in her pastor's presence.

Like vandalizing a tavern.

Like spewing hate and yielding to doubt.

She dropped her head.

"I did something stupid and it took your grandmother's and parents' lives. I may be in jail for years, but I will live the rest of my life with it. I hope you will find it in your heart to forgive me, but I understand if you cannot."

She tried to respond to the pain in his eyes but couldn't. The darkness held tight. The conviction in his words drove her away. Tears blinded her as she raced out of the courtroom. She ran up and down the halls until she found the law library. It would be quiet in there. The door stood ajar.

She searched the shelves. There had to be one there some-where. The law books all looked alike but she couldn't find it, the only book she knew could help her. In the back corner of the library beneath a skylight, sunlight streamed on the black leather Bible. Grabbing it off the shelf, she dropped to the floor in the pool of sunlight.

Quietness wrapped around her. She didn't even open the cover but held it to her heart and felt the power flow into her soul.

She awoke on a couch. Where was she? She jumped up and spun around. One lone desk lamp cast a cone of light on the other side of the room.

Oh yeah, the law library in the courthouse. "Oh my gosh, how long have I been here? What time is it?"

The Bible lay on the floor beside the sofa, and she picked it up. Staring at the dark skylight roof across the room she shook her head. "When did I get to the couch?"

"Oh, I helped with that, miss." The deep voice came from the doorway.

MaryRose froze.

"Ma'am, don't worry none. I came on at six. Not sure how you got locked in here, but they sure have been wondering where you went. Bet my boss will be checking to see if there's a glitch in the security cameras. I always clean in here first and when I switched on the light, I found you. I only carried your Bible to the couch. You got up and walked, kinda like you was sleep walkin' or somethin'. I called my boss and told him about you bein' here, then I went back to work."

"Am I in trouble?"

"No, ma'am. The boss said you was married to his cousin before and told me to leave you on the couch and keep checkin' on you while he got in touch with your family. He said you'd be safe here as long as I kept watch. Said he'd call a Pastor Shane. My name's Micah Staub." He offered her his hand.

"Thanks for watching out for me, Micah. What time is it?"

"It's almost eight. Mr. Shane fella should be here soon."

She brushed hair out of her eyes. "I'm a mess."

He laughed. "No ma'am, you're a pretty addition to this drab room."

After one last hug to her chest, she put the Bible back on the shelf. "I better get out of here."

Papa Shane threw open the door before Micah could respond. "Ya got me heart all worked up and worried, Mary-Rose Elliott. When I didn't see ya outside the courtoom I figured ya walked on home. Been searchin' all your regular places ever since. Thanks be to God that Andrew remembered ya and had the decency to call me."

"I'm sorry, Papa. I fell asleep."

TO FOLLOW A DREAM

"Fightin' with the Holy Spirit is exhaustin' thing. Did ya let Him win yet?"

How to answer? "Let's get going, I need a shower and bed. I'm sure Trudy will be ready to get on the road bright and early."

"Ya'r not fooling me. Answer me question."

She grumbled. "I felt His presence. I heard Him. Papa, forgiveness has never eluded me before. I can't find it. It's like the day my parents died . . . something broke."

"And what would your mama be sayin' to ya right about now?"

Tears filled her eyes. "That's it. I know what she'd say. She'd remind me what Jesus did to forgive me. She'd remind me what He said about forgiving me in the same manner I forgive, but I don't feel like forgiving. I don't want to forgive."

"Feel? Ya be waiting' to *feel* it? Ya don't *want* to? What do ya think would've happened if Jesus had waited till He *felt* like dyin' on a cross? Or waited till He *wanted* to be betrayed? This is not about feeling the forgiveness. It's an action: ya do it. The Lord will bring the feelings when ya use the faith within ya to forgive. He never said ya would feel like it."

He raised his voice at her—something he'd never done before.

He shook his head. "Come with me will ya? It's time we get out of here."

She felt like a child. "Are you mad at me?"

"Mad? 'Course not. Exasperated is more like it. I'm watching ya let this one thing turn ya from the faith and cut off all the blessings waitin' for ya."

"Blessings? What blessings? Sean's gone, Heather never got a chance, and now my parents and Nana are gone. I'm not seeing the blessings here."

"'Course you're not. You're too busy staring at your belly button."

"My what?"

243

He stopped outside the courthouse and pointed at her stomach. "Your belly button. So busy whining about yourself and your hurts ya miss the truth. Ya need to put your focus on the cross, on the power of the cross, what it means to ya and what is expected of ya because of it."

"Maybe I like staring at my belly button."

"Well, I'll not be a part of this pity party. When we get home, I'll be goin' to my chapel to pray and I don't rightly know what you'll do."

They got in the car in silence and headed to the house.

MaryRose barely slept at all. The eight hour drive ahead of them was long after a full night's sleep. Hopefully, Trudy would spell her when she got sleepy. She fastened her seatbelt and pulled the door closed, sealing them in, or so it sounded.

It was hard to say goodbye to Papa Shane. Harder than when she moved away. Her refusal to forgive had somehow hurt him. His sad eyes about broke her. He turned away, shoulders drooping and entered his house. Why did it have to be this way? MaryRose wiped her eyes.

Trudy had been sitting silently on the passenger side, but reached over and patted her leg. "I'll drive if you want, MaryRose. You have to be exhausted. Or we could wait another day before going back."

"No, there's nothing keeping me here. And I'll be all right driving. If I get too sleepy, I'll let you drive."

"Okay then." Trudy took a deep breath. "MaryRose?"

Trudy was wringing her hands in her lap. Her legs bounced a little too. Why was she anxious? "I'm safe driving, honest."

"That's not what has me all befuddled. I can think of one thing to keep you here."

Her hands tightened on the steering wheel. "What?"

"I probably should share the story before I tell you the story. I did something."

MaryRose raised her eyebrows. "Okay."

"It might make you mad."

"At you? Never. You're a godly woman, like Ma. I trust you."

"After you left the courtroom, I asked the bailiff if I could talk to him."

"The bailiff?"

"No . . . Mr. Taylor."

"You what? Why would you do that?" A wave of dizziness played tricks on her eyes. She slowed the car a bit. Maybe her thoughts would slow with it.

"God wanted me to and Mr. Taylor needed me to."

The anger came again; so familiar MaryRose didn't cringe. "I can't believe you did that."

"I think you know why I did. I bet you even know what I said, but I'll tell you. I told him I knew you'd come to a place of forgiveness for him because you have the same Savior he does. I also told him when you forgave him, I believed the Holy Spirit would make his heart know it happened."

"A bit presumptuous of you, wasn't it?"

Trudy stared out the window then turned and looked directly at her. "Was it?"

She opened her mouth, but no words came. It was like a punch to her gut followed by a lump in her throat. Then sweet warmth flowed into her. It touched the depths of her. The road blurred.

She stopped the car.

"I have to get out. I'm choking."

MaryRose jumped out and ran into the field by the highway. Somewhere in the middle of a field of wild daisies, her legs gave out and she dropped to her knees. She'd had many moments in her life when it felt like God was right there helping her. But this time was different. He was filling her, every part of her, with love. So much love it crowded the hate.

The breeze made the flowers surrounding her wave in friendly welcome. She grabbed a handful of the happy flowers and raised them to the sky. As she dropped them into the wind, they fluttered before landing.

The subtle scent of the flowers invaded her senses. Looking down at them, she brushed her fingers across their tops, making them wave back and forth.

Papa Shane knew what he was talking about. Something inside her had been dying.

She raised her hands to heaven and cried out. "Okay, okay, I don't feel it, but this anger hurts. This hatred burns. The warmth of You in me is strong. I forgive him. I won't hold his crime against him anymore. I forgive him."

With a deep breath, she slumped to the ground, ignoring how the morning dew drenched her feet and her knees screamed for her to stop kneeling. Peace still flowed into her like a fresh stream. Bitterness washed from her soul and was replaced with love. The daisies smelled fresh and the soil, rich. She pushed off the ground and brushed the dirt from her skirt.

Then as an afterthought, she bent down and picked a bunch of daisies.

At the car, she handed the daisies to Trudy. "I'm sorry. I couldn't see the road, had to stop. Now I need to go back and talk to Papa Shane. Do you mind?"

"Not at all."

"Somehow I have to get word to Mr. Taylor too."

Trudy smiled. "He already knows."

"Maybe. But I still need to tell him. And I owe the owner of the old tavern for the broken windows."

Papa Shane hung up the phone and brushed his hands together. "Wasn't easy but I got it set up for ya." Papa Shane hung up the phone and brushed his hands together. He turned towards MaryRose. "Tomorrow morning at ten 'o'clock you'll be allowed to see him."

"Hope I'm ready."

He followed her and gently grasped her shoulders. "Ya are. Trudy and I will be there with ya. After you're all done, we'll have us a nice lunch and then I'll be sendin' ya back to your lake and your new family."

"I need a walk. I'll be back by dark."

"Not gonna beat up any more old taverns, are ya?" He winked.

"My vandalism days are over. I promise."

She went to the stream. The old oak tree was still the same. Branches reached out like open arms offering a hug. Swinging onto the lowest branch that stretched over the water was easy. How many times had she sat on it?

She could hear Mom fussing. "MaryRose Elliott, don't go out there and fall in. I'll be purely furious with you."

The only time she ever fell off the branch was the day Sean proposed and in his nervousness dropped the ring. They both fell off trying to catch it. That was a good day.

But now she had to talk to God.

"Your patience with me is far better than mine with You. Teach me to listen more. Help me become the woman You see. I don't much like the one I've been seeing. I've been a poor witness for you. I'm sorry. I will do better from now on. My life is yours again. I don't know how I will face tomorrow. I've never been in a jail before. But I choose to trust You. Thank you, Jesus."

247

At nine-fifty MaryRose stood before the metal detector placing her purse and all the contents of her pockets into a basin with her name on it. This same procedure she followed anytime she went through TSA checkpoints somehow felt more invasive and humbling standing inside prison walls.

The guard pointed to her hair. "I'm sorry Ms. Elliott, but I have to ask you to remove that too."

She touched her hair and frowned. "Remove what?"

"The barrette."

She unclipped the sloppy bun and her hair tumbled loose. "I'm sorry, sir. I should have remembered this. I never use metal clips when I know I'm going through airport security."

"You may pass now." The guard stared through her.

Her legs froze. She turned back towards the door. Papa Shane frowned and wagged his finger at her. "Ya go on in, Lassie. We'll be here."

Big breath. Left foot. Right foot. Step-by-step she made it into the room. It looked like a room within a room. Chairs arranged in a U-shape faced partitioned cubicles. The guard escorted her to a chair. "Sit here until the prisoners come in. When Mr. Taylor comes in, he will sit across from you on the other side of this partition. There is to be no contact—"

"You don't have to worry about that."

He glared at her. "There is to be no contact. You sit here and talk. When you are ready to leave, tell the guard. Mr. Taylor will be escorted back to his cell, but you can't leave until all the prisoners are out of this room. Do you understand?"

Duly chastised, she stared at her shoes and nodded. "Yes sir, I understand."

She sat where he directed as did the variety of men and women escorted to the other chairs. The woman who had been behind her in line nodded at her. No one spoke to anyone else. Her knees bounced up and down like a pogo stick.

A voice came over the speaker. "Inmate Taylor, seat twenty-four."

A large steel door clicked and opened. A man dressed in an orange jumpsuit entered. Her throat closed. Her stomach churned.

Can't do this. Must get away.

She jumped up from her chair and headed to the door. She reached for the handle but the guard stepped in front of her.

"What do you think you're doing?"

"I thought I could do this—I can't ... I—you have to let me out!"

"Ma'am, I cannot open this door. The inmates are in the room. Sit and say what you came to say or not. Either way, you cannot leave until all the prisoners leave. Back away from the door immediately and return to your chair." He held the door with one hand and deliberately placed his other hand on his holster.

She let go.

Look at him.

"Excuse me sir? What did you say?"

The guard glared. "I didn't say anything. I'm waiting for your decision."

Look at him.

"I can't," she whispered.

Look at him now.

She turned toward Mr. Taylor. And in his eyes, she saw hers. Not her reflection, the pain.

Left, right, step-by-step she trudged back to the chair and sat. "I'm MaryRose Elliott."

Tears streamed down his face. Pure emotion flowed from him. Pure compassion flowed into her. When the words come out of her mouth, she wondered who'd said them.

"Mr. Taylor, I forgive you."

Jesus used her mouth. It had to be.

"God bless you."

With a deep sigh, she looked into his eyes and, for the first time, felt the forgiveness inside her. She'd said the words before she felt them like Papa Shane said.

"Mr. Taylor, I have no right for the forgiveness I received after I released my hatred for you. But Jesus expects His children to forgive. Will you forgive my hatred?"

He shook his head. "Me forgive you? Nothing to forgive."

"There is. I detested you. I certainly didn't want to offer mercy, and Jesus says I will receive mercy in the manner I give it. Please forgive me?"

Trembling hands wiped his eyes. "I forgive you."

"God bless you." She bowed her head and closed her eyes as more peace filled her heart. So that's what grace feels like. After a few minutes, she looked up at him and saw his head was bowed also.

"Mr. Taylor, if you become eligible for early parole, they may contact me to speak on your behalf. I will."

"I could never ask that, ma'am."

Trudy's kind words from months ago came to mind. "Didn't hear you ask, Mr. Taylor. I'm offering."

Trudy would be proud of her. She smiled at him. "Peace be with you Mr. Taylor." Then she signaled to the guard. "I'm ready now."

The door clicked and another guard walked in. Mr. Taylor stood and met the guard.

After Mr. Taylor exited, she waited for the others to finish their visits. As she waited to gather her belongings the guard stopped by her side. His eyes no longer held the harsh glare they'd had when she tried to leave the room. "Mighty brave thing you did there, miss."

"It wasn't me. Jesus did it for me."

After the door to the visitation room closed behind her, she ran into Papa Shane's arms. He twirled her in circles. "It's my

MaryRose, back from the dark place. I see it in those green eyes. It's proud of ya I am right now."

"Papa, I feel like myself again."

He put her down and she almost skipped into Trudy's hug. "I never could have done this without you."

"Sure you could."

"No, I couldn't. Thank you, thank you. I'm free of the anger, the hate. Now I think I can get back to my writing. Last week the words stopped flowing. They felt empty." She stepped outside into the sunlight. "I'm ready to go home. Trudy can we leave right now?"

"I'm a mite hungry. Could we have lunch first?"

CHAPTER 24

*M*aryRose hurried home after she dropped Trudy at her house. She willed her eyes to stay open as she rounded the last curve before Lake Nolan Drive. It surely felt like the week had been a long month.

When she parked in the drive, Randall stood from her porch swing and headed toward her. She jumped out of the car, ran to him and leaped into his arms. He kissed her with the passion she'd been dreaming about.

"Welcome home, Pretty Lady."

"Hey, Randall."

He lowered her to the ground, but held her secure in his embrace and nuzzled her neck. "Welcome home."

MaryRose reached around his neck and returned his passion. His arms around her, his kiss deepening, and her body pressed against his. She was home.

He exhaled and released her. Their eyes remained locked. "How are you?"

"I'm wonderful."

"Yes, you are."

She melted into his arms again for one more kiss before they walked up the two steps onto the porch. He sat on the swing and patted the seat beside him. "Tell me all about it."

"I already did, on the phone last night."

"I want to hear it again. I see a light in your eyes I've never seen. It's like I never met the real you. I have to tell you I really liked you before, can't wait to get to know you now."

She rested against his side and told him about the week, even the little details she'd left out on the phone. He tensed when she spoke of running away and taking her frustration at drunkenness out on the tavern.

She looked up at him. "What?"

"I hate that you went through everything alone."

"I had to, don't you see? I had to come to the end of the ugly me to find the way back to myself. I'm not sure vandalism was part of God's plan. And it's going to cost a bit of my savings to pay for the damage. But, it's what God used to get me to the place where my empty was bigger than the anger. I was never alone. God was with me every moment.

"As we drove past the field where I surrendered, Trudy suggested I bring a bunch of the daisies home. We dug a bunch up so I could plant them here. Kind of a personal reminder of my struggle to accept the loss of my family and my unwillingness to forgive. Will you help me plant them?"

"Now?"

"Yes, please. It's a bad time of year to transplant, but they'll do better if we plant them in the cool of night rather than the heat of day."

"Let's get to it. I'll get your bag and the daisies."

"The bag can wait."

"Alright then. The house is open, aired out, and cooled down. Andrea will bring Dapple home tomorrow. Since I didn't know how late you'd be I told her to keep him tonight."

MaryRose stepped inside the kitchen. Home. How good to be back. She grabbed her garden basket from beside the counter, the shovel from the porch and met him by the fence. Randall took the shovel from her and made quick order of digging a hole for the flowers. Removing the daisies from the plastic bag she'd secured them in, she knelt to put the flowers into the ground. He pushed the soil back around them and his hands grasped hers. Leaning around the flowers their lips met.

"Umm. I don't think I've ever been kissed with my hands stuck in the soil." He whistled. "I like it."

MaryRose yawned.

"Sorry if I'm boring you."

"I am far from being bored." She kissed him again. "But I'm also exhausted."

"You go on in. I'll water the flowers and put your tools on the porch."

MaryRose dragged herself inside. Each step stretched to a mile. She barely had the energy to wash her hands and brush her teeth. The heck with sleep clothes, she lay down across the top of her bed in her travel clothes.

It was good to be home.

CHAPTER 25

"*E*xcuse me, Mr. Little, I submitted my article two weeks ago the same day I resigned. Even if I was still in your employ, it would be none of your business that I went out of town."

"I tried to reach you several times during the past four days. You ignored my calls. If I do not have a written resignation from you on my desk by day's end, you will be fired."

Was the man a total idiot? "Sir, you cannot fire someone who has already quit."

He grumbled something.

"Pardon me?"

"Nothing."

"Then I bid you farewell, Mr. Little."

Before he had the chance to respond, she clicked her phone off. With a newfound confidence and understanding that Nana and Mom would be proud of her, she sat on the swing, curled her legs underneath her and opened the journal.

~~~~

August 1, 1866 ILUP

It is awful hot now. My ankles look like I got elephant feet. My belly looks like I swallowed two watermelons whole. Grampa and Patrick won't let me work in the garden. I caint hardly bend anyway. They bring everything in and keep the stove going. All I have to do is the canning and drying. That's enough too.

At night I am either not sleeping, waddling to the outhouse, or waking Patrick to rub my leg cramps. Some days I swear if I could take this pregnant belly off for an hour I'd be mighty fine. And this baby flip flops inside me. One moment I will see a foot pressing on one side of my belly then a minute later, I see it on the other side. I don't think I am big enough for swimming like this inside me.

Patrick loves me. It's what I hold onto most days. He prays with and for me every night. I guess maybe I am not as mad at God now. But I still wish I could have me a heart to heart with him. Who will help me birth this baby out here in the middle of the mountain? I guess I really have to get over my mad and trust God a little more.

Jesus, please you can help me with this. Amen.

~~~~

August 15, 1866 ILUP

Doctor Estep stopped over today. Then three other carriages arrived. Mrs. Estep, Mrs. Atkins, Becky Sue Burnside, Mrs. Porter and Miriam Miller climbed out of

their carriages arms loaded down with packages. Goodness, it felt like Christmas.

Doctor Estep unloaded boxes of meals that he and
Patrick put in the root cellar. Then they wandered into
the barn. All the ladies took me inside and sat me down
in the rocking chair Patrick made for me. They had all
sorts of things for me and the baby. They was clothes,
and blankets, and hats, and booties, so much stuff. Mrs.
Estep made a big meal and we had us a feast. Patrick and
Doc came back in time to eat. Typical.

They all think I will be having this baby soon. And Doc'
told me he will be here faster than his beagles find rabbits
when he hears my time is come. That made me feel a
mite better.

Grampa showed up in time to eat too. Then he brought
in the cradle he made for the baby. It is beautiful. He told
me he didn't want to give me the one they used for my pa
because he figured it should be at his house for when we
bring the baby there.

This was a good day. But I'm plum wore out. Going to
sleep now, if this baby will stop kicking my ribs and my
bladder at the same time.

Jesus it seems I don't know what to say to you these days.
But maybe the Spirit is a speaking for me. Amen.

~~~~

August 25, 1866

The pains have started. Patrick raced out of here on my horse. He sent Grampa to get Doc and hurried back to me. Lord, I don't know if the man will be all right. He ain't never seen a birthing and he is nervous like a sheep standing at a creek's edge.

I can hardly write. I guess when I write again I will be a mother.

Oh Jesus, help me, please. Please forgive me for being so bitter, so mad at you. I know you are in charge. I miss Gramma so much. Please remind me how much you love me when I want to be mad. It hurts in my heart to not forgive. And you didn't do nothing wrong, I know that. But I think you know what I mean when I say, I forgive you. Forgive me too? Amen

That last pain was bad. I spilled my ink on the page.

Gotta let it dry.

Someone's at the door.

I hope it's Doc cause I think this pain will kill me.

~~~~

August 27, 1866

I am sitting on the bed watching my sweet Patrick rocking James Patrick Elliott. He is singing a song from his family's homeland he calls "Hushabye Hush" to him. Watching them makes all the pain worth it. Took me more than a day to get my little boy to join us. I was plum tuckered out and couldn't hardly look at him much less hold him.

Doc says he was inside me all crooked and the worst of my pains was when my body was trying to fix him and push him out all at the same time. They say I passed out at one point. Patrick nearly did too. But they got me awake when it was time to push him out for real.

Now, me and Patrick have us a fine looking baby boy. I caint stop looking at them. My Patrick was made for fathering. I sure hope I was for mothering. And if I thought Patrick looked at me with love in his eyes before, now the love is enough to knock a body over.

I'm real sore and sleepy. Tomorrow Mrs. Estep is coming over to help with the housework and things. She said she will come over every day until I am out and around, like Gramma would be doing if she was still with us.

Oh, yeah. Last night I had Patrick mix my tea for healing. He was like a man with nothing but thumbs on his hands as he tried to mash the comfrey and calendula leaves. Then he brought it to me hot and I hollered when I took a sip. Scared him half to death and woke baby James up. I have to sleep now. Thank you Jesus for my baby, my Patrick, my life. Amen.

~~~~

MaryRose closed the journal. It was the last page of Gramma Rose's first journal. Appropriate to end it with the start of new life. She had no idea which journal to read next. They weren't numbered and none of the others as neatly dated as the first one. Guess maybe that is what happens when you get busy being a mother too.

How she longed to read them in order, but it would take time to thumb through and get the order figured out.

"Come on, Dapple. We're going in."

The puppy raced around the yard and leaped onto the steps. He slid through the doorway and came perilously close to smashing his nose on the frame. His tail wagged so hard it looked like it might shake off his body.

She went inside, grabbed the next journal on the stack. None of the first entries had dates, but the writing looked more mature. The pages had brown stains. Tears? Did she really want to risk reading about the sad days after finishing the other journal with joy? Curiosity got the best of her.

~~~~

ILUPJP

I walk around and cannot think. I clean house, take care of James Patrick, gather my herbs, cook, help people who stop by as if watching myself do it from the outside. Everywhere I look Patrick is here, but he's not. When I realize I will never again touch his hand or kiss his face, or feel his love, I wonder why I am even breathing.

I see him even when my eyes close. He is in my dreams, my every moment. And while there is comfort in that for some people, I find none. James Patrick tries so hard to be the little man. But he's only ten years old. He doesn't know I have seen him out in the barn brushing Patrick's horse and crying. Almost every night he wakes from a nightmare and climbs in bed with me. We don't talk about it, he just does it.

I don't understand hate. Or I thought I didn't. But I am having a mighty battle not hating those feuders. What makes two families so full of anger with each other. And why did they have to bring my Patrick into it? I can't never remember who started the fire and whose house burned down. But the Hatfields and McCoys caused my husband's death. If they hadn't feuded, he'd not have stopped to help with the fire.

I sit here trying hard not to fill up with hate but their fighting killed my Patrick. Left me and James Patrick alone. Yesterday, James and I took daisies up to the cemetery. We put them on Gramma's, Patrick's, and Mary-Rose's graves. Don't guess I will ever get me another daughter after all. Least I held our pretty baby a few hours before she was gone.

Got a letter from James Thomas. He wants me and James to come back to North Carolina. He says the big house is empty with him and Molly Sue there. But they have a baby on the way and it will be busy soon enough. I don't belong there. This is my home, my son's home.

Right now I have to make it through my days. And nights.

Jesus, help me. Amen

~~~~

MaryRose closed the book and held it to her heart. She really hadn't wanted to read the sad things. And thanks to her research she knew Gramma Rose died an old woman, alone. After placing the journal on the coffee table, she grabbed her research notes, the newspaper clippings she'd found and the stories she'd written down all the years Nana shared with her.

So many things connecting. The story Nana told her about how Gramma Rose had dated a local rich man in her later years came to mind. Nana said the man had wanted to marry Gramma Rose but she wouldn't agree. She was missing something. Putting her handwritten notes aside, she picked up another newspaper article.

The headline grabbed her attention. A man named Benjamin Nolan had finally purchased all the land he needed and acquired the permits necessary to begin construction on the reservoir. Nolan. Lake Nolan. The man who bought all of this land and built this reservoir had wanted to marry her great-great grandmother. Oh yeah, Nana also talked about how this man had purchased Gramma Rose's property But the Elliott family had kept life estate on it. And Ruth Cobb said the Nolans were her people. Connectivity.

This meant her family's original property was somewhere around this lake. The realization hit her like a rock to the head. She put the journals away. There would be time to organize them another day.

Today she would write.

MaryRose removed the stack of papers from the printer and stacked them on the desk. She called Randall and his groggy voice greeted her.

"Are you aware it's the middle of the night, babe? Is everything all right?"

MaryRose looked at the clock. Two in the morning. But she wasn't even totally sure what day of the week it was.

"Oh, Randall I'm sorry, I haven't looked at the clock for hours. I wanted to tell you I finished. The last page just printed."

"The book is done?"

"Yes. I haven't done much of anything except write the past ten days."

"Maybe I should take out-of-town jobs more often."

MaryRose rested her chin in her hands and stared out across the lake. Even the water looked lonely. "No, please don't. When will you be back?"

"I gave the construction crew off for the weekend, but I have hours of paperwork and payroll. We should finish the project by Tuesday, Wednesday at the latest."

"I'm going to spend the week with Missy. I guess I won't be here when you get back. Be safe and I'll see you next weekend."

He yawned. "Hey, I really need some more sleep. I'll call you at breakfast. Okay?"

"Sure. I should try to sleep too. Good night, Randall."

Who was she kidding? No part of her was sleepy. Dapple lifted his head from his spot on the loveseat and grumbled. The poor guy had spent most of the past twelve days cooped up inside or alone in the yard as she wrote. But now they could play.

It had actually helped that Randall was on the job down in Kentucky all week. The lonely evening hours when she would have brooded over missing him she spent writing Gramma Rose's and Patrick's love story. She'd admit all of the sweetness of their life together made her more ready to see if what she and Randall had was also a grand romance.

On Wednesday night Luke and Rachel had brought supper over and Andrea joined them. They enjoyed good food and lots of laughter, a pleasant break to her week. She'd been munching on the leftovers ever since. Luke had made her promise she'd bring the manuscript to him for editing. Here she was Saturday morning with the book finished and printed.

But it would be quite rude to take it over to Luke right now. Somehow, she had to sleep. MaryRose finished her glass of milk and walked through the cabin turning lights off. "Come on Dapple, let's go to bed. We'll give the book to Luke later on, and then take Missy up on her offer and go spend the week with her."

Stopping at the desk once more, she kissed her finger and touched it to the title page.

To Follow a Dream
MaryRose Elliott

CHAPTER 26

aryRose carried Dapple inside to keep him from running through every mud puddle between the car and the back door. The lovely weather all week ended in a day long deluge. Wet dog smell filled her house instead of dried herbs.

She dropped her bag inside the doorway. Five days of sunning around the pool, swimming, reading and way too much eating made for good stress reduction. Not to mention she no longer looked like she was afraid of sunshine. A million or so new freckles sprinkled her cheeks and nose.

She barely had the door closed when the phone in her purse started ringing.

"MaryRose? Finally, you're home."

Randall. Aah. She smiled. "I just walked in the door. When did you get back in town? The cell signal at the park was horrid. It wasn't until I got back onto Corridor G that I saw all of the missed calls."

"Got back Wednesday like I said I would. I figured you'd come back from Missy's by then." Anger rang in his voice.

She frowned. "I told you I was spending the week with her.

Jonathon came over for dinner a couple of times, including last night. You could have come with him."

"Wasn't invited."

"So when Jonathon told you he could pick you up on his way, that wasn't an invitation?"

"Didn't feel like one."

MaryRose closed the kitchen door, hard, and then walked into the living room. And people say she's overly dramatic?

"Let's try this again, shall we? Hey Randall, I got in a few minutes ago. I had a wonderfully lazy week with Missy lounging at the pool and snacking too much. Did you get caught up on your rest after all the overtime in Kentucky?"

"What else was there to do?"

MaryRose refused to take the bait. "It's good you rested too. I have to get my laundry started and put the groceries away. Missy and I made cookies this morning. I wanted something to give to Luke when he brings my edits over. Would you like to come over for cookies and milk in a little while?"

"Think I'll pass." He grumbled.

"Okay. Suit yourself. If you change your mind, I'll be here."

She hung up. Why was he so grouchy? He could have come with Jonathon or even on his own. He knew where she was. Instead he stewed. Too bad she hadn't told him she missed him too. It might have melted his hard exterior.

After unpacking and eating supper, she sat on the sofa and started a letter to Papa Shane. Not much past Dear Papa, Luke stood at the front door.

"Can I come in?"

Her heart pounded. What if he hadn't liked the book?

"Well, may I?"

"Yes."

He ambled in and sat on the recliner. He leaned across the end table and handed her the bundle. He didn't release it right away. "Before you look at it, and how much I 'bled' on it, I want to say one thing."

"Which is?"

"This will be a best seller. I've never read anything with more intensity, emotion, and character depth. We have a lot of work ahead of us, but we can do it. MaryRose Elliott, I don't think you'll have to ask Sarah for a job at the diner."

He handed her the bundle. She thumbed through the pages and saw flashes of red everywhere. "You weren't kidding about bleeding on the pages. I'll get started on this today. I can't thank you enough, Luke."

Luke was thorough. "This is amazing. I think you missed your calling. You should be an editor somewhere."

"What, and miss out on all the adolescent angst I get as a middle school English teacher? No, this is the life." He winked. "I promised my wife and daughter my full attention this weekend. Let me know if I can help any further."

"You've already done so much. I think I'll spend my day going over this."

He chuckled as he opened the door. "Then I really better get out of here. By the time you finish reading you may not be so happy with me."

"Yoo-hoo! MaryRose? It's Trudy. I brought tomatoes, peppers, and corn from my garden."

Trudy peeked through the screen door. "You in there?"

MaryRose welcomed her with a hug.

Trudy looked her up and down and frowned. "You all right, honey? I missed you at Sunday services this morning. You're still in your sleep clothes" She reached up and touched MaryRose's forehead. "No fever. What's bothering you?"

"Nothing, really. Luke gave me my manuscript yesterday, and I stayed up all night reading all of his notes and making my own. I lost track of time. Guess I slept right through church time."

"Land sakes, I was afraid you were sick. But, Honey, it ain't right to be still sitting around in your pajamas this time of day. 'Sides, your Randall will stop by soon, I reckon."

"I doubt it."

"Troubles?"

She leaned against the counter and nodded.

"Come sit here and tell me about it." Trudy pulled a chair out and sat across the table from her.

MaryRose relayed the phone conversation and how agitated it made her. Retelling didn't help much either.

"Honey, I think there is something you need to do. Anger is an expression of other emotions, so when you figure out what emotion caused the anger, then you can forgive him and yourself."

"Myself?"

"Yep. That's all I'll say on the subject. You and him have to figure this one out on your own if you want things to work out."

"Maybe I don't want it to work out."

"And you'll have to stop lying too." Trudy patted her hand. "Now, I have more produce to deliver. You finish your reading and think about what I said."

MaryRose stomped around the kitchen a bit and then settled on washing the dishes. How could Randall be jealous of her spending time with her best friend? The only other time she'd been this agitated over a man was when Sean had moped about the time she spent away from him working at the summer camp. Two men she loved wanting to be with her all of the time, which really wasn't a bad thing.

MaryRose made short order of doing the dishes. What she really needed was some time outside.

"Dapple, here boy. Let's go play."

At the lake, Dapple grabbed a stick and dropped it at her feet for her to toss. Fetch was a rather mindless activity, allowing her thoughts free reign. She tossed and he retrieved until he stretched out in the sun beside her. She looked up the hill at the house.

Two bull-headed people. Randall was too busy pouting and feeling left out to call or come over. And she was so busy soaking up down-time she never thought about using the land-line to check in with him. Maybe they had both been solo so long they couldn't remember how to do double. Could this possibly work or should she give up now?

Love is patient, love is kind, it is not envious. Love does not brag, it is not puffed up. It is not rude, it is not self-serving, it is not easily angered or resentful. It is not glad about injustice, but rejoices in the truth. It bears all things, believes all things, hopes all things, endures all things.

MaryRose rested her head in her hands. She loved Randall as she had Sean. "Come on Dapple. I want to go to the cemetery."

He settled in the passenger seat. Before she backed out of the driveway, Andrea knocked on the window. Dapple barked and then covered the window with puppy kisses. MaryRose motioned her in.

Andrea slid into the seat swooping Dapple into her arms in one swift movement.

"I don't know what happened last night, but you have to make up with Daddy. I don't think he slept a wink, and he's walking around the house this morning like an old grumpy grizzly bear. I reminded him about Ken and me going out on the boat tonight and he about bit my head off."

Randall was having a rough day too.

MaryRose patted Andrea's shoulder. "I'm sorry you got the brunt of the temper. Your father has to learn to let some things go."

So do you.

271

She shook her head. Yeah, yeah, yeah.

"Well, I still think you need to talk to him. He loves you, you know?"

"I know."

"Where are you headed anyway?"

"To the cemetery. I need the quiet and peace. You're welcome to come along."

Andrea shook her head. "No. Daddy laid the law down. I had better have every room in my house in order if I want to have this goodbye date with Ken tonight."

MaryRose burst into laughter as the girl did a perfect Randall imitation. "You shouldn't make fun of him like that."

"Go ahead; I see it in your eyes. You can see exactly what he looked like." Andrea snuggled Dapple, then got out of the car. "I'll see you tomorrow."

"Okay. Have fun tonight." She backed out of the driveway.

No matter how hard she tried to force Randall out of her head, he stayed. His eyes called her. His smiles drew her. And memories of each kiss made her tremble. She had it bad. It was similar to loving Sean, but she had to admit, way bigger. It wouldn't matter how long she walked around the graves and talked to Gramma Rose, she would not get the man out of her head—or her heart. Nor did she want to. But what if she lost him too?

I thought you trusted Me.

"I do."

I am faithful.

"But—why bother? Everyone I love leaves me."

I know the plans I have for you. Seek my face and I will hear from heaven. Trust me in all your ways and I will bring you the desires of your heart.

"So, you planned for me to be alone?"

Peace, be still.

"Even when they leave me?"

Lo, I am with you always. I am turning your mourning into gladness. I am giving you comfort and joy instead of sorrow.

Warmth like sunshine filled her chest. It wasn't her fault they all left. And He never left her. She turned away. God said He would restore her joy, her love, but she rejected His help because she didn't trust Him. How was she supposed to deal with this fear of losing the people she loved?

Papa Shane's words came to mind. He'd told her to face her fears with faith.

But her faith was still weak.

I tell you, if you have faith as small as a mustard seed you can move this tree.

She stared up at the ancient oak she leaned against. The canopy covered her in shade as the sunlight sparkled through the leaves. This tree had witnessed the lives and deaths of her family. Gramma Rose's life had been so filled with sorrow. Yet even those final pages of the book sounded full of faith and joy.

"Joy despite heartbreak and sorrow. I want that. I want to count everything joy no matter what happens. God, if You give me love I will accept it. But if You do not, I still accept. I choose to trust You."

I am with you always.

No tears this time, only sweetness enveloping her from the inside out with peace like she'd never before felt.

She needed to talk to Randall and tell him her heart. She drove down the mountain faster than she should have. But the rush was to no avail. Randall's house was dark. His Jeep was not there.

The bell on the door at Sarah's Diner jingled as MaryRose entered. When she discovered Randall wasn't home she couldn't make herself go back to hers. It was too quiet. A slice of 'pie therapy' sounded good. Before she found a table, Vinnie Burns waved at her from across the room.

"Hon, you come on over here and sit with me."

Maybe Vinnie could tell more stories about Gramma Rose. She crossed the room, and before she sat down, Sarah touched her shoulder.

"She's in her happy place tonight. I'm surprised she recognized you because her happy place is way back when she was a young woman."

MaryRose wilted. So much for a story tonight. So much for a quiet piece of pie. She was already at Vinnie's table so she slid into the chair across from her.

"Rose E, why are you looking all worried tonight? Land sakes, I think you get younger ever time I see you. What's got you so all fired sad tonight?" Vinnie put her coffee cup down and stared across the room. "My Billy was supposed to meet me here. I closed the library early and all, but he ain't showed up."

MaryRose had no idea how to respond.

Vinnie looked at her watch. "Who's watching your baby boy with you out this time of night?"

What year was Vinnie in? Maybe she should go along with her to keep from agitating. "Umm, he's already sleeping."

Vinnie reached across the table and patted MaryRose's hand. "That's good. Then you and me can have us a talk. I hear tell they plan to name a road after your Patrick. Right good thing, he was a good man."

"Yes, he was."

Vinnie leaned toward the window and looked up the street again. "Don't know why my Billy ain't here yet." Turning back toward MaryRose, she patted her hand again.

"How long you gonna stay in that house way out there by the creek and all? Not sure a lady and a little boy will be safe way out there."

"We'll be fine." Gramma Rose's house was by the creek. "Which creek? It's not far away, is it?"

Vinnie frowned. "Child, if you don't know how far up the creek your house is who does?" She turned to the window again. "My Billy was supposed to meet me here tonight. I closed the library early. Can't figure where my man is."

"I'm sure he'll be here."

The woman gripped her napkin and tore it in two. She glared. "Just who do you think you are, talking like that? My Billy was a good man, and I been lost ever since he died."

Sarah hurried to the table and placed a slice of cherry pie in front of MaryRose.

She hugged Vinnie.

"I'm sorry MaryRose. This is one of her worst nights in a while. I'll help her get home." She grasped Vinnie's hand and guided her to the door. "Come on Vinnie, it's time for your programs."

"You're right. I'll be seeing you Rose E. Give your sweet baby a hug for me and be careful going over the mountain after dark. You hear me?"

"Yes ma'am."

MaryRose picked at her pie. Seemed like today about all she was good at was making people mad. She put the money on the table and left the half-eaten pie behind.

Loud pounding on her door woke her. She jumped off the sofa and all the notes she'd had in her lap when she fell asleep scattered across the floor. She rubbed her eyes and tried to figure out where the pounding was coming from. It was only ten o'clock but felt like the middle of the night.

MaryRose turned on the lamp and ran to the door. A wet, dirty, hysterical Andrea stood there. After pulling her into the house, MaryRose wrapped her in the blanket from the sofa. Andrea's eyes were wide with panic and she was out of breath. The screaming diminished to whimpers.

Luke stopped inside the doorway. "I heard screaming. What happened?"

Andrea turned away from Luke.

"MaryRose?"

"I don't know. Will you call Randall? He's working late, I guess. Keep him calm, but bring him down here. Have him bring dry clothes for her."

He nodded and rushed out.

MaryRose wasn't sure Andrea had heard them talking. She stood frozen in the middle of the room. MaryRose walked to her and held her. "Can you talk now, or would a shower help?"

"A sh—shower would be nice."

Looking at the torn blouse and the anguish in Andrea's eyes, she took a deep breath. "Wait. Andrea. I have to ask—umm—I should take you to the hospital before you shower if you've been raped. Were you?"

A large shudder racked her body. "He didn't rape me, not for lack of trying though. Is my daddy coming?"

"Luke will bring him. I think a shower is acceptable. You can use the towels on the rack. My robe on the back of the door is clean."

"MaryRose, do you think Daddy will be upset if I talk to you first? Then you can tell him."

"No, I think he'll understand." She hoped. "Go on to the shower. I'll take care of everything else."

"Thanks." Andrea's voice was barely above a whisper now.

MaryRose started coffee and made two mugs of hot chocolate too. Ma had always made hot chocolate when late night soothing was necessary.

Andrea sobbed louder than the shower. The young lady said he hadn't raped her, thankfully. But whatever happened had to be a nightmare. Pounding on the door interrupted her thoughts. MaryRose rushed to the door and opened it quickly.

"What happened? Where is she? Is she okay? I'll kill that boy if he hurt her!" Randall pounded his fist on the side of the house. The man was on the edge of hysteria himself.

MaryRose stood in the doorway and blocked his entry. The last thing they needed was this raging man to come barreling in demanding to know what was going on. Luke placed his hand on Randall's shoulder, almost as if he read her thoughts.

"Randall, I think she's okay, but I don't know what happened. She was wet and upset when she got here. She's in the shower now. She's going to need you, but not like this. Her dad should be a refuge."

His shoulders slumped. "I know, I know."

Luke squeezed the shoulder he held. "I'll stay here with him. You go on back to Andrea."

"I've got coffee on. I'll bring it out to you. Randall, she wants to talk to me first, do you mind?"

He grumbled. "Don't guess I'm much ready to talk yet."

"Randall?"

"Yeah?"

"I didn't hear the boat come back. Maybe you should check the dock. I'll sit the coffee out on the porch."

MaryRose was on the sofa when Andrea came out. She pointed to a stack of clothes on the end table. "Your dad brought these."

"Thanks, but I think I'll stay in the robe for now, if that's okay with you?" Andrea sat on the sofa and curled her legs underneath her.

"It's fine. Here's hot chocolate."

Andrea took a sip.

"Are you really okay?"

"Yeah—I mean—I guess. I mean—I don't know."

"You need your mother right now, don't you?"

"I need you."

MaryRose embraced her. This young woman who was taller than her felt like a child in her arms.

"Tonight was supposed to be special. Ken was so attentive and sentimental when we first got out on the water. He talked about going away to work and missing me. He told me how he worried I might go too far away for vet school. It was fun. I brought snacks. He was supposed to bring tea or something. He brought something all right. Wine. He said it was for a sweet goodbye. I didn't want any but he kept trying to get me to drink it with him. He ended up drinking it without me. All of it. He was freaking me out. I told him I wanted to come back home and that's when he grabbed me and started kissing me.

"I didn't like it. Hard, demanding kisses. I pushed him away."

Andrea sipped a little more hot chocolate. She shuddered.

"That's when he started yelling at me, accusing me of being a tease and mocked me about all of the purity stuff. Then he told me since God made sex He must like it—then he grabbed me again and crushed me against him."

Her breaths became more ragged.

"When I asked him about love and marriage and waiting he told me we'd get to it in time. Then he got crude. Said God gave me this body and these legs. Then he told me to use them on him.

"I slapped him. And when I jerked away my shirt ripped. He laughed. He told me the girls at the beach liked it rough, couldn't get enough of him."

"I asked who he slept with and he actually told me he lost count after three or four." She kicked at the floor, "That's when I jumped off the boat.

"I swam all the way back from the inlet. I have no idea what he's doing—not sure I even care. All I know is he is drunk and I left him out there on Daddy's boat!"

Andrea shrank into a weeping heap on the sofa. "I thought he loved me. How could I be so wrong?"

"He doesn't know what love is. He equates sex with love. Intimacy is a gift God gives a couple on their wedding day. The love is there long before the sex and long after it ends too. Kenneth doesn't see that. He doesn't know Jesus, and in his eyes purity is not important. Sex is what makes a relationship. In reality, it destroyed this one."

"It sure did. I'm hurt, angry, sad, scared. I can't stop shaking. Am I going crazy?"

"You're not going crazy. Go ahead and feel all of those things. God will help you through. Even at times like this, when all the emotions seem to come at once."

"I guess you know what I mean." Andrea's tremors calmed a bit in the warmth of the blanket.

She nodded. "God knows your heart. He is the only One who really knows how to heal you."

MaryRose kissed her cheek.

Andrea lay back on the pillow. "Mommy used to do that."

"I'm going to talk to your dad. I'll be back. If you need me, call."

Andrea curled up on the sofa and MaryRose went to her back door. Before tonight she hadn't seen Randall since he went on the business trip last week. They hadn't really spoken since their difficult discussion on the phone. She needed to apologize to him but hadn't had an opportunity yet. And now she must push it aside and talk to him about Andrea.

When she opened the door, he half rose from his seat on the swing.

"Shh, she's falling asleep. I'll come right out."

Luke got up and patted the seat beside Randall.

MaryRose poured two cups of coffee, and after serving

them, she sat beside Randall. She patted his leg. "Randall, Andrea's had a traumatic night."

His jaws clenched.

"She wasn't raped. But it wasn't for lack of trying. Andrea got away from him, jumped out of the boat and swam home."

Randall stomped across the porch. Then he punched the post. "That boy better not come around here again. I'll put the fear of God in him."

"I guess that's one option." Luke set his empty mug on the porch. "Or we could pray about it and trust God to give us the right words to get through this."

"You really mean that?"

"I do."

"You would." He resumed pacing.

MaryRose went to the door. Not sure how to handle his anger, she chose to go back inside and sit with Andrea.

Luke opened the door for her. "I'll stay with him till he calms."

CHAPTER 27

*M*aryRose stood at the cabinets wiping the counter she'd already wiped. She poured a glass of water and leaned against the counter drinking it. Luke and Randall sat on the porch. Would it be eavesdropping if she listened to their conversation? Probably.

Luke's voice carried into the kitchen. "Buddy, you've got to calm down. You cannot be this agitated when you talk to your daughter. Let's go up to the house. MaryRose will take care of Andrea."

"Sure she will, she'll pray and wait for everything to be hunky-dory again."

"Sarcasm's ugly on you."

Someone stamped his foot. Then Randall spoke. "I'll stay out here and wait until Andrea is ready to see me. You can go on home if you want."

"I'll stay with you."

MaryRose knew she shouldn't eavesdrop. She's just go sit with Andrea. Before she made it into the living room, her driveway was flooded with flashing red and blue lights. Two police cars pulled in behind her VW.

Randall and Luke met the officers as they got out of the car. She stepped onto the porch and backed against one of the posts. She'd be out of the way but could still hear the conversation.

"I'm Officer Rick Rhodes. Is either one of you Randall Cobb?"

Randall nodded. "I am."

"Well sir, we have a plastered young man in our car. He wrecked your boat on the dam head. His parents are meeting us here."

Randall stepped toward the car, but Luke placed his hand across his chest to stay him.

The officer continued. "Kenneth Phillips is in our custody. We need to know what charges you wish to press. He said something about his girlfriend jumping off the boat?"

Randall fisted and un-fisted his right hand at his side. "My daughter, Andrea, is home and safe. Was the boy injured?"

"No. He's drunk and facing some major charges, but otherwise okay. I need to know if you wish to press any charges, sir."

Randall opened his fist. Everything about his posture screamed the need to punch someone or something. "As long as I get my boat back, his family covers the repairs, and I never see him around here again, I won't be pressing any charges."

Another car pulled up and a well-dressed man and woman rushed to Randall. The woman spoke first. "Randall? What's happening? We got a call to come here. What's going on?"

He took a deep breath and answered more calmly than MaryRose thought he could. "Your son was much less than a gentleman tonight. He hurt my daughter. You should go on to the station now. I expect my boat to be repaired and brought back here."

"But what happened—"

"Why not ask your son? Maybe he'll be honest with you. I'm done talking." He turned away from them and strode toward MaryRose.

"Luke?" Kenneth's mom was almost in tears.

"Yes?"

"Did he, did he, oh gosh, I can't say it, did he rape her?"

"No."

"Thank God."

Randall turned back toward them. "Barbara, he was drunk. The only reason he didn't rape her is she got away."

Her hands flew to her mouth. "Not my Kenny. He knows better. Do we want to know what happened tonight?"

Luke shook his head. "I'm sure you don't. And once your son tells you everything—assuming he does—I think you'll agree my cousin has exhibited incredible self-control." He turned to the police officers. "Thank you for your help. I guess you need to speak with Andrea?"

"Yes, please."

"She's in the cabin at the bottom of the hill. We'll go down after the Phillips leave."

After the police left, Randall dropped to the steps on the back porch, head in his hands. Luke stood behind him. MaryRose tiptoed back inside.

Luke followed. "Wait, MaryRose. You two need to talk a bit. I'll go inside and sit with Andrea."

She sat beside Randall and touched his shoulder. He actually relaxed against her hand. "You were amazing."

"Man, that wasn't me. I don't know what came over me. I wanted to slug the boy and punch his Dad for not teaching him better. I wanted—I wanted Andrea to throw the book at the boy for attempted rape."

Silence stretched between them. "Did she do okay talking to the police?"

"She did fine. She's a brave woman."

"Like her mother. I need to calm down more before I see her. Can you go back in and stay with her?"

"Sure. The door's open. Come in whenever." She rose.

He grabbed her hand. "Forgive me for my words yesterday?"

"Already done. Forgive me too please."

"Done."

Andrea was awake and dressed when she got back inside. "Is Daddy out there?"

"Yes."

"Can you go get him, please?"

Randall came in from the kitchen. "I'm here, honey."

"Oh, Daddy." She ran into his arms.

Luke stood at the door. "I'm heading home now. Rachel and Emma are probably about to burst wanting to know what's going on. You go on back in there to Randall and Andrea. They need you."

They needed her? How those words warmed her heart. Entering the living room she interrupted a tender scene. Andrea was curled in Randall's lap. But she smiled at MaryRose. "Could you come up to the house? Andrea wants you to stay with her."

"Randall, do you mind?"

"Not at all."

"Let me change first." Dressed in shorts and a baggy T-shirt, she grabbed her Bible and Dapple and followed Andrea and Randall up the hill. After helping Andrea into a nightgown, MaryRose climbed onto the bed beside her and held her until she fell to sleep.

Sometime later, she sensed Randall come in and place a light blanket over them.

She drifted in and out of sleep. Then Andrea began tossing and fussing. "No. No. How could you do that?"

She struggled, and then sat upright arms flailing. Once she saw MaryRose, she snuggled against her shoulder.

MaryRose rocked her until the sobbing stopped. "Was that a nightmare?"

"No." Andrea grasped MaryRose's hand "I was remembering. There's something I didn't tell you. I couldn't."

"You can tell me anything."

"Ken told me about things he said to you, and the times he touched you. He was all proud of himself. I wanted to puke. Then he insinuated he walked in on you and Daddy one night when he was leaving after one of our dates."

"What?"

"I told him you would never do such a thing."

"Andrea—I never."

"I know. But did Ken really take liberties with you?"

"He tried. I stopped him. Or, I thought I did."

Andrea began sobbing again. "I am sorry."

"It's not your fault. You go back to sleep now."

A light knock sounded on the door, then Randall peeked in. "I heard crying."

MaryRose motioned him in. He pulled a chair across the room and sat beside the bed. She was about to explode, couldn't even trust herself to speak.

"What's going on?"

"She woke briefly and shared something Ken had said to her. Poor girl. Randall, Kenneth Phillips is trouble. I wish I could say we are done with him, but something tells me he is more messed up than anyone realizes."

Randall brushed hair from her face, and then he caressed her cheek. "You are amazing."

"I'm just me."

"An amazing *me*. MaryRose Elliott, I love you."

Andrea sat up and looked at them, then giggled a sleepy sound. "It's about time you admit it." She settled back down on her pillow. "Go on. I'll never get any sleep with all this mushy stuff going on."

MaryRose kissed Andrea's head, and then followed Randall into the hall.

"I'm sorry I was a jerk. You've been an angel in our lives ever since you arrived. Not sure my daughter could have made it through this night without you. Thank you."

"Apology accepted. I'm sorry too. I got mad at you for worrying about where I was and if I was safe. Who does that? For all of my talk of faith and God working all things for good for those who love Him, my faith can be quite weak when it comes to relationships."

"Apology accepted. Looks like we both have things to learn about relationships."

"We're a bit out of practice." MaryRose touched his cheek. "In response to what you said in there? I love you too."

Something hard hit the door. "I can still hear you! Good-night already."

Randall placed his finger over his mouth, "We better hush."

"I should go on home now. We can talk more tomorrow."

"We can and we will. I'll walk you home."

She dismissed him with a wave. "You stay with her. I'm a big girl. Think I can make it down the hill without help."

At the back door, he kissed her soundly. "Good night, Pretty Lady."

CHAPTER 28

$\mathcal{M}$aryRose stretched. A morning spent weeding the flower beds and playing fetch with Dapple had been a good start to a new week. The puppy was currently sprawled under the oak tree in the corner of the yard. His tennis ball was under his head like a pillow.

Gardening had provided her with needed distractions. Andrea was broken-hearted but going to be all right. Randall took a few days off to spend with his daughter. This morning he took her out for breakfast and then to an appointment with her counselor.

The sun was high in the sky and the day rapidly warming. MaryRose raked the weeds into a pile and loaded them into the wheel barrel. Lunch down by the lake would be nice.

The gate squeaked as it opened and then closed. Dapple jumped up and raced around the house barking. MaryRose brushed her hands on her shorts, and then smoothed her braid. Surely they hadn't finished breakfast so soon.

But Dapple's barking stopped with a yip. Silence.

MaryRose ran to the back yard and bumped into Kenneth

Phillips. He held Dapple in a tight grip with hands around the dog's throat. The young man had a crazed look about him. His sneer sent chills up her spine.

"Never did like this noisy dog. I could snap his neck easy as a breath right now."

"You wouldn't."

"Don't tempt me, MaryRose."

"Put my dog down and get off of this property."

"It doesn't look to me like you are in any position to make demands."

MaryRose looked at the back porch. He blocked her way to the door. To her phone. To help. She didn't doubt his threat to kill Dapple one bit. Kenneth's pupils were dilated. He was on something.

He slowly eyed her from head to toe and back again. He licked his lips. "I have yet to see you in anything that didn't look good. Nothing will look pretty good too. But, we'll get to that. I think I'll keep hold of this one for a while."

He put Dapple into a football hold.

"They arrested you."

"Parents with money can pay good lawyers. I bet I was out of jail before you were asleep."

MaryRose didn't know much about drugs, but Kenneth was on something stronger than alcohol. The venom in his eyes was far more frightening than any rattlesnake bite. She sidestepped toward the porch.

He met her steps. "You're going to want to walk easy and slow. Your dog's a squirmer. Wouldn't want him to twist and hurt himself now would you? We're taking us a little ride."

Oh God. Help. MaryRose took another step. "Where's your car?"

"I walked here. Don't want anyone to know I'm not in my room sleeping last night off."

"Kenneth, I don't have my keys on me."

"So come inside with me and your dog. We'll get those keys right now. And don't even try to grab your cell phone or the land line. Keep in mind my grip on this guy's neck is strong. Go on inside, I'm right behind you. No funny stuff."

The screen door banged shut behind them. MaryRose trudged to the table. Her cell phone was still on the nightstand. There was no way she could sprint in there, grab it, and make a call before her dog's neck would be broken. Even the landline across the kitchen was too far away.

"Randall will be here any minute."

He laughed. "You don't make a good liar. Your hero took my girl a while ago. Your neighbors headed out shortly after that. I made sure it's just you and me."

"Kenneth, what do you think you're doing?"

"Getting my vengeance. You've been teasing me ever since you moved in, and now you turned my girl against me. I don't like to lose. Ask anyone who knows me."

"And when I don't check in with them, they'll get worried. You could get out of here and we'll forget this ever happened."

"Oh, you are funny."

He grabbed her keys and shoved her towards the door. Reaching around her, he grabbed a knife from the butcher block on the counter. He held it dangerously close to Dapple.

"Me and your dog are going for a ride. If you don't come along, he'll end up at the bottom of the lake. Your choice."

She pushed her hair back and glared at him. "You'll not get away with this."

"I already have." He squeezed Dapple tighter until the puppy gagged again.

How she longed to charge him and knock him over. But she would fail. He was every bit as large and strong as Randall. There had to be something she could do.

Dapple growled, pulled his head free and bit Kenneth's palm. He swore. While he resumed his grip on the dog's neck Mary-Rose grabbed a sharpie from the pencil box and scribbled Ken on the table. Grabbing and jingling the keys, she faced him.

"Don't hurt my dog. I've got the keys."

At her VW, MaryRose opened the passenger door but he slammed it shut. He shoved her around the back of the car.

"You drive. I'll keep holding your dog. You so much as try to pull something and I will break his neck."

"Where are we going?"

"You don't need to know. Follow my directions."

She backed out of the drive and headed onto Lake Nolan Drive. How could she get Dapple from him and get away?

He hadn't fastened his seat belt. If she got the opportunity to slam on the brakes he'd be hurt. But so would Dapple. She could drive straight to the police station, but when he figured out what she was doing, he'd hurt Dapple. He still held the knife and could easily kill her sweet dog, the last gift she'd ever received from her parents. Hopeless.

At the end of the paved road below the dam, he pointed to a dirt road curving away from the lake and into the woods. "Turn there. There's an old shack at the end of the lane. We'll have plenty of privacy."

By the time they reached the end of the dirt road, she'd better have a plan. His was a pretty good one. No one would ever think to look here. As a matter of fact, right now, this time of day on a Monday pretty much everyone in Lake Nolan was at work. The only thing that might help her was Kenneth's increasing agitation. His legs bounced as his squeeze on Dapple tightened and he kept looking behind them. He might get careless.

MaryRose took her foot off the gas.

"Hey. Did I say you could slow down?"

"Didn't ask. This is my car and it's bottoming out on these ruts. I'll not to ruin my car for you."

"You'll do what I say." He shifted the knife. "I said speed up."

"Okay, okay. Just don't hurt my dog."

His lowered the knife a bit.

Praying for her dog's safety, she hit the next rut in the road hard. His head whacked the roof of the car and the knife slipped from his grip.

Dapple was shivering. If she hit another bump like that, Kenneth might loosen his grip enough so she could get the puppy into her lap. But then what? She sped up slightly before the next pothole. His head smacked the roof even harder.

"You did that on purpose." He let go of Dapple and reached up to rub his scalp.

"Come here, boy." She patted her leg and her dog didn't hesitate to leap from Kenneth's lap into hers. She grabbed him tight.

"Like holding your puppy will save you." He retrieved the knife from the floor. "I have plans you won't mess with. You'll pay for ruining what I had with Andrea."

"You ruined your relationship with her all by yourself. I had nothing to do with it."

"Sure you did. You taught her all the purity crap. She would already have been mine long before last night if not for you."

"She's a young lady, not property you can own."

"That's what you think. I'll soon show you who I can own." An evil laugh slithered out of his mouth.

"So, you think we'll be all alone here?"

"Oh, I know it. Nobody comes here anymore."

"We're not alone right now."

"Oh, you mean your little dog? Ha. He can't stop me. I'll tie him to a tree. Maybe a bear or a wild cat will grab him."

"I am not talking about my dog. I mean Jesus."

He laughed louder. "You really are crazy."

"Am I?"

"Have to be. Jesus wouldn't be here—not with what I aim to do today."

"Why is that, Kenneth?"

He paused. She glanced sideways at him. His brows furrowed. "Stupid question. I'm pretty sure you know what I intend. No room for Jesus in what we're doing today."

"You know, He loves you too. But even if you reject Him, He is here with me. He promised never to leave me or forsake me, so I will not go through anything alone today."

Finally, she felt the bold faith she'd always relied upon, almost lost. This young man beside her was lost, and she actually felt sorry for him.

"You're smiling? Guess you are looking forward to this after all."

"I always look forward to seeing what God has planned for me."

She saw the shack or more like an ancient log cabin. She still didn't have a plan.

Crash into it.

What? The Beetle would crumple up like a foil ball. All of them could be killed.

Do you trust Me?

Yes.

Crash into it.

MaryRose took a deep breath. Kenneth was smirking, even looked a little excited. After placing Dapple on the seat between her thigh and the door, she whispered "stay." With a death grip on the steering wheel she turned the car slightly to the right and aimed directly at the cabin. She floored the gas pedal.

"What the—?"

MaryRose drove right up the front steps and into the old log posts holding the porch up. The car stopped hard and jerked them forward. Kenneth's head crunched into the windshield which shattered into a thousand-piece mosaic. The knife hit the floor. MaryRose's seatbelt cut hard into her abdomen, but stopped her shy of the window. Her forehead hit the steering wheel. Dapple yipped then whimpered. Warmth trickled down her forehead as daylight dimmed.

CHAPTER 29

*M*aryRose couldn't open her eyes all the way. And her head might as well have weighed a hundred pounds. No matter how hard she tried, it wouldn't lift. Dapple whimpered as he moved but somehow squirmed between her face and the steering wheel and began kissing her.

Ouch.

"Help me, Lord."

She finally got her eyes open and raised her head. The world spun a bit. The front of her car, folded like an accordion, rested inches from her lap. And the porch beam had fallen on Kenneth's side of the car. The boy was pinned and unconscious.

She touched his neck and found a pulse.

"Thank you, God."

I am with you always. Now go forth. Step-by-step I will lead you.

"How can I do that?"

Kenneth moaned.

"Okay, I'll do my best."

Her door wouldn't budge. The seatbelt that saved her was locked, and now became her yoke. The steering wheel pushed hard against her chest. But her window was partially down. She turned the crank a bit. Took a breath, and then turned it more. Turn by turn, she lowered it. Miraculously, the seat belt unlatched.

Every part of her hurt. Every breath burned. Legs pinned but she had to get out. Had to get help.

Holding her breath against the pain, she pulled her legs from under the steering column and twisted herself toward the window. Dapple wriggled beside her and jumped up to the window.

"You have to let me get out first, buddy."

Kenneth was still unconscious but for how long?

Even the slightest movement of her legs jarred her with excruciating pain. Her left ankle was messed up. It would be useless in helping her get out of the car. After grabbing the door and pulling on the handled and steeling herself for the impact, she leaned hard on the door. It moved a little and Dapple scooted out the opening.

With one more push MaryRose got the door opened enough to squeeze through. Blood from the wound on her forehead trickled down and burned her eyes. She extended her legs. There was no way she could walk.

MaryRose fell back against the car door.

"I can't do this."

With Me all things are possible.

"Okay, then You have to stand me up and walk for me because all I want to do is lay down and give up."

Be still and know that I am God.

Warmth filled her. No way to describe it. Maybe that's what an adrenalin rush felt like. But she took a deep breath, stood and started hopping. Pain increased with each movement. Her head pounded. Blood trickled down her face, and her stomach felt like she'd been sucker punched. Hard.

Every now and then she heard a car which meant they were

getting close to the paved road. But how close and how long would it take to get there?

Dapple trudged beside her. When she stopped to lean against a tree and rest a bit, he lay on the ground beside her.

Somewhere behind her a horn blew. Oh no. Kenneth was awake. Could he get out and get to her? She'd been so sure he was hurt worse than her.

"Dapple, we must hurry."

MaryRose pushed off the tree and did her best to run.

They made it to the end of the dirt road, and she dropped to the ground in exhaustion.

No cars.

No people.

Nothing.

They hadn't been there long, but every minute meant Kenneth could be that much closer to catching her. She didn't have the strength to get up again. Every thought she had to be pulled it through a dense fog to make sense out of it. And the fog grew thicker every second.

Pushing herself up, she staggered toward the road.

Go up.

"I barely have enough strength to walk at all. And you want me to go uphill?"

Look left.

How had she not noticed the branches strewn on the side of the road; probably from the last wind storm? Walking sticks. After grabbing a sturdy one, MaryRose limped onto Lake Nolan Drive, and began a slow ascent. Up ahead, there was a gas station. Was it even open?

Dapple barked and ran ahead of her into the road. Her voice failed. She couldn't call him back as she tripped into the parking lot and fell down.

A car approached, heading straight toward Dapple.

Tires screeched.

Soft hands touched her cheek. "Oh, dear Lord. Walter, you're right. That's Dapple and here is MaryRose. She's all beat up. Call 911."

Trudy?

"MaryRose, honey, what in the world happened to you?" Fingers touched her lips. "Sh, don't try to answer that. Me and Walter are here. He's got your puppy and is calling the ambulance. Everything will be okay."

MaryRose reached up and pointed toward the dirt road. Caked blood pulled her lips closed, but she had to talk. "Trudy. Two ambulances—down that—"so hard to speak—"dirt road. Kenneth. My car. Crashed." She lowered her head back to the gravel.

"Walt, she says Kenneth is crashed in her car down the old Parson's Rd."

Trudy scooted closer and rubbed her arm. "You be still. The ambulance will be here in no time and we'll be on our way. I'll send Walter to get Randall."

When MaryRose opened her eyes, blue ones looked back at her. Randall reached around the IV line and grasped her hand. "Hey there, Pretty Lady."

"Hey." She croaked.

"You told me you didn't think we had seen the last of Ken. I should have listened to you."

"H-how is he?"

His brows furrowed. "Why are you worrying about him?"

"I intentionally crashed the car into the old house. If he dies it's my fault."

"It's called self-defense. He's banged up a bit but he'll be fine. He has new accommodations in the infirmary at the county jail."

"So young."

"He made stupid decisions, but he really needs help."

"Yes he does. I pray he gets it." She raised the bed a little but even doing so slowly made her head throb. "What about me? The doctor hasn't been in yet today."

He lightly touched the bandage above her right eye. "You have ten stitches up there. Your stomach is bruised from the impact, and your knees got wrenched. Your left ankle has a nasty sprain. The doctor says after a few days here and TLC at home, you will be good as new."

"He knows I live alone, right?"

Randall's laughter boomed around the room. "Missy is already at your house. Rachel and Mom are making meals, and Andrea has Dapple taken care of. You'll not be alone anytime soon."

So different than three months ago when she was in this hospital. Then she was a lonely, bitter widow.

She reached for his hand. "I tried to witness to him."

"Who?"

"Kenneth. He was ranting about what he planned. And I was afraid, but this strange peace came over me. I told him we weren't alone and Jesus would be right there while he did whatever he did."

Randall's eyes widened. "You're kidding?"

"No. I wanted to say a lot more, but he shut me out. Then I knew I had to come up with another idea. God told me to crash my car. I can't believe we weren't both killed. I guess my little car is toast."

"Maybe not. Walt Trumble's son, Bobby, is about the best auto body man around. Plus, he loves to work on classic cars. They towed it to his shop."

She fought to keep her eyes open. Randall kissed her cheek. "Sleep. I'll be here when you wake up."

She liked the sound of that.

⌒

Andrea wheeled the chair to the exit. "Daddy's waiting for you in his Jeep. I'm going home to get supper on the table. We don't want to wear you out, but Gramma made lasagna, and everyone's eating at our house. Missy got her understudy to do the performances so she can spend the weekend with you. Honestly, I think she and Jonathon are both looking forward to her being around all weekend.

"Kenneth's in jail now. I don't know what will happen with him. Daddy told me what you said to him. I got to thinking and have decided the best thing I can do is pray for him. When I do, it sure helps my angry moments."

MaryRose had never welcomed Andrea's chatter more. The girl appeared well recovered from the traumatic week. At the exit, Andrea kissed her cheek and stepped away as Randall scooped MaryRose into his arms. He planted a solid kiss on her lips.

"Good thing you're holding me, kind sir. A kiss like that would make my legs give out."

Andrea giggled. "You two are cute. See you at home."

Once she was fastened in, Randall kissed her again. "We have one stop to make on the way home. I have a surprise for you."

He got in his seat and whistled as they drove toward home. Beyond Bill Mack's gas station, he turned onto Parson's Road. Her heart checked. Why would he bring her here?

"I know what you're thinking. I'm pretty sure you'll be glad we came back."

As they pulled in front of the house, the demolished front

porch made her shudder. Then she looked at the sun sparkling in his eyes and the smile on his face. Something was up.

He stopped the car beside the house.

MaryRose opened the car door and looked around at things she hadn't noticed during her ordeal. A stream babbled around the back of the house. There was a dilapidated smokehouse by the car and an outhouse at the edge of the clearing. Something strangely familiar struck her. Other than the crunched up porch, why would she recognize this place?

Randall helped her out of the car and carried her inside. He carefully placed her into a rocking chair facing a huge fireplace.

He winked. "I brought this chair here before I came and got you. I didn't want to wear you out. I'll open the shutters and let the sunlight in."

Randall walked around the house opening shutters. Cozy place. Why had the owners let such prime property fall into disarray? It could be a charming home with a lovely location.

"Randall, should we be here? I mean, I need to find the owner and pay for the mess I made."

He placed his fingers over her mouth. "Shh. The name of this road is Parson's Road. Did you happen to notice that?"

She nodded.

"It was named for a beloved minister who used to live here."

Her heart hitched again.

"After he passed, the people of the little community wanted to do something to honor him, so they named the road after him. I've always known this part of the story. The only things left of him and his family are the road, this house, a few graves, and many memories. Can you stand?"

"I can try." She pushed herself up to stand and he was at her side. With one arm around her waist, he helped her to the fireplace. He pointed to letters carved into the wood of the ancient mantle.

MaryRose read them. "P.E., R.E., November 1865."

She frowned. Then she inhaled sharply.

Parsons Road. 1866.

Randall's smile filled his face.

"I lied. There is one family member still around."

"It isn't—it can't be."

She traced the initials with her finger.

"Patrick Elliott, Rose Elliott. This is—"

"Their house."

MaryRose sunk back into the rocking chair. Her breath was a knotted ball in her chest. Of all the places on the mountain, Kenneth brought her to her homestead. Something evil turned into beauty.

"I—um—"this was too big to grasp—"when did you find this?"

"Vinnie Burns called my house the other day. She was going on and on about the old house on Parson's Road. She told me she knew Rose E was there all alone with her baby. I ignored it.

"As I watched the Trumbles pulling your car off the porch, I got to thinking about her words. They didn't make sense. My Mom always told me there are no coincidences only God-incidences. Of all the hollers and back roads around here, why did Kenneth choose Parson's Road?

"Then, while I was standing there, Officer Rhodes came up, and we got to talking. He mentioned the property belongs to the Lake Nolan Water Authority, but the rights to the house belong to the Elliott family. Since the Elliott's own the house, the water authority can't touch it. He asked if I knew how to reach the family."

"I crashed into my own house."

"Yes, you did. And I happen to know a really great guy who can fix this place up good as new. Should I call him?" He winked.

"I want to kiss him."

He knelt in front of her. "Kiss me. I'll see he gets it!"

She leaned into the sweetest kiss she'd ever experienced.

After he pulled away, he reached into his pocket. "I've been waiting for the perfect moment and this is it." He opened the box.

"MaryRose Elliott, will you marry me?"

"Thought you'd never ask. Yes. Yes. Yes."

He slid the ring on her finger then took her into his arms.

No, *that* was the sweetest kiss she'd ever experienced.

EPILOGUE

$\mathcal{M}$aryRose ripped the page off the calendar, November 6, her wedding day, exactly one-hundred and fifty years after Gramma Rose and Patrick's wedding. The morning of her first marriage she'd been a knot of nerves. Not this time. She was excited, ready, and confident. Gramma Rose's dress—cleaned, pressed, and tailored hung on the peg in the bedroom waiting for her. Miss Ruth, soon to be Mom, had outdone herself making it so MaryRose could wear the dress.

Today she would marry Randall in Gramma Rose's yard. Everything was decorated for a small family wedding, but in a few weeks, the house would convert to her office and work-shop. Randall's idea to use the house this way was perfect.

They talked about living there, but as nice as the brook was, she loved living on the lake.

MaryRose had showered and twisted her hair into a bun. She wanted to sit in her rocker and be with Gramma Rose a few minutes before everyone arrived to prepare for the ceremony. She sipped coffee and opened the last of Gramma Rose's journals. Soon she would read all of the ones in between, but today, as a new chapter in her life started, it made sense to read the last chapter in Gramma Rose's.

~~~~

July 4, 1951

I held my great-grandson, Samuel James Elliott today. What a grand joy for this old lady. He looks so much like my James Patrick did when he was a new one. It took me back to those happy days. I am pleased Samuel decided to bring his new family to come meet his old grandmother.

That was a long journey for a family with a baby. But Samuel has always been the sweetest grandson. And his dear wife, he could not have married better, Elizabeth is the perfect wife for him. And, my oh my, she is plain absorbing everything I can teach her about plants. Reminds me of me, except she is way more willing to learn than I was.

Today she asked me about what I did when my James Patrick moved back to the old family place in Hertford. I told her I cried for days. I walked around this little house and fussed at God so loud it was good I didn't have neighbors. If anyone had come around and heard me yelling at my God, they would surely have taken me to the county home.

But God, you have always known me to be fully honest with you. Then Elizabeth asked why I didn't go with James Patrick. I looked at her and said true as could be that this is my home. I have belonged here since I came here a scared girl about to be married. I couldn't no more move away from here than stop watching the sunrise every day.

It did help me get through the lonely years writing and making things for all the people around here. I wonder how many medicines I have made in this life. It helped that my James and his family came to see me so much and stayed a few weeks every year.

Samuel loves to come here and so does his wife. I told them last night that I want them to take my journals with them. I don't need them a cluttering my shelves and maybe sometime somebody in our family would get a chuckle out of my lifetime of rambling. Samuel is the kind, sweet husband and father my Patrick was. He will raise his little Samuel James to be a man of faith and love. And I could ask for no greater legacy than that.

~~~~

Had Gramma never written any more journals after she gave them to Nana? Or had they disappeared? MaryRose held the journal to her chest. Seeing her grandfather as a new father. Amazing. Thinking of her Gramps holding her father in his arms conjured a beautiful image. Here she was in the house where Gramma Rose had penned the words. Her eyes filled when she pictured Gramma Rose in the room rocking and cuddling Pa. So this is what it felt like to come full circle. She looked back at the last words in the journal.

~~~~

Tomorrow they must go back to the coast. As usual they begged me to come with them. As usual I told them this is where I belong. These mountains are my home and the only place I want to be. Well, except for the grand day I get to go before my Lord in heaven and see my sweet, sweet Patrick waiting for me.

Thank you Jesus. Amen.

~~~~

Approaching footsteps interrupted her. MaryRose inhaled a whiff of the best scent in the world. Randall's frame filled the doorway.

"You shouldn't be here. They say it's bad luck. I disagree."

He winked, crossed the room in two long strides, took the journal from her hands, and placed it on the table. Then he swooped her into his arms and planted a huge kiss on her lips.

"I snuck out. I know this is a breach of the wedding rules, but as soon as Jonathon and Dad went to the bathrooms for their showers I snuck out. Figured if I hurried I could get here before Mom, Missy, Andrea, and Rachel descended upon you."

"I'm glad you came. I read the last pages of Gramma Rose's journal. Read about her holding Dad as a baby, and when she gave all of the journals to Nana. So sweet and right. You know, when I first started reading the journals and learned about Patrick dreaming of her and following the dream, I thought it was crazy. But now I don't."

"Why not?"

"All of those years ago one man made a choice to follow a dream, and, because of his decision, today I marry the love of my life."

He kissed her nose. "I'll have to remember to thank that man when we meet in heaven." He stood and backed toward the door. "Now, I better get out of here before the ladies show up and give me all kinds of grief for coming here to see you before the wedding."

She stood on tiptoes and kissed him.

He cupped her chin in his hand. His eyes darkened with the promise of things to come.

~THE START~

AUTHOR'S NOTE

While Lake Nolan is fiction, the beauty of the West Virginia Mountains and lakes is real.

I love creating locations for my novels almost as much as the characters. Lake Nolan is one of my favorites. In the past seventeen years I've had many wonderful getaway weekends visiting my dear friends in West Virginia. Picnics and hikes at Kanawha Falls, New River Gorge, Hawk's Nest State Park, Chief Logan State Park, and the views of Cheat Lake and Lake Stephens all serve as inspiration for my lake and town of Lake Nolan, West Virginia.

I have been to summer theatre performances at Theatre West Virginia, in Beckley, and Liz Spurlock Amphitheatre in Chief Logan State Park. They serve as inspiration for the outdoor theatre and park in this novel. If you're ever in West Virginia in the summer, I highly recommend treating yourself to the outdoor dramas. They are well worth the trip.

To Follow a Dream is a complete work of fiction. However, the inspiration for this book comes from a story in my family history. John M. Davis—who from Mama's best recollection was my great-great-great-uncle—had a dream about his future bride. He dreamt who she was, where she lived, and what dress she would be wearing. He rode his horse the seventy miles to the location of his dream, met Thomas E. Everette and told him he'd come to court his daughter—whom he'd never met. On December 24, 1839, John M. Davis and Elizabeth Everette were married. My ancestor following his dream inspired this novel. By the way, when John met Elizabeth she was wearing the *exact* dress he'd seen in his dream. The record of John M. Davis's story is described in detailon page 201 of The Heritage of Lenoir County 1981, published by The Lenoir County Historical Association, Kinston, North Carolina in 1981.

ABOUT THE AUTHOR

Chandra Lynn Smith is a professional dog trainer by trade and a writer by heart. *To Follow a Dream* is her third novel. Chandra, a 2015 American Christian Fiction Writers Genesis Contest, and the owner of Best Friend Dog Training and lives on a small farm in South Central Pennsylvania with her husband and two dogs. Their house is often filled with the glorious chaos of any combination of four sons, two fiancés, two daughters-in-law, precious granddaughter, and nine grand-dogs. Her other novels, *Turtle Box Memories,* and *The Light Holding Her* in *Coming Home; A Tiny House Collection* can be found on Amazon.

Visit Chandra's website at
 www.ChandraLynnSmith.com
 Feel free to post reviews of this book and purchase others at:
 www.amazon.com/author/chandralynnsmith
 Look for her weekly posts on life and dogs at:
 www.chandralynnsmith.blogspot.com

COMING SOON

Stay tuned in 2020 for Andrea's story in book two of Lake Nolan Summers Series.

... Can a veterinarian and an artist, both successful, but empty, learn to trust each other in time to prevent more dogs from disappearing during the next full moon?...

Made in the USA
Monee, IL
07 December 2020

50244586R00184